CHRISTMAS
AT THE
LAKE

Also by Anita Hughes

Christmas at the Ranch
A Magical New York Christmas
Christmas in Vermont
Christmas at the Chalet
California Summer
Christmas in London
Emerald Coast
White Sand, Blue Sea
Christmas in Paris
Santorini Sunsets
Island in the Sea
Rome in Love
French Coast
Lake Como
Market Street
Monarch Beach

005019232483
2 shoes
1 socks famous
4/8

CHRISTMAS
AT THE
LAKE

A Novel

ANITA HUGHES

ST. MARTIN'S
GRIFFIN
NEW YORK

First published in the United States by St. Martin's Griffin,
an imprint of St. Martin's Publishing Group

CHRISTMAS AT THE LAKE. Copyright © 2023 by Anita Hughes.
All rights reserved. Printed in the United States of America. For information,
address St. Martin's Publishing Group, 120 Broadway, New York, NY 10271.

www.stmartins.com

Library of Congress Cataloging-in-Publication Data

Names: Hughes, Anita, 1963- author.
Title: Christmas at the lake : a novel / Anita Hughes.
Description: First Edition. | New York : St. Martin's Griffin, 2023.
Identifiers: LCCN 2023016791 | ISBN 9781250871923 (trade paperback) |
ISBN 9781250871930 (ebook)
Subjects: LCGFT: Romance fiction. | Christmas fiction. | Novels.
Classification: LCC PS3608.U356755 C4615 2023 | DDC 813/.6—dc23/eng/2023
LC record available at https://lccn.loc.gov/2023016791

Our books may be purchased in bulk for promotional, educational, or business
use. Please contact your local bookseller or the Macmillan Corporate and
Premium Sales Department at 1-800-221-7945, extension 5442, or by email at
MacmillanSpecialMarkets@macmillan.com.

First Edition: 2023

10 9 8 7 6 5 4 3 2 1

To my mother

CHRISTMAS
AT THE
LAKE

Chapter One

It was Christmas Eve and in six hours, Rebecca Huntley was going to marry her college sweetheart, and the love of her life, Ben Cole. They had planned for the ceremony to be held in the small chapel at Grace Cathedral with its mosaic tile floor and stained-glass windows, where Rebecca had listened to the San Francisco Boys Chorus sing Christmas carols every year since she could remember, followed by an intimate yet lavish reception at the Four Seasons Hotel. After their send-off, Rebecca and Ben planned to climb into the vintage car she had rented from a local film company for the three-hour drive to Christmas Cove Lodge in the quaint village of Christmas Cove on the shores of Lake Tahoe.

Rebecca was looking forward to the honeymoon more than anything. More than cutting the strawberry-infused wedding cake with lemon-buttercream frosting ordered from their favorite bakery on Fillmore Street. Even more than seeing the expression on Ben's face when she walked down the aisle in her oyster-colored silk Mikado gown. The honeymoon was going to be seven days of ice-skating, exploring the Christmas market, and strolling along the lakefront. Rebecca had even booked a sleigh ride with real reindeer.

The best part about the honeymoon was that it would be just her and Ben together. They had both agreed on a strict no-work policy. No phones, no laptops, and no late meetings that started at 5:00 p.m. and somehow lasted so long that when they arrived home at 10:00 p.m., they ate whatever they could find in the fridge, standing up at the counter, before falling into bed.

They had been working too hard lately. The company they started eight years ago when they were students at UC Berkeley, a dating app called Dealbreakers.com that matched up couples by the things they hated, instead of what they had in common, was about to go public. Their days were filled with meetings with venture capitalists.

It hadn't helped that Rebecca decided not to hire a wedding planner. She didn't want to simply show up at the church in her gown and have some woman in a severe black dress point her down the aisle when the organ music started. And she loved choosing the decor for the reception. She loved seeing the flower arrangements she had sketched for the florist become vases filled with crimson and white pansies. She had painstakingly picked out the party favors: small jars filled with coffee beans at each place setting.

All the weekends spent designing place cards, deciding on lighting and tablecloths, had been worth it. It was their wedding day, and they were going to remember it forever.

There was a knock at the door. The makeup artist wasn't due for two hours. It was probably the bellboy delivering more wedding presents to be stacked on the dining table and delivered to their apartment after the wedding.

Rebecca opened the door, and Ben stood in the hallway. He had spent the night at their apartment, while she stayed in the Four Seasons bridal suite. It had been odd waking up alone, and she wasn't used to staying somewhere so luxurious. The few times they'd allowed themselves proper vacations since founding their company, it was more fun to stay at Airbnbs or quaint hotels where they could soak up the local culture.

But Rebecca had made herself give in and enjoy the beauty and luxury of the bridal suite decorated for Christmas. The walls were paneled wood, and the carpet was a thick wool, the seafoam green of the San Francisco Bay. A white grand piano stood next to the window and there was a Christmas tree strung with colored lights. Linen sofas faced each other and the stone fireplace was hung with stockings. Vases of red and white Christmas roses stood everywhere: on the bar, in the bedroom, and on the giant coffee table carved from the base of a redwood tree. How often would she have the chance to stay in a place this beautiful?

"Ben." Rebecca ushered him inside. "Are you all right? You look terrible."

Ben had left the rehearsal dinner early, saying he felt a migraine coming on and that he didn't want it to get worse. A sheen of perspiration stuck to his forehead, and his blue eyes, usually as bright as the bay on a clear day, were tired and missing their usual shine.

"I didn't sleep," he admitted.

He followed her inside and sat down on the sofa. Even when he was sick, he was still incredibly handsome. His light brown hair was parted to the side and he had a dimple on his cheek.

Ben had been the captain of the soccer team at UC Berkeley. When they'd first met—standing at the counter of a burger place near campus—the first thing Rebecca noticed was how muscular and athletic he was, with broad shoulders and strong thighs.

They'd both put in their order at the same time. Cheeseburgers with steak fries and mayonnaise instead of ketchup.

The waitress had picked up her notepad and glanced from Rebecca to Ben.

"Is this together?"

"No, we've never met." Rebecca shook her head and turned to Ben. "I hate ketchup. It's always too watery and the fries get soggy."

"Ketchup is the worst," Ben agreed solemnly. "I've lost an entire burger to ketchup that pools on the bottom of the plate."

The waitress finished scribbling on her notepad.

"Well, perhaps you should eat together."

That's when Rebecca glanced over at Ben and noticed his radiant smile. She knew right away that something important had happened. That she'd met someone who would change her life.

Ben almost never got sick. In all the years of building the company, he only had the flu once. Even then, he kept working until Rebecca threatened to call his mother to come and take care of him unless he put away his laptop. But this was different. He couldn't stand at the altar in his tuxedo if he was about to faint.

"Rebecca, we need to talk," he began.

He twisted his watchband, the way he did before having a difficult conversation. Rebecca used to think it was odd that Ben wore a watch when everything he did was on his phone. The watch wasn't about telling the time, it was like one of those rubber stress balls many CEOs kept on their desk.

He pushed his hair over his forehead. "I can't get married."

"I'll call Kimi. She invented this drink for when she's coming down with something before an important presentation. A seaweed and cauliflower-rice smoothie, with a spoonful of cocoa powder. It sounds awful, but it works." Rebecca rushed to find her phone.

Kimi had been Rebecca's best friend ever since Kimi was hired as a senior programmer at Dealbreakers.com. Rebecca and Kimi bonded over a love of shopping at the Anthropologie outlet store and drinking cold-brew coffee. Over the years they had shared everything. Kimi's nine-month-old daughter, Leila, had just started day care two days a week, and Kimi wanted to make sure she and her husband, Andy, stayed healthy.

"I mean I can't marry you ever." Ben looked up at her. His mouth sagged at the corners and his expression was anguished. "You must have seen it coming, Rebecca. We've both changed. We couldn't even agree on the number of guests to invite to our wedding."

Ben had wanted to get married in Grace Cathedral's main sanctuary followed by a reception for three hundred in the Four Seasons' grand ballroom. They were one of Silicon Valley's power couples, so it was expected that they have an over-the-top celebration. Rebecca had no problem with large groups; she had given countless speeches at tech conventions. But this wasn't an industry event, as it was their wedding. Finally, they agreed on fifty guests, but with a surprise musical guest. Adam Levine from Maroon 5 was scheduled to perform.

But Ben was right, they hadn't agreed on many things recently. For years, they lived frugally and poured all their money into the company. Lately, Ben was more interested in the trappings of success. He had ordered one of those German cars you built out online, and then took months to arrive. He wanted to put down a deposit on a penthouse in the newest skyscraper being built South of Market. Rebecca longed to buy a house near the water in Sausalito. Luckily, they both fell in love with a Bernadoodle puppy named Oliver, and it was impossible to have a dog when you lived thirty floors up in the sky. They compromised and made an offer on a sweet Victorian house in the Castro district.

Rebecca had always appreciated the simple things. Her bedside table held a forever-growing stack of books she was reading. Her favorite activity on the weekends was simply walking with Ben along the pier. And she was most excited about moving into a house because they could have a garden. But Ben hadn't minded before. It was only in the past few months that the things she enjoyed weren't enough for him.

They'd been together for most of their twenties. Of course they had changed. That didn't mean they'd stopped loving each other, Rebecca thought.

The words tried to register in her brain. Whatever Ben was going through could be fixed. As long as they faced it together.

"We can postpone the wedding and go to therapy. Kimi and Andy went through a rough period a year ago, and now they're happier than ever."

"You know I don't believe in therapy," Ben said. "And this isn't the kind of thing that can be fixed. I am sorry, Rebecca."

Rebecca was alarmed by the change in his voice. It was stern and almost businesslike. A heavy feeling settled on her chest. Once, she read that long-term relationships based on mutual love and respect didn't break up. Unless one of the couple fell in love. With someone else.

Ben had developed feelings for another woman. Rebecca knew exactly who.

"It's Natalie, isn't it?" she breathed.

Natalie Gordon was the head of legal. She had only been at the company less than a year, and even Rebecca was intimidated by her. Natalie had graduated from Duke undergrad and Columbia Law School. She'd even won Miss Teenage Louisiana, which she'd only entered so she could donate the prize money to charity.

Natalie was instrumental in their public offering, so it made sense that Natalie and Ben spent so much time together. Rebecca had noticed the proprietary air Natalie assumed about Ben when they were all in the conference room together. And there had been late meetings that Rebecca didn't attend. She had her own work, and there was often some wedding detail that she had to take care of.

She tried to think of any times when Ben and Natalie had been alone. There were a few Saturday mornings that Ben met Natalie at a café to talk strategy. Ben went jogging first, and he always invited Rebecca to join them. Rebecca declined; she was happy to spend the extra hours in bed and make her own leisurely coffee when she got up.

And there was one Friday night a couple of weeks ago, when Ben skipped their cherished Friday-night ritual of eating takeout and watching a cheesy movie on Netflix and worked late at the office. He had been so stressed, Rebecca hadn't said anything even though she was disappointed. Should Rebecca have volunteered to pick up the takeout and bring it to the office?

Had Natalie been with him then?

Why hadn't Rebecca noticed the cracks forming in their relationship, the differences in their goals, like hairline fractures in a piece of pottery? If she had, she could have tried to smooth them over before Natalie filled them in herself.

A thought flashed through her mind, and she pushed it away. If she hadn't insisted on doing the planning herself, would this wedding have gotten as far as it did?

Ben looked at her guiltily.

"It's nothing either of us planned. Natalie almost quit because she didn't want to come between us." He spread his hands in his lap. "I convinced her to stay. It wouldn't have helped." He hung his head. "The kind of thing Natalie and I have, it doesn't go away."

Suddenly, Rebecca was so angry, she could barely breathe.

"Of course you fell for Natalie. It's a chapter in a psychology textbook." Her eyes flamed. "The hotshot attorney who pushes a computer screen across the table promising you the payoff for all the years of twelve-hour days. It doesn't hurt that she looks like Hailee Steinfeld."

Rebecca hated commenting on another woman's looks. And she adored Hailee Steinfeld; she was a gifted actress. But she had to say something—Natalie had stolen her fiancé.

"It's not like that," Ben said quietly. "I thought you more than anyone would understand. Haven't we always said that the only thing we care about is each other's happiness?"

Rebecca felt as if she had been punched in the stomach. When they'd first started dating, Rebecca had confided her nervousness about getting serious. Her parents had divorced when she was ten. Her parents almost never fought, so it was a surprise to Rebecca. Later her father explained they got married too young. Her mother was in her last year in art school and her father was a newly graduated engineer. They grew apart until her mother fell in love and moved to a cattle farm in Argentina. It was just Rebecca and her father for a long time and Rebecca often felt lonely. It took years to repair her relationship with her mother and they still weren't close. When she was in her senior year of high school, her father remarried and now he lived in Seattle with his new wife and twin sons. Rebecca visited twice a year, but her father was usually too busy to spend quality time together.

Ben had simply kissed her and said he would never hurt her.

She believed him, and for the last eight years he had been her family.

They had solved so many crises together. There was the time when Dealbreakers.com was about to go under and they finally secured an investor. They had been about to sign the deal when they discovered a company in the investor's portfolio with questionable ethics. They spent two sleepless nights and went through six bags of Trader Joe's plantain chips, trying to decide what to do. Eventually, they decided to turn down the investor. It was better to let Dealbreakers fail than to be part of anything they didn't approve of.

And there had been crises outside the office too. Like when their beloved Biggles, the beagle mix they rescued from an animal shelter, had to be put down. They held each other so tightly, Rebecca thought she'd suffocate and choke on her own tears at the same time. It had taken until recently for either of them to be ready to get another dog.

This wasn't something they could solve together. Now it was Rebecca who was standing between Ben and what he wanted.

"How could you wait until today?" Rebecca demanded. "We're supposed to get married in six hours."

"I thought if I ignored my feelings, eventually they might go away," Ben sighed. "I finally came to terms with the fact that it was impossible at the rehearsal." He rubbed his chin. "I couldn't start our marriage by living a lie. I didn't want to tell you at the rehearsal dinner, I thought it would be better if we were alone."

Did that mean Ben was with Natalie last night? Had he gone home, or had he stayed at her place instead?

"Natalie and I are going to leave tonight for three weeks in

St. Barts," Ben said, as if he could read her mind. "Her parents rent a villa at a resort there every Christmas, and I found a last-minute flight. I'll e-mail the guests before we go. They all signed nondisclosure agreements about the wedding. None of this will leak out and affect the public offering. When we return, we can all get on with our lives."

Rebecca wanted to say she couldn't care less about the public offering. But it wouldn't help.

"We still haven't closed on the new house, I'm sure we can get out of it." Ben kept talking. "And you can have Oliver. Natalie doesn't like big dogs, and I know how much he already means to you."

They were supposed to pick up the new puppy when they returned from the honeymoon. Rebecca had pictures of him on her phone. His adorable black-and-white face, the white tip on his tail. Every time she looked at it, she felt happy. How would she look after a dog who would one day grow to be sixty pounds in their eight-hundred-square-foot apartment? She didn't care, it was love at first sight.

Ben stood up and walked to the door.

"I should go." He stuffed his hands in his pockets. "I'm really sorry, Rebecca. One day you'll see that it was the right thing to do."

And then he left, closing the door behind him.

The suite was completely quiet. The lights on the Christmas tree twinkled and Rebecca could smell pine needles and roses. She stood up and walked uncertainly into the bedroom. Her lace veil sat on the dressing table, and her shoes—the most romantic shoes she'd ever owned, satin sling-back heels with pearl-encrusted bows—stood next to the bed.

She sank down onto the floor and hugged the shoes to her chest.

Then she let the tears come, until her shoulders shook, her T-shirt was wet, and she thought she'd never stop sobbing.

An hour later, Kimi arrived. Rebecca had sent her a flurry of texts.

"So many men get cold feet before their wedding," Kimi said when Rebecca had repeated the whole story.

They sat in the suite's living room, drinking vodka and orange juice from the minibar. For once, Rebecca didn't care what the minibar cost. She only wanted something to numb the pain.

"And all couples disagree on things," Kimi continued. "You know how I felt about having a baby. Now I'd walk on hot coals to get Leila's favorite teddy bear if she dropped it."

Kimi's husband, Andy, was thirty-four and anxious to start a family. Kimi wanted children too, but she preferred to wait a few years. Her parents had emigrated from South Korea when Kimi was a baby so she could have every opportunity. Kimi had worked hard to get into UCLA, and then went to Stanford for her master's degree in computer science before accepting the position at Dealbreakers.com.

She didn't want to put a child in day care full-time, but she loved her job and cherished her time with Andy. They went to therapy and came to an agreement. Andy would work from home three days a week, and they'd leave Leila with Kimi's parents every Friday evening so they never missed a date night.

"You would not risk third-degree burns to give Leila her stuffed animal." Rebecca smiled for the first time since she'd spoken to Ben. "And Ben won't go to therapy. You work with Natalie every day; I can't compete with her."

In the magazine profiles about Ben and Rebecca, the writer

usually described Rebecca as "attractive" and "engaging." She had inherited her mother's fine light brown hair and her father's brown eyes. Her body was lean from years of running. But she couldn't compare to Natalie's beauty and charisma.

"Looks have nothing to do with love. I loved Andy even when he went to that barber in the Mission District and got a haircut that embarrassed his own mother."

"It's not just Natalie's looks, it's the way she carries herself," Rebecca reflected. "As if she knows how special she is, and everyone in the room should be grateful to be around her."

"That sounds exhausting," Kimi said sullenly. "Marriage isn't about winning some sort of prize. It's about doing the hard work together. The week after Leila was born, my boobs stuck to anything I was wearing, and I made coffee in the Instant Pot instead of the coffeemaker. We ate coffee-infused chicken and rice for days, neither of us could sleep because we were loaded up with caffeine. Finally, Andy insisted we order takeout and send our clothes to the cleaners. We spent the whole week holding Leila and watching *The Bachelor*. It was the best week of my life."

A pain shot through Rebecca's shoulders. She and Ben had wanted children. A girl and a boy, and a third baby if the first two were the same sex.

"I'm sorry." Kimi noticed Rebecca's expression. "Being a parent isn't all about those adorable winter jackets with ears, and cute booties with matching scarves in the Christmas windows at Macy's. Leila is teething. She's like a little beaver, I have bite marks on my shoulder."

Rebecca set her glass on the coffee table. Getting drunk would only delay the pain. It was better to feel it and get it over with.

"I don't want to be married to someone who doesn't love me,"

12 | ANITA HUGHES

Rebecca conceded. "But you can't imagine how it feels. In a few hours, the Four Seasons' white Rolls-Royce was supposed to take us to the church. The window would mist up because it's so cold outside, and I'd keep rubbing it with my glove because I wouldn't want to miss seeing the eighty-foot Christmas tree in Union Square or City Hall lit up for Christmas on my wedding day. At the reception, Ben was supposed to give a toast"—her eyes filled with tears—"and after the reception, we were to go down to the parking garage and get into the car for our honeymoon. The car was going to be a surprise for Ben. A silver 1963 Corvette that was used in a *Fast and Furious* movie. It took me ages to track it down." Rebecca kept talking, as if it was the only way to stop the images of her wedding day from disappearing forever. "It would be so late when we arrive at Christmas Cove Lodge that we'd both be tempted to crawl into bed. But when we were escorted to our suite, and we saw the crackling fire in the fireplace, and the tray of champagne, hot chocolate, and pumpkin bread on the coffee table, we would decide to stay up all night and talk about the wedding instead." She gulped. "By the time the fire would go out and we'd eaten the last bite of pumpkin bread, we'd fall asleep together on the sofa. I'd still be in my going-away outfit and Ben would be wearing his tuxedo. Except without the tie," she finished bravely. "Ben hates wearing a tie. He'd probably take it off the minute the reception ended."

Kimi ran her fingernails over the rim of her glass.

"You can still go on the honeymoon. There's no point staying in San Francisco," Kimi suggested. "Instead of listening to tourists ring the bells of the cable cars all day, you can relax in an indoor Jacuzzi overlooking the lake."

"I can't go on my honeymoon alone," Rebecca objected.

Kimi jumped up. Her sleek black hair swayed at her shoulders and she paced around the room.

"I'll go with you. Andy is off all week, he can take care of Leila." Her tone grew excited. "We'll go snowshoeing and eat at those funky little diners where they don't even have a menu, and the cook serves whatever he likes."

"The suite only has one bed," Rebecca said doubtfully.

But deep down, she knew it was a good idea. She wasn't ready to go back to the apartment. And she didn't want to be alone in San Francisco at Christmas. Her mother hadn't even come for the wedding. She was going to watch it on FaceTime from Argentina. Rebecca had been upset; she'd even offered to buy plane tickets for her mother and her husband, Carlos. Her mother explained it wasn't the cost. Carlos had injured his back and couldn't sit in a plane for so many hours. Carlos was in a lot of pain, and her mother didn't want to leave him. Her father and his family had come for the wedding, but they were treating it like a Christmas vacation. They were so busy sightseeing, she had barely seen them. In the morning they were leaving to spend a few days in Carmel before returning to Seattle.

"I'd be happy to share the bed, or I can take the sofa," Kimi said cheerfully. "Anything will be better than sleeping with a bit of drool on the sheets and waking up with a crick in my neck because I fell asleep while I was nursing."

Why shouldn't Rebecca use their reservation for a vacation? Lake Tahoe was her favorite place in the world. It had been her idea to spend their honeymoon there. Ben had wanted to go skiing in the French Alps, or rent an overwater bungalow in Tahiti with a Plexiglas floor, so you could see all the fish.

Rebecca didn't want to do something so extravagant when they were buying a house and paying off Ben's new car and also had all the expenses of a new puppy. And Lake Tahoe was special to them. It was where they'd gotten engaged two summers ago.

It had been the Fourth of July weekend. They'd spent three nights at a charming Airbnb. On the last evening, Ben packed a picnic and they ate it on the shores of the lake. He chose all their favorite foods: focaccia and tomatoes and mozzarella with pesto.

"We don't have the time or money to go to Lake Como in Italy, so I thought we could have an Italian picnic instead," he'd said, filling two glasses with cabernet.

It was almost sunset, and the lake was infused with a pink-and-gold light. A layer of fog settled on the water, and the air smelled of primroses and pansies.

"I can't think of anyplace I'd rather be," Rebecca said as she stretched her legs.

They had spent the whole day bicycling around the lake. Her calves ached, her shoulders were slightly sunburned, and she'd never felt so happy.

"You have to try the dessert." Ben handed her a white ceramic cup. "It's tiramisu. The bakery on Main Street uses all local ingredients."

Rebecca ate the tiramisu. At the bottom of the cup were the words "Will you marry me?"

She put her hand over her mouth and gasped. They had talked about getting married for a while, but there was always so much to do.

"I know we said we wouldn't think about getting married until we felt the company was stable"—Ben was kneeling on the picnic blanket—"but I don't care if we never travel farther than here, or if we live in the same one-bedroom apartment for the rest of our lives. All I want and need is right in front of me." He took a velvet box out of his pocket. "You make me happier than I ever thought possible. Rebecca Huntley, will you marry me?"

Rebecca nodded yes, and Ben slipped the diamond solitaire ring on her finger. Then they kissed for so long, her lips were numb. They only parted when a pigeon came dangerously close and threatened to eat the leftover pesto.

How had Ben gone from arranging something so simple and sweet to wanting products and experiences that were promoted by influencers with millions of followers? And how had he fallen in love with Natalie? Most importantly, how had she missed the signs?

"You can spend the whole week crying on my shoulder," Kimi said, interrupting her thoughts. "That's what a mother's shoulder is for." She grinned.

Rebecca stood up and hugged her friend.

"I'd love to go together, and I promise I won't cry." She wiped her eyes deliberately. "How can I, when I'm lucky enough to spend Christmas week with my best friend in Christmas Cove?"

Chapter Two

Rebecca and Kimi drove to Christmas Cove in Kimi's car. Kimi apologized for the plush animal toys that could practically fill a cage at the zoo and were scattered over the seats.

"It's a wonderful way to introduce Leila to animals from different countries," Kimi said, removing an orange-and-gold lynx and a black bear from the passenger seat. "But the subscription service sends five animals a month. I already have a family of Siberian musk deer and three mandarin ducks. We're running out of room; I may have to cancel the subscription."

Rebecca didn't mind the toys. And she was grateful for the heated seats when the temperature dropped as soon as they left the city. She tried not to think about the honeymoon playlist she had put together with her and Ben's favorite artists; Beyoncé, Drake, Ed Sheeran. Instead, she focused on the changing landscape and the winter setting sun that turned the sky a buttery shade of yellow.

Christmas Cove's website described it as "the brightest little town on the shores of Lake Tahoe during the holiday season," and when they arrived, as the clock in the village square chimed 5:00

p.m., and the storefronts turned on their lights, Rebecca wasn't disappointed.

Lights twinkled everywhere. Silver lights were entwined in the lampposts and looped around old-fashioned street signs. The skating rink was ablaze with lights, and Santa Claus's sleigh was painted fire-engine red and trimmed with gold and silver light bulbs.

Rebecca pressed her face against the glass to take it all in. There was a chocolate shop and a bakery and a gift shop, the window of which was crammed with wrapped boxes. A giant Christmas tree stood in the middle of the square. It was strung with ornaments of candy canes and snow skis and topped with a gold-and-white star.

"At midnight on Christmas Eve, carolers sing Christmas carols in the pergola," Rebecca said, pointing to a white structure in the middle of the square. "They serve hot toddies for the adults, and hot chocolate and gingerbread cookies for the children. Santa Claus makes an appearance and all the children get so excited to see him."

Rebecca remembered how excited she'd been about the Christmas events.

"On Christmas Day, the diner on Main Street serves a special Christmas breakfast: sweet potato hash with eggs and sausages, French toast made with real maple syrup, and pancakes with blueberries," she said.

"Since Leila was born, breakfast at our house is coffee and cereal straight out of the box. It takes too long to make a bowl of cereal." Kimi sighed.

Couples strolled hand in hand along the sidewalk, and the restaurants began to fill up with young families eating early dinners. Rebecca bit her lip. It wouldn't help to feel sorry for herself; she could have done that alone in her apartment.

The car pulled into a long driveway. At the end was a two-story wooden building with a peaked roof. A fir tree was decorated with Christmas ornaments and there was a wraparound porch.

A bellhop in a red uniform opened the car doors. Rebecca caught a glimpse of a boat dock and the path that led down to the lake. Even at night, the view was glorious. The water was inky black, and the surrounding mountains were a powdery white. A wooden steamboat chugged along the shore, and there was a forest of pine trees.

"Oh, it's beautiful," Rebecca breathed.

For a moment she forgot Ben and Natalie, she forgot the guests who a few hours ago had received the e-mail canceling the wedding, and she even forgot the feeling of desperation and grief when she gathered her overnight bag and shut the door of the bridal suite.

Lake Tahoe at Christmas was even more stunning than during the summer.

The lobby had tall windows overlooking the lake. The ceiling was timbered wood and the stone floors were covered with red carpets. A huge fireplace took up one wall and deep, comfy sofas were scattered around the room. The Christmas tree was at least fifteen feet high and the smell of pine needles filled the air. There was a wooden front desk and, in the corner, Rebecca caught sight of the bar.

Rebecca gave her name to the bellhop and he led them to their suite without stopping at the front desk. She took a glance around the space—high ceilings and a fireplace in the living room, a king-size bed with a quilted headboard in the bedroom, a picture window overlooking the lake—and allowed herself a small sigh.

Ben would have loved the clawfoot bathtub and spa shower in the bathroom.

After the bellhop left, Kimi poured a cup of hot chocolate spiked with brandy and handed it to Rebecca.

"I'd join you, but first I have to pump." Kimi sat on the sofa in the living room. "When you're pregnant, no one tells you how difficult pumping is. It's all the work of breastfeeding, with none of the satisfaction of hearing Leila burp or having her snuggle against me."

Rebecca sipped the hot chocolate and looked worriedly at her friend.

"I shouldn't have taken you away from Leila on her first Christmas."

"That's the beauty of babies, they don't remember anything of their first year." Kimi waved her hand. "Andy will understand, he knows that we're best friends. That's what best friends do for each other. Besides, it's not as if Andy and Leila will be alone. During the holidays, we're always racing between our families—it's a Christmas version of the Indy 500. You're saving me from a week at the gym working off Christmas dinner. All the relatives bring a dish to my parents' house: kalbi, which are Korean BBQ ribs; pajeon, which are green onion pancakes; and japchae, which are sweet potato noodles."

Rebecca had reserved a sunset sleigh ride followed by Christmas dinner at Christmas Cove's nicest restaurant. Dinner came with a complimentary bottle of champagne and a special gift for the couple.

How were Ben and Natalie going to celebrate Christmas? The resort in St. Barts probably served a buffet on the beach with cocktails served with paper umbrellas. Or they'd have a candlelit dinner on their terrace overlooking the ocean, and afterward they'd walk barefoot on the sand.

She had to stop thinking about Ben and Natalie.

Rebecca went into the bedroom to unpack. She stacked her books on the bedside table and hung her dresses in the closet.

"I finally got through to Andy." Kimi stood at the door. "Leila's teething is worse. Andy's been trying to get her to stop crying for hours. He can't take her to my parents' house. My mother's aunt and uncle are visiting from South Korea. They want to meet Leila, but they just arrived and have terrible jet lag. Andy wants to wait until tomorrow to see them. And Andy's mother is hopeless with babies. She's terrified of dropping her."

Rebecca folded her sweaters into the drawer.

"You have to do what's best for Leila. You have to go back to San Francisco."

"I can't." Kimi shook her head. "I promised I'd be with you."

"And you did. If you hadn't suggested it, I'd be sitting in my apartment, drinking straight bourbon and deciding which of Ben's clothes I should donate to Goodwill." Rebecca smiled thinly. "Instead, I'm in a gorgeous suite facing the lake. The bed has a goose down comforter, and the TV has every streaming service available. If I run out of books to read, I can borrow more from the lodge's library. And when I get tired of walking around Christmas Cove, I'll rent one of those fat-tire bikes and explore the lake shore."

"You'll be alone on what's supposed to be your honeymoon at Christmas," Kimi said doubtfully. "You're my best friend, I can't desert you."

"I'm your boss and Leila's godmother," Rebecca said with a smile. "You have to do what I say."

"Are you sure?" Kimi asked.

"Perfectly sure." Rebecca nodded with more courage than she felt. "If you leave now, you won't even have to pump again." She returned to the living room and handed Kimi a bottle of wine. "Take this to Andy as a Christmas present."

"I'll FaceTime you every day," Kimi said and hugged Rebecca. "You can always stay at our house if you get lonely. We don't have a guest room, and the adult furniture in the living room has been replaced by a tummy time activity mat, but we're happy to have you."

Kimi left and Rebecca returned to the bedroom. She hadn't eaten anything since breakfast and she was hungry.

She'd do her hair and makeup and go to the lodge's restaurant.

There was a sound in the living room. Kimi must have forgotten something. Or the bellboy had knocked and she hadn't heard him.

A man of about sixty stood in front of the fireplace. He was very tall, with gray eyes and salt-and-pepper hair. An overcoat was slung over his arm, and he wore a red Christmas sweater and loafers.

"Who are you, and what are you doing here?" Rebecca asked.

"I could ask you the same question," the man replied. "This is my suite."

"You must be mistaken," Rebecca objected. "I checked in an hour ago."

He held up an old-fashioned room key. "I have the key right here. The Santa Claus suite. I booked it through New Year's."

Rebecca picked up the house phone. There must be some mix-up. She had specifically asked for the Santa Claus suite.

"I'm afraid Mr. Brewster is correct," the man at the front desk said. "Mr. Cole called a few hours ago and canceled your reservation. We called Mr. Brewster and he paid for the week in advance. He's been trying to book a room for weeks."

"There must be another available suite," Rebecca insisted.

"There isn't an available room on Lake Tahoe," the man apologized. "I'm terribly sorry, the bellhop shouldn't have taken you directly to the suite without checking you in first."

Kimi had driven back in her car; Rebecca didn't even have a way to get back to San Francisco.

She hung up and turned around. She had almost forgotten the man standing by the fireplace.

"Howard Brewster." He held out his hand. "I take it the front desk agreed with me."

"Rebecca Huntley." She shook his hand, but she wasn't listening. She glanced down at her phone. There was a text from Ben saying he called the lodge and canceled their booking. He must have sent it while they were driving and Rebecca hadn't seen it. Would she have come to Lake Tahoe if she had? And what would she do now that she was here?

"It looks like you need another one of these." Howard poured a shot of brandy from a bottle on the sideboard. "Drink this; I'll join you."

"No thank you." Rebecca shook her head. "I've had too much to drink already."

"Then why don't you sit down and tell me what's wrong," Howard said kindly. "I lead travel groups all over the world. I'm good at listening to people's problems."

Rebecca wasn't used to confiding in strangers, but suddenly it was all too much. She had been so hopeful when she arrived, and now she was stranded with no place to stay. She sank down on the sofa and let it all pour out. The months of wedding planning, Natalie, and Ben's betrayal. Her entire future being pulled from under her.

"I'm sorry. I guess that's why I've never married," Howard said when she finished. "You can be in love, but how do you know if the other person feels the same?"

Rebecca had been a psychology major. It was one of the reasons she felt confident about starting Dealbreakers with Ben. Ben ran a successful car wash business during high school and had interned at a tech start-up while at college, so he had some entrepreneurial experience. And Ben's roommate, Brian, was a genius at computer programming. Rebecca prided herself on being familiar with the human side of the business. She loved psychology and spent years learning how to understand people. But she had missed the signs in front of her.

Is that what always happened in a relationship? You concentrate on the special moments, the ones that made you feel meant for each other—like the year when she and Ben gave each other the exact same Valentine's Day card—and brushed away the ones that were a warning that something was wrong. Usually on Halloween, Rebecca and Ben attended a Halloween party and wore matching costumes. This year, they had been swamped at work and decided not to attend any parties. If they had, what would they have worn and would that have been a sign that something was off between them?

"I've had a rotten day myself," Howard said as he sipped his brandy. "Every year for the last twenty years I've hosted a New Year's Party on the night after New Year's Eve. In the beginning, I held it on New Year's Eve, but people often had other plans so now it's on the following night. It's my favorite event of the year and I always look forward to it. This year it's at the log cabin I just bought on the lake. Yesterday, my party planner broke her leg and had to cancel. I've got six days to turn the cabin's boathouse into a winter wonderland. The main house is being remodeled, and I can't stay there. So I need this suite."

Just then, the room's phone rang. Rebecca picked it up.

"Ms. Huntley, it's Gerald at the front desk," the man said. "I've been thinking . . . we hate to disappoint our guests. The lodge has a converted equipment room. You have to climb a ladder to the loft to reach the bed, but it's heated and there's a bathroom. You're welcome to stay there."

"Thank you," Rebecca said into the receiver. "I'll think about it and call you back."

Rebecca hung up and told Howard what Gerald said.

"It's a nice offer, but it has a sleeping loft and I'm afraid of heights." She sighed.

"You said you planned your entire wedding yourself," Howard remarked.

"Even the nuts sprinkled on the ice cream sundaes." Rebecca nodded ruefully.

She'd spent an entire afternoon sampling different kinds of nuts. Roasted pistachios tasted the best, but the green clashed with strawberry ice cream. Finally, she settled on pecans. They went with all ice cream flavors and were perfect for Christmas.

"I have an idea," he said as he rubbed his chin. "If you plan my New Year's Night party, I'll stay in the equipment room and you can have the suite."

Rebecca's eyes widened. Howard was a stranger; why would he make such an offer?

"The vendors have been hired; they just need to be supervised," Howard continued. "I'm going to be busy with the remodeling all week, and I'm hopeless at that kind of thing."

"I've never planned a party for someone else, and I don't know anything about you," Rebecca protested. "Is the party for family and friends, or business associates? Will there be dancing, and what are the most important things to you?"

Howard set his glass on the coffee table.

"I don't have any family. I give the party every year for my friends and as a thank-you to all the people I work with." Howard ticked items off on his fingers. "There will be a DJ, as the boathouse isn't big enough for a band. I've hired someone to set off fireworks from the dock. The most important thing is that the guests have a good time. Isn't that the reason anyone throws a party?"

Ben and Rebecca had loved having parties. They'd had a housewarming party when they moved into their apartment, even though the space was so small. The guests ended up hanging out on the staircase. Last year, Rebecca threw Ben a surprise party at their favorite Thai restaurant. He expected a surprise party when he turned thirty, so she decided to hold it a year early.

A party was an expression of love. That's why planning their wedding had been the most important thing in the world.

Perhaps planning Howard's New Year's party would keep her mind off Ben and Natalie.

"We just met; how can you trust me?" Rebecca wondered.

"You don't look like someone who would run off with my Christmas ornaments," Howard chuckled. "And anyway, I believe in chance, especially at Christmas."

Rebecca would have to stay in Christmas Cove an extra night but there was nothing waiting for her in San Francisco.

For the first time since Ben walked out of the bridal suite, Rebecca felt a pinprick of excitement. She held out her hand.

"You have a deal."

Howard had a firm handshake. "Great! And I'll tell the front desk about the switch, as well, so they can find you if need be. We'll start in the morning. I have a feeling it's going to be a good Christmas after all."

Howard left, and Rebecca walked through the lobby to the hotel's restaurant. Thankfully, Ben hadn't canceled her dinner reservation. He must have forgotten about it.

The kitchen was open to the dining room, which had floor-to-ceiling windows. The fireplace was hung with stockings, and a sideboard was set with silver serving dishes and crystal wineglasses. A white Christmas tree stood in the corner and there was a fish tank with all kinds of fish.

Rebecca stood near the hostess's desk and waited for her table. The other diners were festively dressed, and she was glad she wore the green velvet dress she'd bought for the honeymoon. She paired it with ballerina flats and a silver bracelet.

A dark-haired man about her age caught her attention. He wore a white shirt and thin black tie and was standing near the bar. Their eyes met and they recognized each other at the same time.

"Rebecca Huntley, this is a surprise." He approached her. "It's nice to see you."

His name was Zach Mason and they had been in the same film class her senior year at UC Berkeley. Rebecca needed four credits in the arts to graduate. She signed up for an introductory film course, but had been placed in the advanced class instead. Zach was the only student who didn't completely ignore her. She remembered him as being quite handsome. He had worn his hair a little longer than now, and he had hazel eyes under thick lashes.

"I'm surprised you remember," she said. "It was a long time ago."

"We made that film together," he reminded her. "It won the award for best editing."

"No one wanted to be my partner," she recalled, smiling. "You let me assist you on location. If it wasn't for you, I wouldn't have graduated."

Zach smiled back at her.

"I read an article about you and Ben online. Your company is a huge success and you were getting married." He glanced down at her left hand. "You must be here on your honeymoon."

Rebecca had forgotten to take off her engagement ring!

She'd probably never see Zach again. And this wasn't the time or place to tell the whole story. It would be easier to tell a little white lie, and less painful.

"We just arrived." She nodded. She turned the conversation onto Zach. "Are you staying here?"

Zach glanced around the dining room. He sat down at an empty table. "I was about to have dinner."

Rebecca was about to ask about his films when a woman appeared next to her. She was in her forties and attractive, with thick auburn hair and blue eyes. She wore a red silk blouse and a long, flowing skirt.

"Meredith Moran." She shook Rebecca's hand and sat opposite Zach. She smiled coyly at Zach. "I'm sorry I took so long. Did you order without me?"

Zach pushed his hair over his forehead.

"Not yet," he said, picking up the menu.

"Good, I never order until I hear the specials." She turned from Zach to Rebecca. "Though they're always overpriced. The chef buys too many steaks and it becomes a special at twice the cost of anything else."

"I'm sure that's not the case," Zach said hastily.

"So, tell me," Meredith said, turning her attention to Rebecca, "how do you two know each other?"

"Rebecca and I were at college together," Zach answered for her. "We haven't seen each other in years."

The hostess approached Rebecca, and she excused herself.

She remembered the last time she saw Zach. He asked if she wanted to grab a burger after their last day of filming, but he never showed up. Ben had been at the burger place and they got into the discussion about ketchup and mayonnaise. Zach had been kind and good-looking; she may have had a small crush on him. But then she and Ben fell in love, and she never thought about Zach again.

Her phone rang and she hoped it was Ben.

"Rebecca, it's your father," a male voice said over the line. "I got the e-mail about the wedding being postponed. I tried calling you earlier."

"I'm in Lake Tahoe. The reception isn't very good up here," Rebecca answered.

"You and Ben are in Lake Tahoe?" her father asked.

Her father and Ben had only met a few times, but he had admired Ben's ambition and focus. Rebecca didn't want to tell him everything that happened.

"I'm alone," she said into the phone. "Ben and I broke up."

The phone line went quiet. Rebecca hoped that her father would say that he and his family would join her, or invite her to go with them to Carmel.

"I'm sorry. I want to hear all about it," he said after the short silence. "Jane and I are leaving with the kids in the morning. I'll come back to San Francisco soon and you and I can catch up."

Rebecca hung up and glanced around the restaurant. Christmas music played over the speakers and the scent of roasted vegetables drifted from the kitchen. Every table was filled with couples and families. Even Zach was having dinner with an attractive older woman.

The air was charged with the anticipation of waking up on Christmas morning and sharing presents and hot apple cider with family and loved ones. Rebecca felt like she was the only guest at Christmas Cove Lodge who was completely alone.

Chapter Three

Zach loosened his tie and sank onto a stool at the lodge's bar.

It was almost midnight on Christmas Eve and the last guests had finally finished eating.

Zach couldn't wait to go to bed. At least he didn't have to get up early. His next shift wasn't until the following evening.

Zach's older brother Cory thought Zach was crazy to work over Christmas. Zach should be home with the family. But Zach's parents lived in San Diego, and Zach didn't have the time or money to visit. He needed to finish the film by the contest deadline in January. If he didn't, he had promised himself he'd set aside his film camera forever and join his father and Cory running the family sports camp. His father had started the camp when Cory was born, and Zach worked there over the summers during high school. But he never enjoyed it, and it was the last thing he wanted to do now. His father and Cory didn't need him. They'd only be including him because he failed at filmmaking and couldn't figure out what else he wanted to do.

God, what a mess he'd made of the night.

Seeing Rebecca after all these years, looking even more beautiful than he remembered and knowing she was so successful, made him act like an idiot. Instead of admitting that he was a waiter, he told her he was meeting someone for dinner. He sat down at an empty table, and it wasn't until that stranger introduced herself to Rebecca that he realized the table was occupied and the diner had only gone to the ladies' room.

Thank God the woman named Meredith had played along. It had still been embarrassing. And what if he bumped into Rebecca again?

Zach sipped his glass of water and reflected over the last eight years. His career had started off so well. After graduation, he received a grant to shoot a film in France. From there, he'd made films in Berlin, and for a while he was involved in the film community in Prague. But getting your film screened at international festivals didn't pay anything. Eventually the grants dried up and he packed up his gear and returned to California.

Now he was in Christmas Cove because Sofia Coppola, the renowned director, owned a cabin on Lake Tahoe. Every year, she held a contest for aspiring filmmakers. First prize was twenty thousand dollars and a chance to have the film produced by Coppola's production company.

At the same time, Zach was volunteering at Christmas Cove's community kitchen. It provided free hot meals to children at the local schools. Zach was making a film about the kitchen in order to attract more sponsors.

His boss, Edward, appeared in the doorway. Edward was in his fifties, with dark eyes and a perpetual frown.

"Zach, I'm glad I found you." Edward approached him. "I need to talk to you."

Zach gulped. He'd heard from other waiters that Edward only wanted to talk to you when you were in trouble.

"I saw you sitting at a table with a guest," Edward continued. "That's against the rules."

"I wasn't dining with her; I didn't even know it was her table."

"That doesn't make it better." Edward's eyes narrowed. "When you're working, you should either be in the kitchen waiting for plates or delivering the plates to the tables."

Edward had hired Zach even though Zach's experience was limited to working at a pub in Prague. But it was the Christmas rush and he'd needed a waiter.

Now Edward was probably ready to fire him. Zach's only option was to tell the truth.

"I was waiting for an order of drinks at the bar, when I noticed a woman I had known in college. I hadn't seen her in years and she's really successful." He smiled as if he and Edward were old friends. "I couldn't let her think I'm a waiter. I said I was meeting someone for dinner and sat down at an empty table. At least, I thought it was empty, but Meredith was in the ladies' room."

Zach wished he had a cocktail. Edward was staring at him and he didn't look happy.

"Do you always know the names of strangers?"

"Meredith introduced herself." He gulped. "For some reason, she thought it would be fun to play along."

"Probably so she can give a more interesting one-star review on Yelp," Edward barked. "I'm sorry, Zach, you're fired. And you'll need to leave the employee housing."

Zach's stomach dropped. He wished he had ordered a drink while he still had the employee discount.

"I know it was wrong, and I promise it won't happen again," Zach begged. "You said yourself, the lodge is understaffed."

"My nephew just arrived from Oregon. He's happy to take your place." Edward stood up to make it clear the conversation was over. "If you leave a forwarding address, we'll send your last check in the mail."

Edward left and Zach rested his elbows on the bar. Even if he could afford a room, there probably wasn't another place to stay in Lake Tahoe. But he couldn't leave Christmas Cove, he had commitments. Besides the film contest, the community kitchen was depending on him.

He had no one but himself to blame. Seeing Rebecca in that green velvet dress, her light brown hair falling to her shoulders, made the last eight years fall away. He remembered when they met on the first day of the advanced film seminar.

"Try not to look so anxious. Film professors can smell fear," Zach whispered to the girl sitting next to him. "It's how they keep the class size down. They fix newcomers with an icy stare until they give up and switch courses."

Zach knew almost everyone else in the room; they'd all been in film classes together since freshman year. This girl was new. She wore a summery yellow dress and sandals, and her light brown hair was scooped into a ponytail.

"I'm not supposed to be here," the girl groaned. "I signed up for introductory film and ended up in this class instead."

Somehow she was even prettier when she frowned. Her brown eyes widened and her mouth curled down.

"Everyone is looking at me as if I crashed a party," she continued. "There's nothing I can do; it's the only section that fits my schedule."

"It's the way you're dressed," he commented.

"What am I supposed to wear?" the girl asked.

Zach pointed to his own dark-colored shorts and black T-shirt.

"Most filmmakers wear black because they can't afford a lot of clothes. I own two black T-shirts. One to wear and one to toss into the laundry."

"Well, I don't have anything black, and I can't afford new clothes," she shot back.

"Zach Mason." He held out his hand and smiled. "For what it's worth, I like your dress. Filmmakers can also be gloomy. We need some bright colors around here."

"Rebecca Huntley." She shook his hand. Her frown faded and she smiled back. "Making films seems so hard, so why do you do it?"

Zach didn't even have to think about it.

"Most of the time, it's the most frustrating activity in the world. On location, it's either too bright or too windy, and you worry that you'll never get the footage you need. Then you spend double the amount of time budgeted in the editing suite, and everything you think was good ends up in the deleted file on your computer. At the end of the day, you're tired and hungry and you resolve to choose any other career." He fiddled with his laptop. "Just when you've given up hope, you click on a scene that comes straight from your heart, and you can't wait to share it with an audience. That's when you know you're doomed. Nothing else could ever feel so good."

Zach could kick himself. Rebecca had asked a simple question and he'd rambled on like an anxious schoolboy.

After class, Rebecca was the first to leave. Zach slowly gathered his things. They probably wouldn't sit near each other again and he'd missed his chance to learn anything about her.

But when he walked outside, she was sitting under a tree, reading a book.

"I take it you didn't like the class," he said, joining her. "You couldn't leave fast enough."

"It wasn't the professor; it was the other students. When the professor announced we had to work in pairs, they avoided me as if I had the chicken pox."

Zach tried to hide his smile. She hadn't left because of him.

"We can work together," he offered.

"I can't let you do that, you're the only person who's been nice to me." She shook her head. "I'll bring down your grade."

"You can assist me on location," he offered. "Anything that doesn't work can be fixed in the editing suite."

Relief flooded her features and she smiled.

"If you really don't mind," she said eagerly.

He wanted to stay and talk to her, but he had to get to his next class. He'd get to know her better when they were filming.

"We'll start tomorrow," he suggested.

"It's a deal," she said and put down her book. "I don't know how to thank you."

The sun reflected on her tan shoulders, and Zach felt the beginning of something new. For the first time, since she sat next to him, his confidence returned.

He slung his backpack over his shoulder.

"I promise that by the end of the semester you'll love filmmaking as much as I do."

* * *

Footsteps sounded behind him, and Zach pulled his mind to the present.

Meredith approached the bar. She had changed out of the blouse and skirt she wore at dinner into slacks and a sweater. A scarf was wrapped around her neck and she wore après-ski boots.

"I saw the manager, he didn't look happy," she said, joining him. "I hope I didn't get you into trouble."

"I got myself into trouble," Zach sighed. "Edward fired me. And I lost my housing. It's my fault; it's against the rules to sit with guests."

"Oh dear, I was afraid that might happen." Meredith sat on a stool. "I should have known right away by the suit he was wearing. Anyone who uses so much starch is bound to be uptight."

Zach smiled despite himself. He looked at Meredith curiously.

"Why did you play along?"

Meredith set her purse on the bar. She had long, pink finger-nails and smelled of a floral perfume.

"I recognized you when you were standing by the bar. You might not remember, but we met briefly at a film festival in Brussels. My ex-husband is a film producer and one of your films was being screened."

Zach had a film accepted to the Brussels Film Festival two years ago. After the screening, many people congratulated him and he thought it was going to be his ticket to Hollywood. But no one picked it up and the film ended up gathering dust with his other projects.

"I don't expect you to remember me. You had lots of admirers," she said, as if reading his mind. "Tonight I was only having some fun. And I thought I was helping. You didn't look like someone who would lie without a good reason."

"I hardly ever lie, but I couldn't tell Rebecca I was a waiter." Zach fiddled with his water glass. "The last time we saw each other, I was twenty-two and on my way to Europe with a grant and a promising film career. Now I'm thirty, and I've got nothing to show for the last eight years except a few awards and posters from film festivals."

"There's nothing wrong with being a waiter," Meredith countered. "I live in Beverly Hills. Everyone in Los Angeles is a waiter-slash-scriptwriter, or a waiter-slash-actor. Some have two slashes. My hairdresser is a waiter-slash-hairstylist-slash-costume designer."

"I agree, but I gave myself a deadline," Zach said. "I entered a filmmaking contest. If I don't win, I'm going to quit filmmaking and work for my family's company."

"You should never give up doing what you love," she counseled. "Then you stop being who you are."

"I can't live on rice and beans forever," he sighed. "And it's too cold to sleep in my car. I'm going to have to beg every business in Christmas Cove for a job and a place to stay."

Meredith studied Zach thoughtfully.

"I doubt anyone is hiring, it's already the last week in December. I have a two-bedroom suite at Christmas Cove Lodge through New Year's. You can stay with me. I don't usually do this sort of thing with strangers, but we have met before. I know how hard it is to be a filmmaker."

A blush crept over Zach's cheeks. Meredith was attractive but even if he was interested, he didn't have time for a relationship.

Meredith noticed his expression.

"I didn't mean romantically," she assured him. "You're too young for me, and anyway, I've sworn off men for a while. I'm going through my second divorce."

"You don't look old enough for two divorces," Zach said gallantly.

"I'm forty-three. My first marriage didn't work out," Meredith said. "The second time was my fault entirely, I should never have married Josh in the first place." She squared her shoulders. "But I refuse to be lonely. That's why I have Buttons."

"Buttons?" Zach repeated, puzzled.

"My Yorkie. That's why I saw you just now, sitting at the bar. I brought Buttons back from his walk."

"It's a kind offer, but I can't accept." Zach smiled and shook his head.

"I told you, I feel guilty," Meredith urged. "And I don't need such a big suite. I only took it because it's all they had and I didn't want to spend Christmas in Los Angeles. You can't have a proper Christmas with palm trees, and sand between your toes."

Zach usually didn't mind rooming with strangers. Living in Europe, he often had roommates of both sexes. This was different. He was accepting charity.

"I'll tell you what," Meredith said, as if reading his mind. "You can walk Buttons for me. Buttons gets up early, and I like to sleep in. It's the only thing Buttons and I disagree on."

The opportunity was too good to pass up.

"All right, I accept." Zach nodded.

Meredith reached into her purse and took out a key.

"It's the Reindeer suite," she said, handing it to him. "I'll get another key from the front desk while you get your things."

The Reindeer suite was furnished in whites and blues. A white Christmas tree was decorated with silver and blue ornaments and there was a glass dining table with blue upholstered chairs. The bedrooms were on opposite sides of the living room and Zach was amazed to find his own bathroom, complete with thick, white towels and a navy robe.

For a moment, he wondered which suite Rebecca and Ben were staying in. Then he put the thought out of his mind. There wasn't time to think about Rebecca.

He set his computer on a desk and tossed his bag in the closet. The only good thing about being fired was he now had all day to work on his film.

He had planned on staying awake until Meredith appeared, but the bed was too tempting and he was tired.

He stripped off his shirt and climbed under the soft, white comforter. Then he closed his eyes and, for the first time since he arrived in Christmas Cove and entered the contest, he let himself relax.

Early the next morning, Zach headed out of the lodge toward the lake. Early morning was his favorite time of day. Wherever he was, he started it the same way; with the darkest coffee he could find and some kind of sweet pastry. It didn't matter if it was day-old doughnuts wrapped in cellophane and sold at the counter of Dunkin Donuts for half price, or a flaky chocolate croissant from a patisserie in Paris. The caffeine and sugar were essential to allow him to spend the next six hours at his computer.

But today, the coffee and pastry would have to wait. He'd promised Meredith he would take Buttons for a walk. Buttons was the smallest dog he had ever seen. He was dressed in a red snow-flake sweater and red booties, and when he walked next to Zach, the bell around his neck tinkled.

He bent down to pick Buttons up and almost collided with a woman wearing pink running shoes.

"Zach!" Rebecca said. "What are you doing here? And what a sweet dog."

"His name is Buttons," Zach said.

Zach noticed how pretty Rebecca looked in the daylight. Her cheeks were flushed from the cold, and she wore gray jogging pants and a ribbed turtleneck.

"I love dogs. Somehow I pictured you as someone with a bigger dog. Something more . . . masculine." Rebecca reached out and petted Buttons. She smiled teasingly and he wondered whether she was flirting.

But Rebecca was married; he was imagining things.

"Buttons belongs to Meredith," Zach said before he could stop himself.

Zach hadn't meant to mention Meredith. But if Rebecca and Ben were staying at Christmas Cove Lodge, they'd probably run into each other. And he couldn't tell Rebecca he'd been fired, when he had lied about being a waiter. He would have to keep up the charade.

For a moment, Rebecca seemed shocked. Then she quickly recovered herself.

"Last night, I thought you were having dinner. I didn't realize you were staying here."

"We're staying in the Reindeer suite," he went on, setting Buttons down. "There's a Christmas sing-along in the village square this afternoon followed by fireworks over the lake. You and Ben should go."

"Actually, Ben had to go back to San Francisco," Rebecca replied. "It's a work thing, he'll be back in a few days."

Zach was about to reply, but Rebecca was climbing the steps to the lodge's entrance.

"Well, it was nice to see you," she said and turned around. "Have fun with Buttons."

The path around the lake was already crowded. Couples bundled in sweaters walked hand in hand, and a small boy held a muffin while his mother juggled a tray of coffee cups. There was a group of skiers carrying skis and poles.

Zach had so many things he wanted to ask Rebecca. What kind of work could Ben have on Christmas Day, and how could he leave his own honeymoon? But Rebecca had left so quickly, and it was none of his business.

Still, just seeing Rebecca and knowing she was here alone was unsettling.

"Come on, Buttons. After our walk, I'm going to treat us to cinnamon bear claws from Christmas Cove Bakery." He leaned down and patted Buttons's silky head. "It's Christmas and we deserve it."

Chapter Four

After Rebecca finished her morning run, she changed into a sweater and jeans and strolled down Main Street.

Christmas Cove had that wonderful small-town holiday feel one couldn't find in San Francisco. It was as if she'd stepped inside the pages of a Christmas story, with life-size illustrations. There was a gingerbread house with a graham cracker roof and white vanilla icing windows and a front door made entirely with M&M's. She passed a shop that sold teddy bears and a gardening store that had a sleigh made out of ivy, and chrysanthemums in red pots.

The concierge gave her brochures of the week's activities. She could take a horse-drawn tour of Lake Tahoe, which stopped at all the resorts and taught you the lake's history. Like the story of "Snowshoe Thompson" who, in the 1850s, delivered the mail while wearing a pair of homemade snowshoes.

Rebecca could watch performances by Tahoe Jazz Orchestra on a stage overlooking the lake and make s'mores in the lakefront firepits. The ski slopes were open for night skiing and every night there was a Christmas torchlight parade.

Rebecca had accepted the brochures and stuffed them in her

purse. She wasn't ready to sing Christmas carols, or ice-skate to the melody of "Jingle Bells." First, she needed some time alone. She felt as if she had been run over by one of those snowmaking machines that scaled the mountain, and she had to put the pieces back together.

A proper, hot breakfast would help. She scanned the restaurants until she found what she was looking for: a diner with an overpowering smell of bacon and sausages wafting from the doorway.

"Fried eggs with extra bacon, please," Rebecca said to the waitress when she was seated at a table. "And a side of monkey bread." She handed back the menu. "And the strongest coffee you have. With cream and sugar."

If Ben heard her order, he would say she was trying to give herself heartburn. He ate the same breakfast every day: coffee with two percent milk, whole wheat toast, and one banana. The whole wheat toast was for fiber, and the banana provided potassium for optimum brain functioning. One cup of coffee per day actually helped digestion and promoted good heart health.

It was Christmas and she was on vacation.

Then she reminded herself that it didn't matter what she ordered. She'd never sit across from Ben at breakfast again.

Somehow, she had hoped that yesterday was some crazy dream caused by wedding stress. Maybe she'd spent too much time deciding on varieties of roses, or she'd eaten too many slices of chocolate cake at cake tastings. She'd wake up in the bridal suite of the Four Seasons and the whole day would play over again. This time it would include the officiant pronouncing them husband and wife and instructing Ben to kiss the bride.

For a moment, she recalled the floral arrangements and the cake she had chosen and felt a small pang. Giant balls made entirely of white and red roses, scattered around the reception. And the blackberry mousse and chocolate fudge cake that had been Ben's favorite. Rebecca ordered it as a groom's cake. The blueberry icing read "To My Best Friend" and it was going to be a surprise.

Or perhaps, Ben would call or text and say he'd made a terrible mistake. That it was wedding nerves combined with stress about the public offering. That nothing had happened between him and Natalie, and he was going to drive up to Christmas Cove. They'd do something wild and impromptu like drive across the state line to Nevada and get married in one of those wedding chapels where the officiant sprinkles you with glitter after the ceremony.

Then they'd go back to Christmas Cove Lodge and they wouldn't ride in a sleigh or see a single firework display all week. Because all they wanted was to stay in bed with their arms wrapped around each other, and whisper they were never letting go.

But her phone stayed silent except for a late-night text from Kimi saying she'd arrived home safely and instructing Rebecca to call if she needed her.

The waitress brought the coffee and Rebecca stirred in cream and sugar. Her mind went to running into Zach on the lodge's steps. She hadn't meant to say that Ben had gone back to San Francisco. But Zach looked so handsome and confident, and he was staying with that glamorous older woman. She couldn't admit that Ben jilted her hours before their wedding. Plus, if she told Zach the truth, she would have to admit she'd lied last night at dinner.

There wasn't time to worry about Zach. After breakfast, she was meeting Howard at the boathouse.

Her phone buzzed and Kimi appeared on her screen. Kimi wore red-and-white candy cane pajamas. A baby carrier was strapped over her chest, and Rebecca saw Leila's dark, wispy hair.

"Merry Christmas," Kimi said. "I'm checking that you're not lying in bed with a pillow over your head, because after I left you finished the entire bottle of brandy and plate of pumpkin muffins."

"I didn't touch the brandy." Rebecca turned her phone to display the plate of fried eggs and green salsa. "I'm at a diner, having breakfast."

Kimi's eyes opened wide.

"If I eat one bite of fried food while I'm nursing, Leila starts burping. And forget salsa. A few weeks ago, Andy brought home tacos, and I added one teaspoon of salsa. Leila's stomach got so upset, Andy and I spent the night taking turns carrying her. It's the only thing that calmed her down.

"Thank God Leila's teething is better this morning. This thing is a lifesaver." Kimi pointed to the baby carrier. "All I have to do is figure out how to shower and get dressed without taking it off. I should have been a kangaroo."

"Can't Andy help?" Rebecca laughed.

"He has a project he has to turn in for work, and then he has to buy some last-minute presents for all the nieces and nephews. Tell me about you. How was your first night at Christmas Cove?"

Rebecca told her about meeting Howard and her promise to plan his New Year's Night party.

"I don't know what I was thinking," Rebecca groaned. "I've never planned a party for someone else."

"You'd never been on a dating site before you started Deal-breakers," Kimi reminded her.

Kimi was right. For a long time after her mother left, Rebecca didn't believe in love. She had seen photos of her parents and they had looked so happy. But in college she'd read too many novels to think true love never happened. Instead, she believed her parents had been too young when they'd gotten married to make it work. As long as Rebecca waited to fall in love, she'd be fine.

Then she met Ben, and the promises she made herself—she wouldn't start dating until she graduated and found a job, she wouldn't commit to a serious relationship until she was twenty-five and no longer living with roommates—all dissolved.

"I have to go," Kimi said, interrupting her thoughts. "Leila can tell when I stop moving. She's like one of those infrared security systems they install at museums."

Rebecca said goodbye and hung up. She couldn't help thinking about what Kimi said about Dealbreakers.

What would it be like working with Ben now? Could she sit across from Ben at a brainstorming session, wondering if he ran his ideas past Natalie the way he used to when he and Rebecca were together? Would she keep asking herself if she should have known that Ben was unhappy, and if she could have done anything differently? Seeing Ben and Natalie together all the time would be like checking under a Band-Aid every day to see if a wound was healed, just making it worse.

Dealbreakers was half Rebecca's company, and she couldn't think of anything else she wanted to do instead.

And would she ever allow herself to fall in love again? She had believed that what she and Ben had was special, but she'd been wrong. What if she made the same mistake yet again?

Howard was waiting for her at the log cabin. The cabin wasn't large and imposing like some of the others on the lake. Howard's cabin resembled the cottage in "Hansel and Gretel," with a peaked roof and heart-shaped windows. There was a white picket fence and small garden. The boathouse was to the side of the house. Rebecca couldn't see inside, but from the outside it looked to be a simple tin structure.

"Welcome to the Gingerbread House," Howard greeted her. He noticed Rebecca's perplexed expression and grinned. "The previous owner loved fairy tales."

"All that's missing is the licorice stick front door," Rebecca said, laughing.

"It's the perfect winter cabin." Howard ushered her inside. "I can practically heat the whole downstairs with the fireplace, and it's too small to feel lonely."

The interior was a construction zone. The plank floors had been ripped up, and the kitchen appliances stood unmoored in the living room. Rebecca could tell it would be lovely when it was finished. There was a picture window overlooking the lake, and behind the house were forests of pine trees.

"I shouldn't have made you work on Christmas Day," Howard apologized. "But the party is in six days. I'm running out of time."

"I don't have anything else to do." Rebecca shrugged. "And I'm used to working on holidays. Ben even worked on Thanksgiving."

Rebecca bit her lip. She had to stop talking about Ben.

"Why don't we see the boathouse," Howard suggested.

The boathouse was reached by a stone path. There were roll-up metal doors where the boats were brought in, and hooks for the boats on the ceiling. The floors were cement and the walls were covered in plaster.

"I rented space heaters, and I gave the party planner carte blanche. She could do whatever she liked."

"Did she have a theme?" Rebecca asked, making mental notes. The fluorescent lights would make the guests' skin look green. Even with space heaters, the room might still feel cold. It would need rugs and something on the walls to warm it up.

Howard rubbed his chin. He was dressed in a flannel shirt and blue jeans.

"She showed me some sketches," he said and shrugged. "Flower arrangements on the tables and a chandelier hanging from the ceiling. And a Christmas tree, of course, with ornaments that the guests could take for gifts."

It sounded pretty, but similar to every holiday party she and Ben had attended. The flowers were either poinsettias or, if the party planner was trying to do something different, tiger lilies or African violets. The party favors were often part of the table setting: a piece of jewelry for the women, a tie or money clip for the men.

Rebecca felt a small twinge. Had their wedding reception been unique? Rebecca chose every detail to reflect something about her and Ben. There was nothing wrong with appreciating good wines and fancy coffees. And the guests would expect to receive expensive gifts, as she and Ben were an internet power couple.

She turned to Howard.

"A party should reflect who you are. If you could have or do anything, what would it be?"

Howard thought about it for a moment.

"The most important thing to me is adventure," he mused. "The world is a big place and there are so many interesting places and people."

Rebecca thought about what Howard said. She had an idea.

"The party can have a western theme, like an adventure from the Wild, Wild West," she said eagerly. "We'll set up a saloon to serve drinks, and a tarot card reader to tell the guests when they'll fall in love. The floor will be covered in straw-colored rugs, and at each place setting there will be a blanket, so the guests stay warm.

"The food will be western," she continued. "Honey-glazed ham and potato casserole and biscuits and corn on the cob. For decorations we'll have snowshoes hanging from the walls, and a dogsled."

Rebecca sketched out her ideas. She'd go to the hat store in Christmas Cove and buy cowboy hats for the guests. The band would play cowboy songs you'd sing around a campfire, and a fiddler would play the violin during dinner. The party favors wouldn't be extravagant. Horseshoe-shaped cookies from the bakery, or a coffee mug wrapped with a red bow.

"I love it," Howard said when she finished. He led her to the storage room. Boxes were piled in the corner and there was a closet with empty hangers. "I might have a cowboy hat somewhere. In the boxes are things I brought up from San Francisco. Use whatever you like."

"I'll get started," Rebecca said.

"Are you sure you don't want to wait until tomorrow?" Howard asked. "It *is* Christmas Day. There's a parade on Main Street."

Rebecca flashed on the young fathers balancing toddlers on their shoulders, the happy couples deciding where to eat breakfast. She shook her head and turned the page of her notepad.

"I'd rather stay here."

Howard went to run some errands and Rebecca opened one of the boxes. There was a box with holiday china, and another with board games. One box held dusty guidebooks and wine bottles.

She opened a rectangular box and peered inside. There was a man's Shetland sweater. Underneath the sweater was a dress, wrapped in tissue paper.

Rebecca took the dress out and unwrapped the paper. She rocked back on her knees and gasped.

It was one of the loveliest wedding dresses she'd ever seen. The fabric was Belgian lace and it was tea length with a satin sash and capped sleeves. The bodice was adorned with appliquéd flowers and the skirt had a satin trim.

It was the kind of dress Rebecca had longed to wear at her own wedding.

Rebecca's wedding dress was one of the first things she and Ben disagreed on. If Rebecca had sensed then that Ben was different, that something had changed between them, could she have avoided the pain?

"I don't plan on seeing the dress before the wedding," Ben said, sitting in their living room last August. "But I should know what style of dress you're going to wear. We have a certain image."

They were eating Thai takeout and catching up on work.

Rebecca had been scouring vintage dress shops for weeks, but she hadn't found what she was looking for. Something elegant but whimsical with a history.

"This is our wedding, it's not an industry presentation," Rebecca reminded him.

"Here, take this card." Ben took a card from his wallet. "It's a bridal salon on Sutter Street. Natalie says it caters to all the high-end San Francisco weddings."

"Why were you discussing my wedding dress with the company's lead attorney?" Rebecca asked, puzzled.

"The wedding is an excellent chance for publicity before the public offering." Ben leaned forward and kissed her. "And you can't blame me for boasting about my bride-to-be to everyone at the office."

The bridal salon was so exclusive, there was no sign; one only heard of it by word of mouth. Inside, it resembled a Fabergé egg, with padded satin walls and jewel-colored geometric rugs. Every dress looked as if it stepped off a Paris runway. Organza gowns with endless chiffon trains. Silk sheaths with slitted skirts and pearl buttons.

The saleswoman convinced Rebecca to purchase a chemise gown with fake fur trim and a matching fake fur muff. Rebecca liked the gown but she didn't want to wear any type of fur, even if it was fake. What if some of the guests thought it was real? But the saleswoman assured it was all the rage at Christmas.

It wasn't until Kimi saw the dress that Rebecca burst out crying and explained the whole story.

"Did you know that Audrey Hepburn refused to wear the wedding gown her fiancé picked out for their wedding?" Kimi asked. "It was while Audrey was filming *Roman Holiday*. The dress was made in Rome by some fabulous Italian designer."

Kimi's mother had learned English by watching American movies. She was obsessed with Audrey Hepburn.

"Audrey insisted the dress be worn by a girl who couldn't afford it—'the most beautiful, poor Italian girl you find,'" Kimi quoted. "It was worn by a girl named Amabile Altobello at her wedding on a farm."

"How do you remember these things?" Rebecca grinned, already feeling better. Even though they had only known each other a few years, Rebecca and Kimi were almost as close as sisters. Kimi instinctively knew what Rebecca needed, and she always made Rebecca laugh.

"You'd remember them too if your mother was an encyclopedia of Hollywood facts." Kimi folded the wedding dress carefully back in the box.

"What are you doing?" Rebecca demanded.

"We're going to return this dress. And you're going to choose the dress that in thirty years your daughter will want to wear, because she'll see pictures of you looking so happy when you walk down the aisle."

The oyster-colored Mikado gown that Rebecca bought instead wasn't quite what she had envisioned, but the color and fabric were lovely. And the shoes—satin slingbacks with a pearl-encrusted bow—made her feel like Cinderella at the ball.

She stroked the Belgian lace dress and wondered who it belonged to and how it had ended up in the box. She found a hanger and hung it in the closet. She'd ask Howard about it later. Right now, she had a party to plan.

Chapter Five

Meredith wasn't in the suite when Zach returned from walking Buttons. He was glad to have some time alone. He could reflect on bumping into Rebecca on the lodge's steps.

What was it about Rebecca that made him keep lying? One of the things he loved about being a filmmaker was it taught him to be honest. The best movies came straight from the heart.

Rebecca had assumed that he and Meredith were a romantic couple and he didn't correct her. Then he would have had to explain that he got fired, when he lied about being a waiter in the first place.

Rebecca had looked so sleek in her running clothes, with her hair scooped into the same ponytail she'd worn in college. He recalled reading that Rebecca and Ben were both serious runners. He remembered other things from the article: they were passionate about giving back to the community. Every Thanksgiving they volunteered at the homeless shelter. Their company made a commitment to hire first-generation college graduates and partnered with other start-ups to sponsor STEM programs in local high schools.

When he read the article, Zach wondered if some public relations department dreamed it up. But seeing Rebecca again, Zach knew instinctively it was true. She had an earnestness about her. And she was spending her honeymoon in Christmas Cove, when she could travel anywhere in the world.

He shouldn't be thinking about Rebecca—he had to edit his film—but he couldn't help it. In college, he had a crush on her. And he envied Rebecca and Ben for finding each other. His own relationships since he graduated had been almost nonexistent.

When he'd first arrived in Paris, he thought he'd meet someone as easily as picking out a loaf of fresh bread at a boulangerie. But most women expected to be taken somewhere nice on a date. Even if they offered to pay for themselves, they still didn't expect to share a sandwich on a bench in the Bois de Boulogne. It wasn't any different in Brussels or Prague. If he dated a filmmaker, she was as broke as he was and they couldn't afford to do anything fun. If she wasn't, she became impatient with the long hours he spent in the editing suite.

Moving from city to city and never having any money was the worst recipe for falling in love.

Eventually he gave up. He would have time for love once he was a successful filmmaker. Except soon he wouldn't be a filmmaker at all. Instead, he'd be an unemployed waiter who would end up working for the family business and living in his childhood bedroom.

The door opened and Meredith entered. Her hair was hidden by a scarf and she wore a down jacket and knee-high boots.

"You're back," she said, as Buttons jumped into her arms. "I had the most wonderful morning. I slept until ten a.m. and then went sledding. I grew up in upstate New York. Living in Los Angeles, I miss the snow, especially at Christmas. You can't drink hot chocolate when it's seventy-five degrees outside, and Christmas isn't the same without icicles clinging to your clothes."

"Buttons and I brought you cinnamon rolls." Zach pointed to the bag on the counter.

"Thank you, but I already had breakfast," Meredith said. "This afternoon I'm going cross-country skiing. You're welcome to join me."

Zach shook his head.

"The contest deadline is in two weeks. So far, I just have a bunch of scenes strung together."

"Would you like me to look at it?" Meredith asked, lowering Buttons to the floor.

"You want to see my film?"

"Why not? I told you my ex-husband is a producer. I'm very honest," she said and smiled. "Directors always cringed when they came to our screening room. But what would be the point if I lied and said it was fabulous and then it failed at the box office."

"If you're sure," Zach said, but he was already going into his room to get his laptop. He was too close to his own work to tell if it was good.

Meredith sat at the dining table and Zach hit Play.

"The camera work is good, and the sound is excellent," she said when the final scene dissolved. "But it doesn't say anything."

"What do you mean?" Zach asked, puzzled.

"It's about saving the redwood trees," she said as she tapped her fingernails on the table. "It's a noble cause, but I don't know how you're personally invested in it. So your viewers won't either."

Meredith was right. Saving the redwood trees was important. But he was more interested in helping people, like the film he was making for the Christmas Cove community kitchen.

"Sofia Coppola is a big fan of the redwoods," Zach explained.

"Your film should tell a story. Often the best stories are about finding love and then losing it. You could interview me," Meredith suggested. "Falling in love is my Achilles' heel."

"You're willing to be in my film?"

"Why not?" Meredith shrugged. "When I lived in New York, I was a therapist. I listened to other people's stories for hours. And I'm a good storyteller, I volunteer at the children's hospital at UCLA."

Zach's mind started working. It could be a good idea. Was it enough to capture the judges' attention?

"When Josh and I arrived in Hollywood, everyone said the biggest movie audiences were teenage boys," Meredith reflected. "That's changed. Many producers and directors today are women. They don't want to see cars being blown up; they want to make movies that will touch people."

"Like a modern-day *When Harry Met Sally*," Zach said, excitement creeping into his voice. It was such a simple concept. But the best things in life were simple. Sneakers instead of fancy loafers that got ruined the minute you walked in the rain. Chocolate chip cookies made with butter and sugar instead of vegan sugar-free cookies that were healthy, but weren't tasty enough to eat in the first place.

"Let's try it," Zach said enthusiastically.

He grabbed his camera and tripod from his bedroom.

"I'm wearing my sledding clothes and I haven't fixed my hair," Meredith protested.

Zach placed a chair in front of the window overlooking the lake.

"You're the one who said it should be authentic. Start talking and let the camera work its magic."

Meredith recounted how she had grown up in a small town up-state and moved to New York City after college.

"I was like every twenty-four-year-old living in New York. I worked two jobs and rented an apartment with too many room-mates, and ate nothing but peanut butter sandwiches because I didn't have any money. I was a hostess at a French restaurant in the West Village. One evening, a guy stood outside, looking through the window.

"Even through the glass, I could tell he was incredibly hand-some.

"He had the kind of warm brown eyes that wouldn't let you look away. And wavy, dark hair that curled around his ears. He wore a navy turtleneck and a scarf was wrapped around his neck.

"I walked outside and handed him a menu. The owner taught us that was the best way to attract customers.

"'Would you like a table?' I asked.

"He turned his attention from the restaurant window to me.

"'The food won't be good.' He shook his head. He had a French accent.

"He started walking away, but I stopped him. It wasn't just that the restaurant needed customers, it was something about him. An arrogance mixed with an easy confidence.

"'How do you know if you haven't tried it?' I called out.

"He turned and walked back to the restaurant. His eyes had yellow flecks under the streetlamp.

"'Because you're too thin,' he announced.

"'I'm too thin?' I repeated.

"I was wearing a tube dress that belonged to my roommate. Jane worked as a stylist and got clothes at sample sales. She was taller than me and her clothes hung on me a little, but they were styles and fabrics I couldn't afford.

"'If the hostess is too thin, the food must be terrible,' he reasoned.

"'Hostesses don't get free food, only the waiters. The chef doesn't like too many people in the kitchen.'

"He looked at me for so long, my cheeks turned hot and I looked away.

"He reached into his wallet and took out a card.

"'My name is Phillippe,' he said and handed me the card. 'I was a chef at a Michelin star restaurant in Paris. One day, I'm going to open a restaurant in New York. Everyone who works there will eat for free.' He smiled and his teeth were straight and white. 'A smart chef wants everyone to love his dishes. Especially a pretty American girl.'"

Meredith blinked in front of the camera. Her mouth pursed together and she instinctively touched her hair.

"Later I found out Phillippe hadn't been a chef in Paris. He was a line cook, and occasionally he suggested a dish for the menu. And he wasn't anywhere near to owning a restaurant. He was twenty-five and didn't have much money." She let out a sigh. "All I knew then was that I had met the man of my dreams and I'd never be the same."

Zach glanced up from his camera. He had been so engrossed by Meredith's story, he almost forgot he was filming.

"What happened next?"

Meredith glanced at her watch.

"I have to go. I'm taking Buttons to see Santa Claus before I go cross-country skiing." She tapped her knee and Buttons jumped into her lap. "Why don't you edit the footage, and we can shoot more later."

Zach spent the next few hours editing the footage. It was good. He had that heady feeling he got when he knew a project was going to work. Like drinking one glass of wine with dinner, so that it delivered a pleasant buzz without making him drunk.

Then he pulled on a sweater and headed down Main Street. There had been a light snow, and the sidewalk was covered with a white film. He was going to spend the afternoon preparing Christmas dinners at the community kitchen.

Rebecca was coming out of a gift store. Her arms were laden with packages and she wore a red ski parka.

"Zach!" she greeted him in surprise. "I've only been in Christmas Cove for two days, and I've run into you three times."

Zach was about to say it was purely a coincidence, he hadn't been stalking her. But that would make it seem like he was apologizing for something he hadn't done.

"It's a tiny village, and we're staying at the same lodge," he said instead.

"Of course, it's just so different than San Francisco," she agreed. She pointed to her packages. "I thought I was finished Christmas shopping, but I couldn't resist. My goddaughter is nine months old and the gift shop has the cutest gifts. A teddy bear on skis, and a moose stuffed animal."

Zach suddenly had an idea. Rebecca was spending Christmas alone. Why shouldn't he ask her to join him?

"I'm on my way to prepare meals at the community kitchen,"

he said before he could talk himself out of it. "Would you like to come?"

"Now?" Rebecca frowned.

What had he been thinking? Rebecca was on holiday, and she had plenty of money. She probably booked one of those mini-coach tours, where you sit in a Mercedes SUV and sip champagne while the driver takes you to spots around the lake. Afterward you dine at one of the high-end resort restaurants. The tables are lit by candlelight and there's a sommelier to help guests choose the best wines.

Zach let out a small sigh. He'd never eaten at a restaurant like that in his life, and he probably never would.

"It's Christmas Day, you must have plans," he apologized, starting to walk away. "Maybe another time."

"I don't, actually," she said quickly. She reached out and touched his sleeve. "I'd love to help."

Zach hadn't considered what would happen if she said yes. What would they talk about? Rebecca might ask him about Meredith. But he couldn't back out now.

"Jerome runs the community kitchen. He'll be thrilled to have extra hands," Zach said, walking beside her. Somehow he felt less nervous when he was in motion.

"You wouldn't think there's a problem around here, with all the huge cabins"—his arms swept over the view—"but the local workers get small salaries, which can't support a whole family. And many of them are undocumented, so they don't qualify for food stamps."

"One of my favorite things about Dealbreakers is helping others," Rebecca said. Her eyes lit up and Zach noticed how lovely she looked when she was excited. "The first charity we were involved in was Big Brothers Big Sisters. The company wasn't even making money, but helping children is so satisfying. You're not just doing something for now, you're shaping their future."

Zach turned to her curiously. He'd never heard anyone put it so well.

"The community kitchen also donates meals to the local schools," Zach said. "I'm making a film to help them attract more sponsors."

"I should have brought my checkbook," Rebecca said with a laugh. Her tone grew serious. "It's great that you're doing those things, you must be so successful. Where are you based in Europe?"

"In Europe?" Zach asked, puzzled.

"I haven't seen your name on any movie credits, so I assumed that you must be living and working in Europe. I don't see many foreign films," she said apologetically. "Ben hates subtitles."

Zach felt as if he had been in a race car speeding around a track and had suddenly slammed into a tree. He had forgotten about Ben. Now he had to start lying again.

"The usual places. Paris, Berlin," he said evasively. "But I'm here for a while."

"How did you and Meredith meet? Not that it's any of my business." She smiled almost shyly. "I do own a dating app. I'm always curious about couples' stories."

"At a restaurant," Zach said.

God, how had that slipped out? Why hadn't he said at a film festival, which was the truth? But did it count if Zach hadn't remembered her?

"In Hollywood; Meredith lives in Beverly Hills," he added quickly. It was one more lie, but at least the restaurant part was true.

"Most couples don't meet in person anymore," Rebecca reflected. "That's why the app is so successful. At first, I thought dating apps were sort of cheating. You know, people were too lazy to go on traditional dates. But people work from home and shop from home. I have friends who don't go to bars, they make cocktails themselves. How else will people meet except online?"

"I've never used a dating app," Zach admitted. "I don't even have Instagram."

"Well, you're a big-shot filmmaker," Rebecca said. Her feet crunched in the snow and she grinned. "Women probably line up to talk to you."

The Christmas Cove community kitchen was in the back of a church. There was an industrial-size stove and double refrigerator. A wooden island took up the middle of the room and pots and pans hung from the ceiling.

Zach introduced Rebecca to Jerome. Jerome was from Trinidad. He was in his midtwenties, with thick locs, and he wore a white apron over baggy pants.

"You do a wonderful thing here," Rebecca said.

Jerome flashed a white smile.

"It's my fourth Christmas in America," he said. "Growing up in Trinidad, we had different traditions. Instead of going door to door singing Christmas carols, groups serenade their neighbors with lots of different instruments. Women spend the whole month cooking, and often families repaint their houses or at least clean them from top to bottom. In December our flat was cleaner than the royal palace."

Jerome went to get more supplies and Zach stood next to Rebecca at the counter. He told her the things that Jerome hadn't mentioned.

Jerome's father had worked in the oil industry. When oil prices fell internationally, he lost his job. There was no other work and a cousin agreed to sponsor him to come to America. It took him five years to save enough money to send for his family. Jerome received a scholarship to college, and now he was in his first year of law school in San Francisco.

"I'm not a good cook," Rebecca said when Jerome returned.

Jerome set aluminum trays on the counter.

"No cooking required," he replied. "Just fill the trays with peas and mashed potatoes. Zach can slice the turkey."

Zach and Rebecca washed their hands and put on aprons, then Zach picked up the carving knife. He turned to Rebecca.

"We talked enough about me. Tell me about Dealbreakers."

"In the beginning, hearing from the app's users was the most exciting part." Rebecca ladled peas from a large pot. "We received e-mails describing couples' first dates. They sent wedding invitations and birth announcements. It felt wonderful to make a difference in people's lives."

"And now?" Zach prompted.

Rebecca looked up from the peas. Her cheeks were flushed from the heat of the stove and talking about Dealbreakers.

"It's like running any successful company. You outgrow the dorm room or garage where you started. The late-night brainstorming sessions that had been so much fun because it felt like you were staying up past curfew turn into meetings that go on so long that you miss dinner and end up eating crackers and cheese from the sideboard in the boardroom. You don't have time to do things you used to love—getting the app into users' hands, always making it better—because you're consumed with sales projections and growth charts. If you did have time, you couldn't do them anyway because you've hired someone to do them who's an expert. Instead, you find other ways to be fulfilled. You buy a house and a dog and take trips to places you didn't know you wanted to travel to . . ." She suddenly stopped talking. "It's all great, of course, you can't believe you're so lucky. Especially if you have someone to share it with."

Zach didn't know how to answer. Rebecca had a far-off look in her eyes, as if she was thinking out loud.

"Is that why you came to Christmas Cove for the holidays?" he asked tentatively. "Because it's not the kind of place you'd normally go?"

Rebecca filled a container with mashed potatoes. She lightly wiped a small line of sweat from her forehead with her apron.

"No. Ever since we got engaged, I wanted to spend our honeymoon in Christmas Cove." She turned to Zach. "I'm glad I'm here. It's every bit as quaint and picturesque at Christmas as I imagined."

They finished filling the trays and said goodbye to Jerome. The midafternoon sun was a milky white ball, hovering halfway down the sky. A few boats were out on the lake, and there was the sound of horse hooves clopping along the pavement.

"It's like a scene from a Christmas card," Rebecca commented. She rubbed her hands together. "I booked a private sleigh ride for later this afternoon. It takes you along the route of the old Pony Express and you stop at the Pony Express Inn. The tour guide tells you the local history and leads you in singing Christmas carols," she said. "Since Ben isn't here I wondered if you'd . . ." She stopped to tie the lace on her boots.

Zach waited expectantly. Was she going to invite Zach to join her?

Rebecca straightened up.

"If you and Meredith would like to take my place," she finished. "It would be my treat."

Of course, Rebecca wasn't inviting him. She was a married woman.

"Meredith already made plans for this afternoon," he answered. "But thank you for the offer."

Rebecca slung her bag of packages over her arm.

"I should go, I want to do a little more shopping." She smiled at Zach. She held out her hand tentatively. "Thank you for a lovely time."

When Zach shook her hand, her palm was warm and soft under his. He watched her go and felt a sharp pang of disappointment. Then he turned and walked back to the lodge.

Chapter Six

Rebecca had had such a pleasant afternoon helping Zach at the community kitchen. He was handsome and charming and easy to be with. So why was she was sitting in her suite now, scrolling through Instagram for photos of Ben and Natalie?

There were so many things in the suite she could be doing instead. The maid left a tray of chocolate truffles. It came with a note from the staff thanking her for spending the holidays at Christmas Cove Lodge.

Usually, she ate anything chocolate on the spot. Ben used to laugh that other women expected perfume or flowers. He just had to appear with a paper bag containing one hazelnut truffle or a peanut butter and marshmallow s'more, and Rebecca smiled from ear to ear. Ben was the same. How many Sunday evenings did they spend watching Netflix and sharing a bag of dark chocolate almonds with chocolate that was so strong and bitter it was almost like drinking dark-roasted coffee?

Eating chocolate truffles without someone to share them with wasn't the same.

Would she ever find someone who loved the same foods as she

did? Who liked to eat them the same way? Sucking the orange out of the rind instead of peeling off its skin, eating noodles with chopsticks because the extra work made them taste better.

She told herself it was completely fair that she checked Instagram for photos. Her fiancé had run off with another woman. She couldn't help being curious.

Ben was right, none of the guests had leaked the news. There was nothing about the canceled wedding, and no photos of Ben and Natalie in St. Barts.

The last photo on Ben's Instagram was a picture of Ben and Rebecca at the rehearsal dinner. The dinner was held in the dining room on the fifty-second floor of the Bank of America building. They could have picked a trendier location: Foreign Cinema in the Mission District where guests watch a private screening of a movie during dinner. Ragazza, where dinner is served in a see-through, weatherproof tent set up in the restaurant's Italian garden. But there was nothing better than being high up with a view of San Francisco at Christmas.

Everything about the location had been perfect. The cocktail area, with a stone fireplace and a glass bar, and a Christmas tree strung with ornaments. The dining room itself, lit only with candles, and near the city lights twinkling outside the window.

And the view! Coit Tower, wrapped in layer upon layer of silver and gold lights, City Hall with its marble dome and columns bathed in a red-and-green glow. The pink and yellow lights on the cable cars snaking up and down the hills like neon-colored inchworms.

Rebecca and Ben had sipped the Christmas cocktails created for the occasion—Fireball hot toddies topped with cinnamon sticks and anise—and greeted their guests. Ben kept his arm draped around Rebecca and she couldn't stop pinching herself. It was finally their rehearsal dinner and the next day they were getting married.

Ben must have known then that it was a sham. That he'd leave before the dinner was over. Had Natalie been waiting for him in the apartment? Or did he spend the night at her loft?

Her phone buzzed in her hand.

"So, you're at the stalking stage in the breakup," Kimi said when Rebecca answered.

"What are you talking about?" Rebecca asked.

"I can tell by how quickly you picked up. You were scrolling through social media, looking for photos of Ben and Natalie."

Rebecca started to argue, but Kimi was her best friend.

"Guilty," she admitted. "I don't believe that Ben decided at the rehearsal dinner that he couldn't go through with the wedding. Ben doesn't do anything on impulse. He spent three weeks picking out the leather for his custom-made Porsche."

"The good news is you never have to drive in it," Kimi said cheerfully. "You get nervous in cars that are close to the ground."

It was true. Rebecca hated sports cars. She used to laugh with Kimi that one of the best things about becoming a mother would be having an excuse to buy a sensible car: a station wagon or an SUV.

Rebecca sank miserably against the cushions. When would she have children now? She was thirty and single.

"There has to be something better you could be doing," Kimi said, cutting into her thoughts.

"I was going to go on the sleigh ride," Rebecca answered. "And afterward I booked Christmas dinner at a restaurant on the lake. But I don't want to go alone."

"Of course you do!" Kimi insisted. "The sleigh driver might be some gorgeous Austrian ski instructor moonlighting in Lake Tahoe. Or the restaurant might seat you opposite a sexy, young writer who is suffering writer's block and came to Christmas Cove for inspiration. He'll see you sitting across from him and suddenly have the heroine for his next novel."

"I don't have any interest in ski instructors, and I don't want to be in anyone's novel," Rebecca said, laughing.

"I never told you how I met Andy," Kimi reflected. "I had just gone through a breakup with a guy named Jae-sung. Jae-sung was Korean, I was madly in love, and my parents were happy. But we attended graduate school on different coasts, and a long-distance relationship didn't work. Six months later, I met Andy. He was a year out of college and living at home.

"The first three times he asked me out, I said no. We finally agreed on one date, then he'd leave me alone," she recounted. "Even that date wasn't a success. The restaurant was noisy. When he walked me home, it started raining and we got soaked. But there was something between us," she finished. "You never know when you'll find love."

"We should put that on the site," Rebecca remarked, grinning. She stared out the window. "It's too early to think about men."

"It's never too early to be happy. Put on your warmest sweater and those knee-high Vince boots that make your legs go on forever and have some fun."

Kimi was right. She didn't come to Christmas Cove to sit in her room.

"All right, I will." Rebecca took the phone into the bathroom and turned on the bath.

"And one more thing," Kimi said. "Leave your phone in your

suite. I promise I won't call. I'll either be in a Christmas coma from eating too many of my mother's fried rice cakes, or Leila will be asleep on my chest because she'll be exhausted from getting her cheeks squeezed by the aunties, and I won't want to go near my phone."

Rebecca walked through the village square. It was late afternoon and the square teemed with activity. Carolers dressed in velvet costumes and little caps sang "Silent Night." Santa Claus waved from his sleigh. Mrs. Claus handed out candy canes and reindeer wearing red sweaters tapped their hooves on the pavement.

The sleigh that Rebecca had reserved was an antique European sleigh, drawn by a blond Belgian horse. The driver's name was James. He was in his midfifties with a stocky frame and a short, white beard. He presented Rebecca with a thermos of hot chocolate and a picnic basket stocked with ham sandwiches and gingerbread snaps. Rebecca wasn't the least bit hungry. After the sleigh ride, she would take the basket to the community kitchen instead.

The horses trotted along the lakefront and then headed into a pine forest. Rebecca had never been anywhere so beautiful. The trees were thick with icicles and the sleigh's wheels dug into powdery snow. The air was crisp and fresh, and there were no sounds except for a few squirrels scurrying into the bushes.

Just when she thought they'd be in the forest forever, they reached a clearing. The lake spread out below, and behind it the mountains were craggy and blanketed with snow. Log cabins were tucked into microforests and she could see ski gondolas climbing up and down the slopes.

They stopped to take photos and James told her about the Pony Express. It operated from April 1860 until nearly the end of 1861 and stretched from Missouri all the way to Sacramento.

During the winter, the route over the Sierras had been almost impassable, but nothing stopped the riders and the mail was delivered without interruption. It was rumored that Wild Bill Cody was one of the riders when he was only fourteen. James handed her a copy of the original ad. It was shaped like a Wanted poster and read: WANTED. YOUNG, SKINNY, WIRY FELLOWS. NOT OVER EIGHTEEN. MUST BE EXPERT RIDERS. WILLING TO RISK DEATH DAILY. ORPHANS PREFERRED.

Rebecca tucked the paper into her purse. It would make a perfect decoration for Howard's New Year's Night party. Perhaps she could pay James to come to the party and tell the story to the guests. There could be a map of the route on the wall. After dinner, the guests could play a game similar to Pin the Tail on the Donkey.

Rebecca snuggled in the blankets and felt a jolt of happiness. She was in a beautiful place and she had things to look forward to.

It was only after the sleigh ride, after she had dropped off the picnic basket at the community kitchen, that things started to go wrong. First, she fell on the icy sidewalk, and her pants were damp. If she went back to the lodge to change, she'd probably curl up in her suite and make do with whatever was in the minibar for dinner instead of going out to eat.

Christmas dinner at The Landings had already been paid for and she didn't want to waste it.

"I have a reservation," Rebecca said to the hostess when she arrived at the restaurant. "Rebecca Huntley."

The hostess scanned her computer screen.

"I don't have anything under that name."

"Look under Ben Cole," Rebecca suggested.

The hostess clicked on the screen. She smiled at Rebecca.

"You're our honeymoon couple." She gathered two menus. "Please follow me."

Rebecca was about to explain she was eating alone. But the hostess was already pulling the table slightly from the window and arranging the wineglasses.

It was Rebecca's fault. She had booked the most romantic restaurant on the lake and forgotten to change the reservation to a party of one.

From there, the evening grew worse. A couple snuggled in the firepit right outside her window, toasting marshmallows on long sticks and smiling at each other over the coals. The woman at the next table asked Rebecca to take a photo of her and her husband. Rebecca handed back the woman's phone and the woman gushed that it was their tenth anniversary.

And just as Rebecca was about to eat the first bite of beef Wellington, hot and sizzling on her plate, a guy wearing a navy suit and skinny red tie presented his date with a diamond engagement ring and the whole room erupted into applause.

Even when the engaged couple left, trailed by a flurry of clapping waiters, Rebecca couldn't concentrate on her food. Beef Wellington was Ben's favorite meat dish and Rebecca had specifically requested it. She had picked everything on the menu. The pumpkin soup that Ben's mother served every Thanksgiving. Yorkshire pudding because they had seen it on a British baking show and it was the sort of thing one should eat at Christmas.

Rebecca drank two glasses of wine during dinner, but instead of them giving her a warm feeling, tears sprang to her eyes.

Her father was with his family in Carmel, and her mother was with her husband Carlos in Argentina. Rebecca had FaceTimed with her mother earlier in the day. The call didn't go very well. Carlos had run out of pain medicine and it was difficult to get more over the holidays. Her mother was too distracted to talk and Rebecca hung up feeling more alone than before she'd called. Even Kimi and Andy and Leila were with their families. She was the only person she knew eating Christmas dinner alone.

She was about to ask for the check when the hostess appeared at her table.

"You can't leave yet," she said, noticing her gathering her purse. "You haven't had dessert."

The hostess disappeared. She returned a few minutes later with a pumpkin cheesecake drizzled in white chocolate.

"I didn't order this. I requested the pecan pie." Rebecca frowned.

"Your husband called and changed the order," the hostess explained. "And he wanted you to have this."

She set a flat, wrapped box on the table.

Rebecca gasped at the box in surprise.

"When did he call the restaurant?" she asked.

"A month ago," the hostess said as she glanced at her notes. "It's a pity he couldn't be here tonight. He must be a thoughtful guy."

Rebecca had forgotten about the gifts included with the meal. They were supposed to be small things, chosen by the restaurant. A scented candle or a souvenir ornament. Except that Ben called the restaurant and sent the gift himself. It's true that he was thoughtful; it was one of the things she had loved about him.

The hostess left and Rebecca drew the cheesecake closer. The drizzled chocolate read: *Rebecca, on our one-day wedding anniversary.*

Her throat closed up and she tried to swallow.

A month ago, Ben had still wanted to marry her. What had changed? Or had he ordered the dessert to reassure himself he was making the right decision? Ben hated doubting himself, he always liked to feel in control.

Rebecca was tempted to donate the wrapped box to charity, but she couldn't resist opening it.

Inside was a photo in a silver frame. Rebecca and Ben were holding a small puppy with a black-and-white nose.

The photo had been taken about a month ago, when they'd picked out Oliver, their Bernadoodle puppy.

She tucked the photo into her purse, then she walked quickly out of the restaurant. She walked past the skating rink, where children made circles on the ice, and past the pergola, where the carolers were singing "The Twelve Days of Christmas." She passed Mrs. Claus, who was handing out cups of hot apple cider, and Santa's reindeer, who were eating sugar cubes from Santa's hand.

She kept walking until she entered the lodge and collided with Zach.

Her purse fell open and the contents spilled on the ground.

"Rebecca, are you all right?" Zach asked, helping her up. He reached down and collected the items.

"I'm fine," Rebecca answered. She had slipped twice walking home and her sweater and scarf were damp.

"You're all wet." Zach straightened up. "Why don't you sit by the fireplace and I'll get us some drinks."

Rebecca debated going up to her suite and taking a bath. But she didn't feel like being alone, and the fireplace looked so inviting. Deep leather armchairs had been pulled up around it and there were bowls of oranges and mixed nuts.

"What about Meredith?" Rebecca asked.

"She wasn't feeling well, so she went to the suite." Zach pointed to his laptop case. "I was catching up on some work."

Rebecca sat by the fire and waited for Zach to return. He looked handsome in a white button-down shirt and navy slacks.

"Here, you dropped this." Zach handed her the silver frame. He set two glasses on the coffee table. "What a beautiful puppy."

"That's Oliver." Rebecca took the photo. "We're supposed to pick him up next week."

"He's going to be as big as Santa's reindeer." Zach grinned, sipping his drink.

They talked about Rebecca's sleigh ride. She told him about the view of the lake from the clearing, and the story of the Pony Express.

"Snow is wonderful as long as your fingers don't freeze, and the boots you invested in are actually waterproof," he said with a laugh. "Once, I got caught in a blizzard in Prague. The trams weren't running and I had to deliver my film before the festival deadline. I carried my laptop through an unfamiliar city in the middle of a snowstorm."

Rebecca had always wanted to go to Europe. She couldn't afford it during college, and afterward she and Ben were too busy with the company. They had planned on going next summer after Dealbreakers went public. She'd hoped to get pregnant in Italy, and they'd give the baby an Italian name; Enrico if it was a boy and Francesca if it was a girl.

She had to talk about something else. She pointed to Zach's laptop.

"Are you working on a film now?"

Zach nodded.

"It's about how couples meet and fall in love," he said, his eyes brightening. "I should interview you."

"Me?" Rebecca repeated.

"It wouldn't be anything about the company, just a personal piece about how you and Ben fell in love."

"Ben isn't here," she reminded him.

"It would be your side of the story," Zach urged. "It's easy, all you have to do is talk to the camera. You'd be doing me a huge favor."

In the morning, she had planned on going straight to Howard's boathouse and the last thing she wanted was to talk about Ben in front of a camera. But Zach had done her a favor years ago. She would have failed the film class without him.

And it was Christmas. The whole idea was to help people.

She took a long gulp of her hot toddy.

"All right," she agreed reluctantly. "But it's the same as any love story."

Zach set his glass on the coffee table. He pushed his dark hair over his forehead.

"You'd be surprised, every love story is different," he replied, his features alive with excitement. "That's what makes love so fascinating."

Chapter Seven

When Rebecca woke up the following morning, she felt different. At first, she thought it was from sleeping under the down comforter. Ben preferred a weighted blanket. The weighted blanket was cozy in winter, but Rebecca missed the lightness of down. The way it kept her warm but breathed at the same time. Then she guessed it was the winter sun peeking through the curtains. San Francisco was always covered in layers of fog; even in the summer it never burned off until noon.

But even after she'd peeled off the comforter and opened the drapes to reveal white clouds settled over the lake, the feeling didn't go away.

She knew what it was. It was the feeling of relief coupled with a new determination.

She had survived Christmas without Ben.

Last night, she and Zach had sat in the lobby for ages. Zach was easy to talk to and they discovered they had things in common. When they were children, they'd both had black Labradors named Dusty. Rebecca laughed that half the black Labradors in America were probably named Dusty but it was still a coincidence. And they both grew up loving Choose Your Own Adventure books. Rebecca used to have a stack on her bookshelf, next to the Sweet Valley High series she adored so much, she sometimes thought about writing one herself. And she couldn't deny that he was good-looking. He was different from Ben. She found his dark hair and hazel eyes attractive.

After they drank a second round of hot toddies, she finally went to her suite and took a bath. Sitting in the vanilla-scented bubbles with Christmas music playing softly on her phone was heavenly. She even made a list of things she was going to do when she went home.

She'd stop running in the mornings. She hated waking up at 5:00 a.m. She'd leave work earlier so she could run in the evening instead.

And she'd buy groceries once a week instead of picking up takeout. The takeout places Ben liked were expensive. Rebecca had always wanted to learn to cook, but there was never time.

The most important decision concerned Oliver.

Even if Oliver's crate and dog bed took up the bedroom, and even if she didn't have anyone to help her take care of him, she was still going to get Oliver. The last time she and Ben visited the breeder, Oliver licked her hand as if they already belonged together.

Oliver needed her and she needed him. She wasn't going to disappoint either of them.

She took a quick shower and wolfed down the muffin that was waiting on a tray outside her door. Then she pulled on jeans and a sweater and started for Howard's boathouse.

The first two hours were spent meeting with the florist. Rebecca knew exactly what she wanted. Pots of Christmas cacti scattered around the room. Vases of red and white roses and Christmas chrysanthemums. And on the tables, vegetables arranged artfully on platters. Flowers weren't the only things that were beautiful. The vegetables grown in local greenhouses—plump red tomatoes, purple eggplants, sweet yellow peppers—were bright and colorful too.

After the florist left, Rebecca returned to the storage room. She found Howard's cowboy boots and a Stetson hat. Inside a second box were some maps and a snow globe. It was the strangest snow globe she had ever seen. There was no festive holiday scene, only snowflakes inside an empty globe.

"It looks like you've been busy." Howard entered the storage room. He held up two cups. "I brought coffee."

Rebecca accepted the cup gratefully. The boathouse wasn't heated and she was freezing.

"The heat lamps should be here on Thursday," Howard said apologetically.

"I'm fine, I'll wear two sweaters tomorrow." Rebecca grinned.

She was feeling happy and excited. The meeting with the florist had gone well and she couldn't wait to meet with the caterer.

They sipped their coffees and talked about Christmas Day. Howard had spent the day making last-minute adjustments to a tour of the underwater caves in Vietnam. He was so busy, he'd skipped lunch altogether and eaten takeout pizza for Christmas dinner.

"Who eats pizza on Christmas?" Rebecca laughed.

"I've never had anyone to celebrate Christmas with," Howard said and shrugged. "And I hate buying a traditional Christmas dinner. There's always leftover mashed potatoes and Brussel sprouts in my fridge for days."

"Never?" she asked in surprise.

Howard fiddled with his cup. He was perched on a box, his long legs stretched out in front of him.

"I spent Christmas with my parents when they were alive. But no wife or serious girlfriend. That's one of the reasons the New Year's Night party is so important to me. Besides showing my guests a good time, of course. It's the thing I look forward to most about the holidays."

Christmas had always been Rebecca's favorite holiday. The first few years after her mother left, her father had made sure it was special. Every year, they cut down their own Christmas tree the day after Thanksgiving. They visited the reindeer at Golden Gate Park and never missed a tree lighting ceremony at Union Square.

Even during college, when her father was living in Seattle, Rebecca made it festive. The first two years, her roommate was British and didn't go home for the holidays. They bought tickets to *The Nutcracker* and had their own feast with a Costco turkey and sticky toffee pudding her roommate's parents sent from London.

She had survived one Christmas without Ben, but she couldn't imagine spending every future Christmas alone.

"Some of my best memories are of traveling at Christmas in the early days of starting my company," Howard went on. "You'd be surprised how empty airplanes are on Christmas Day, and the airlines used to serve a decent pumpkin pie." He smiled ruefully. "Now they expect you to eat peanuts for Christmas dinner."

Rebecca showed him the Stetson hat and went over her ideas for party games. Howard noticed the snow globe and picked it up.

"I haven't seen this in years." He turned it over. "It's from a street market in Brussels. It's empty, because you're supposed to shake it and make a wish. If you believe hard enough, the scene will appear in the snow globe."

"Can I use it at the party?" she asked eagerly. It would make a fun party game.

"I don't see why not," Howard said, poking around the boxes.

He pulled out some postcards and a stack of notebooks. They were wrapped in a thick elastic band.

"These things are ancient. I wrote in dozens of travel journals. I thought I'd publish them someday."

Rebecca glanced at the notebooks curiously.

"Do you mind if I go through them? They might give me some ideas."

"Be my guest," he said, and handed them to her.

Rebecca sat in a coffee shop on Main Street. Howard's notebooks were spread out on the table. A postcard was taped to the top of the page at the beginning of each entry.

The first postcard was of a canal in Amsterdam at Christmas. Boats were strung with colored lights and the pavement was filled with bicyclists. There was a square with a palace and a church and the tallest Christmas tree Rebecca had ever seen. Below the postcard was a journal entry. Rebecca started to read.

November 25th, 1990, Amsterdam, the Netherlands

I've only been in Amsterdam for four days but already, I'm acting like a local. I rented a bicycle and toured the entire city. Dam Square is the most beautiful square in Amsterdam. During the holidays, they erect a Christmas tree grown in the Ardennes Forest in Germany. It's sixty-five feet tall with forty thousand lights!

The Royal Palace was built in 1808 and the Dutch royal family still holds receptions there. And the church is called the New Church even though it was built in the seventeenth century. My history professor would smile if he read this, I was never the best student. It's different to see the salon where King Louis Napoleon Bonaparte entertained guests, rather than reading about it in a textbook.

The only thing that locals like more than bicycling is sitting in cafés. No one orders lattes with five different names and ingredients like they do at home. Instead, they drink coffee black or with skim milk, and with a cookie on the plate. If there's no cookie, you send it back! And the coffee cup never holds more than six ounces. The coffee is made in an espresso machine. If you drank more, you wouldn't sleep for days.

When it rains or snows, it's almost impossible to get a table. Yesterday, I waited for thirty minutes and even then, I made a mistake. A girl was sitting at the table. An American girl with wavy red hair tied with a multicolored scarf.

"You can't sit there," she objected. She had bright green eyes and light freckles on her nose. "The seat is taken."

The table was for two. A copy of the new Stephen King book rested on the empty seat.

"I just need the chair," I explained. "I found a table, but there's no chair."

"I'm sorry, but I need this chair." She went back to her guidebook.

"Your book doesn't need its own chair," I tried again. "It's not a very good book anyway. Stephen King's last book was better."

"I didn't ask for a critique of my reading material." She set her cup on the table. "I need the chair. If I go up to the counter to order another coffee, someone might take the table."

"Why not leave the book on the table?" I asked logically.

She glared at me. Her eyes were fiery as a cat's. She wore an angora sweater over a yellow turtleneck.

"Because then someone will steal the chairs."

We had reached an impasse. I was cold and wet and desperate for a cup of coffee.

"I'll make you a deal," I offered. "I'll go up to the counter and order for you. I'll even pay for your coffee."

She studied me curiously.

"You'd buy me a cup of coffee?"

"I'll buy you a Danish too, if you want. I was bicycling, it started raining, and I'm freezing. If I don't sit down soon, I may never feel my calves again."

"The Danishes are too sweet, they remind me of Krispy Kreme doughnuts back home," she deliberated. "I wouldn't mind a bowl of soup. I haven't eaten all day; I've been saving my appetite for dinner."

I ordered a bowl of pea soup and a meatball sandwich for myself. The sandwich was huge. I could eat half now and half for dinner.

The girl invited me to sit at her table, and I accepted. Her name was Kat. I tried talking about the usual things young people talk about when they're traveling. The hostel where I'm staying. Which cities I planned to visit and the cheapest buses and trains.

Kat was different. She didn't give much away. The only thing I learned was that she was from Chicago and studied art history at university. That and the fact that she hated cell phones.

"The whole point of traveling is to leave everything behind," she said, scraping the last drop of soup from the bowl. "If anyone wants to get in touch with me, they can send a telegram."

I wrapped up half my sandwich and tucked it inside my backpack.

"You can't save the sandwich," she objected. "The meatballs will make the bread soggy."

"I have to save it, it's my dinner."

She looked at me as if I was crazy.

"It's Thanksgiving, you can't eat a meatball sandwich on Thanksgiving."

"They don't celebrate Thanksgiving in Amsterdam. And you said you wanted to leave everything behind," I reminded her.

"The holidays are the best time of year," she objected. "For the next month it's perfectly acceptable to spend your time baking cookies and writing to Santa Claus. It's like being a child all over again."

"I promise I'll start on my Christmas list tonight." I grinned. "But I'm still going to eat this sandwich."

"No, you're not. You're coming with me."

"Where are we going?"

She stood up and gathered her books. Her smile was brighter than the lights in the boats on the canal.

"You ask a lot of questions. You have to learn to trust people."

We walked to the hostel where she was staying. She went into the kitchen and made me wait in the common room.

An hour later she pulled me into the kitchen. The table

was covered with a tablecloth and there were two place settings.

I sat down and she handed me a plate with sliced turkey and stuffing and cranberry sauce.

"Where did all this come from?" I asked, eagerly spooning stuffing and sauce.

Ever since I arrived in Europe, I'm always hungry.

"I bought the ingredients at the outdoor market but I made it all myself," Kat said, sitting opposite me. She poured two glasses of wine and handed me one.

"You made all this?" I inquired.

"I started cooking yesterday." Kat nodded. "I was going to eat it for dinner tonight, but you look like you needed a proper Thanksgiving meal." She raised her glass to her lips. "Anyway, it's better this way. I hate to waste food and I didn't have anyone to share it with."

Something about the way she said it made me feel as if she wasn't telling me something. Perhaps she left a boyfriend at home or just went through a breakup. I didn't ask questions. We hardly knew each other.

"I'm glad we met, and I don't know how to thank you," I said, taking another bite of stuffing. "And you're right. No one should eat soggy meatball sandwiches on Thanksgiving. This is much more festive."

The journal entry ended there. Rebecca couldn't wait to read more. She tried to imagine Howard in his midtwenties, traveling through Europe and meeting an interesting American girl.

Suddenly she had an idea for the party. Postcards papering the walls, with descriptions of each place underneath. It would tie in to Howard's belief that life was a great adventure.

It was late afternoon. Zach was waiting for her at the lodge to film the interview. She chastised herself again for agreeing to do it. Now she had to keep lying about being married.

But Zach had been so kind, buying her a hot toddy on Christmas Day. And at the end of the week they'd probably never see each other again.

It couldn't be that hard to keep telling one small, white lie. She survived her first Christmas without Ben; she could do anything she set her mind to.

Chapter Eight

Zach inspected the lens on his camera and checked the microphone for sound. It was the third time he had checked it. He couldn't help himself. He was meeting Rebecca in an hour and he wanted everything to be perfect.

He still couldn't believe he'd asked Rebecca to be in the film. It was the two hot toddies they'd drunk, combined with the cheerfulness of Christmas. Everyone in Christmas Cove, from the shopkeepers giving out free samples to Santa Claus waving from his sleigh, was warm and friendly. It was impossible not to get caught up in the Christmas spirit.

But now it was the day after Christmas. The buzz from the bourbon had worn off and Zach had no idea what he was going to ask Rebecca. The only person he had interviewed was Meredith and it had been her idea. What if Rebecca froze up, or there was a glitch in Zach's equipment?

"If you polish that lens any harder, the glass might break," Meredith said, entering the suite's living room. She wore a green parka and white après-ski boots. Buttons jumped out of her arms and ran to lick Zach's pant legs.

"Dogs are so clever." Meredith took off her parka and hung it on a chair. "Buttons has only known you for a few days and he's already attached to you."

"I did something stupid." Zach sighed, setting the camera on the table. "I asked Rebecca to be in the film, and I didn't tell her it was for a contest. She probably thinks I've already got a production deal, and it will be in movie theaters across America."

Meredith took a dog biscuit out of her pocket.

"Do your parents know that you were working as a waiter?" Meredith inquired.

"Of course." Zach nodded. "They sent me a check for a hundred dollars for Christmas. I spent it on a new white shirt and tie for the job."

"Over the years, have you ever lied to your friends about your career?"

"I've never hidden anything from anyone." Zach was slightly indignant. "You're the one who said everyone in Los Angeles has two jobs. Being a waiter isn't a crime."

"Except you lied to a woman you haven't seen in eight years."

Zach shifted uncomfortably. His collar suddenly felt too tight.

"What are you saying?" Zach asked.

"It's obvious; Rebecca isn't the only one you're lying to. You're fooling yourself," Meredith declared. "Once you probably had feelings for Rebecca. You probably still do."

How could Zach not have had a crush on Rebecca in college? She appeared in his film class like the sun on a bright summer day. And she was a psychology major; she was interested in people. So many film majors were wrapped up in themselves.

But that was years ago. If only she had changed. Turned into the kind of successful businesswoman one saw photos of online, with an expensive hairstyle and a perfectly contoured body that could only be achieved by working with a personal trainer.

But Rebecca looked exactly the same. The perky brown ponytail, the minimum of makeup, and most importantly her smile. It wasn't the smile of someone who was jaded by having everything she wanted. Rebecca's smile was tentative and uncertain. It came and went like the clouds over the lake.

"That's ridiculous," Zach objected. "I haven't thought about Rebecca in years."

"Not consciously, but she was in the back of your mind," Meredith replied. "Now she suddenly appears and you want to impress her. Like the knights in medieval literature. They wore all that armor to impress the women at home."

"And I thought the armor was to protect them in battle." Zach smiled.

He had wanted to impress Rebecca. He told himself it was because of the articles he'd read about her and Ben, and the huge diamond ring on her finger. But he had other friends who were successful. His best friend from high school owned a pool company and the girl he took to prom was an attorney at a high-powered law firm. He still told them how difficult it was being a filmmaker, that he practically lived on rice and beans and didn't have his own apartment.

"The question is what you're going to do about it," Meredith said, interrupting his thoughts.

"There's nothing I can do. Rebecca is married—she's on her honeymoon."

"Married to a husband who isn't here on his own honeymoon. There is something very odd about that. Why isn't Ben with her?" Meredith folded her scarf into a neat square. "I was a therapist for years. Sometimes it was like being an archeologist on a dig. When you start digging, you never know what you'll find."

Meredith went to her room. Zach remembered back to college when he thought he had a chance with Rebecca and hoped she had feelings for him too.

Zach decided to make a film about Fisherman's Wharf in San Francisco for the group project. Where else could you find an amusement park built right on San Francisco Bay? He wanted to show adults having fun: riding bumper cars, visiting the sea lions, watching chocolate being made at the Ghirardelli chocolate factory. Zach and Rebecca spent three days on location shooting the footage. Each day after they finished filming, they strolled along the waterfront, inspecting the tall ships and eating fish and chips.

They talked about everything. Zach's hopes to get a film grant after graduation. His goal to one day help people through his films by raising awareness of important causes. Rebecca told him why she studied psychology. She wanted to do something to make a difference in other people's lives.

And they talked about things they had wanted when they were younger. Zach always wished he had a sister. Rebecca dreamed of being a writer and filled notebooks with the first chapters of stories.

Then Zach started editing the footage, and they didn't see each other for days. The times that Zach invited Rebecca to join him in the editing suite, she had a lecture class she couldn't miss. Until the day when the film was due and they agreed to meet at a burger place near campus.

* * *

"I need to borrow your bicycle," Zach's roommate, Raymond, said, bursting into Zach's room.

Zach was standing in front of the mirror, deciding on a shirt. He was meeting Rebecca. It wasn't exactly a date; it was the middle of the day and they were going to discuss last-minute changes in the film. But he wanted to look good. He had changed three times, finally deciding on the only clothes he owned that weren't black. A yellow T-shirt his mother sent for his birthday and a pair of blue shorts.

"What's wrong with your bike?" Zach asked.

"The tire is flat, and I'm meeting Marella and her parents at the Bancroft Hotel."

Raymond had been dating Marella for three months. Her parents lived in the Philippines and she refused to get serious without her parents' blessing.

"I'm sorry, I need the bike." Zach shook his head. "I'm meeting someone at Burger Shack."

"I'll bring it back in an hour," Raymond pleaded. "I have to make a good impression. Or Marella's parents will go back to the Philippines and our relationship won't progress any further."

Zach wasn't meeting Rebecca until 2:00 p.m. That would give him plenty of time.

"All right. Bring me some of the Bancroft Hotel's breadsticks," Zach relented. "I'm spending all my money on a burger and fries; I won't have any money for dinner."

An hour and a half later, Raymond hadn't returned. Zach sent him a text, but there was no reply. Finally, Raymond texted back and said Marella's parents were bombarding him with questions and he couldn't leave. He was sorry and he'd make it up to Zach later.

The Burger Shack was on the other side of campus. The buses were unreliable and if he walked, he'd be late. He replaced his one good pair of loafers with running shoes and jogged all the way there.

When he arrived, Rebecca was sitting at a booth and she wasn't alone. Zach was about to enter when he noticed the guy she was with. His name was Ben Cole. He was the captain of the soccer team and a member of the coolest fraternity.

It was Zach's fault that he was late. Rebecca probably thought she had been stood up. Why shouldn't she grab a burger with another guy?

He could go inside and interrupt them. But Rebecca wasn't the kind of girl who would abandon the person she was eating with. Plus, this was Ben Cole! Every girl on campus wanted to spend time with him.

Zach turned around and walked home. He tried calling Rebecca but her phone went straight to voicemail. Eventually, he changed back into his black T-shirt and watched the film one more time before sending it to the professor.

The film won the award for best editing and they both received As on their midterm grades. By the time Zach worked up the courage to call Rebecca to celebrate, she and Ben were a couple.

Rebecca was already waiting in the village square when Zach arrived. She looked particularly lovely in a camel-colored coat and knee-high boots. Her hair was looped in a ponytail and she wore a beige sweater and wool gloves.

They strolled down to the lakefront and Zach set up the camera in the cove. The sky was pale blue and there was a fresh layer of snow on the mountains. He could see the ski gondolas and children spiraling down the slopes on toboggans.

"I don't know what to talk about for the camera," Rebecca said nervously.

Zach attached the microphone to her collar.

"Start at the beginning," he prompted. "How did you and Ben meet and fall in love?"

Rebecca thought about it for a moment.

"I don't believe in love at first sight," she said. "When I was a child, I wrote dozens of stories. They were never the kind where the heroine meets the handsome prince at the Christmas ball and falls in love. They were more boy meets girl and they become friends. It's only after they share adventures—getting caught in a raft rushing down the river, being stuck in a tree because they were both trying to rescue a cat—that they realize they're in love."

She stopped to drink the coffee she was holding.

"True love is strong enough to survive anything: when you both have the flu at the same time and you take turns making hot soup and going to the store for more Tylenol. When both sets of parents surprise you at Thanksgiving and you have to order Chinese because the grocery store ran out of turkey. It's impossible to know if it's love right away." She looked searchingly at the camera. "It's like trying to predict what the weather will be like at Christmas in July."

"So, when did you know you were in love?" Zach asked.

Zach stepped back and admired the way Rebecca was framed by the camera. Behind her, the sun reflected on the lake and the water was as smooth as butter.

Rebecca started by describing how she and Ben met over a shared dislike of ketchup. They never went on a proper date. But they were together twelve hours a day, hashing out ideas for Deal-breakers.

"We both graduated in May, but we had twelve-month leases on our student apartments. We still ran Dealbreakers out of Ben and his roommate Brian's kitchen. It was the end of summer and we didn't know what was going to happen next.

"Brian was leaving to go home and then start MIT. If we didn't get funding soon, Ben and I would have to get jobs. He was going to work in finance in New York and I wanted a job at a residential psychiatric facility in Oakland."

"Even though you were a couple?" Zach said in surprise.

Rebecca shifted on the bench.

"That's the thing. I thought we were a couple, but I wasn't sure." She frowned. "We didn't do any of the usual dating rituals, all our energy was focused on Dealbreakers.

"Then we got a meeting with a venture capital firm. We re-hearsed our speech for days. Ben splurged on a haircut for himself. He insisted we get a Nordstrom credit card to buy clothes, even though there was no money to pay it off.

"The day of the meeting came. I woke up with a pain in my lower stomach. We thought it was from the takeout we ate the night before. Ben said he'd go ahead, and I'd come as soon as I could.

"I ate a packet of Tums, but it only got worse. I went to the hospital near campus and found out I had a ruptured appendix. I tried to call Ben but his phone went straight to voicemail. Then I called Brian and left another message."

Rebecca paused to drink her coffee. Then she recounted the rest of the story. Ben appeared at the hospital that evening. He was still wearing his new suit and he had a sheaf of papers under his arm.

"'How did you know I'm in the hospital?' I asked him.

"I tried to sit up, but I was groggy with painkillers.

"'Brian texted while I was in the meeting,' Ben said, and pulled up a chair next to the bed. 'I came as soon as the meeting was over.'

"He handed me the papers. 'We got the funding! And this is for you.'

"It was a lease agreement for an apartment in San Francisco. Both our names were written on the top.

"'You rented an apartment for us?' I asked in shock.

"'I looked at apartments last week,' Ben replied eagerly. 'It's a few blocks from the office space we saw for Dealbreakers. It's on the third floor and there's no view. We won't need a car to get to work, we can ride bicycles.'

"I tried to read the details. How much square footage, was there a washer and dryer. But everything was blurry.

"I was thrilled, of course, but it was so sudden. We hadn't talked about moving in together.

"'What if we hadn't gotten the funding?' I inquired.

"Ben did that thing he does. Instead of answering a difficult question, he smiles as if all you have to do is believe, and everything will work out.

"'We did get the funding,' he said, and he leaned forward and kissed me. 'And now we're going to live in the same apartment complex as the CFO of Salesforce.'

"That's when I knew I was in love. The whole time that I thought Ben was completely wrapped up in Dealbreakers, he was also thinking about us. He planned our whole lives together. We signed the lease and moved in the following month."

Zach hit Stop and stepped back from the camera.

"That was fantastic," he offered. "You were perfectly relaxed."

"It's easier than I thought," Rebecca said with a smile. "You're so good at what you do. I forgot all about the camera."

"Why don't we break and continue tomorrow," Zach suggested.

"Do you really want to hear more?" Rebecca questioned.

"Definitely." Zach nodded. "That is, as long as you want to keep going."

She took a moment to answer and Zach was afraid she'd say no.

"Yes," Rebecca said as she pulled on her gloves. Her eyes lit up and she looked at Zach for a moment longer than was necessary. "I think I'd like that."

Rebecca left to run some errands and Zach packed up his gear. There was a sharp feeling in his gut, like when he was in the editing suite and forgot to eat all day.

Except this time, he was certain it wouldn't go away by raiding his refrigerator for anything that wasn't rice and beans. He shouldn't have asked Rebecca to be on camera, and he definitely shouldn't encourage her to keep going. But she seemed as eager as he was to continue.

It wasn't entirely his fault. Rebecca didn't have to say yes. And how could he have known that when he turned on the light and hit Record, she would become almost another person?

Someone raw and vulnerable. Someone he cared about and didn't want to see hurt.

Zach was being ridiculous. Rebecca had everything. A handsome, successful husband, a million-dollar company. Christ, she was even about to get the kind of puppy Zach dreamed of.

But her story moved him in a way he hadn't expected.

For some reason he felt angry at Ben. If it had been Zach, he wouldn't have waited until the meeting was over to dash to the hospital. He would have gone as soon as Brian texted. And he would never have rented the apartment without Rebecca's approval. More importantly, he wouldn't have waited months to tell Rebecca he wanted a future together. He would have told her on their first date.

None of this was about him. Rebecca and Ben loved each other; they were married.

Meredith said the best films came straight from the heart. He was simply getting the footage he needed.

He slung his camera bag over his shoulder and headed to the community kitchen. An hour of working on the kitchen's film would clear his mind.

Jerome was rinsing utensils when he arrived.

"Hey, man." Jerome looked up from the sink. "I'm glad you're here. I need a favor."

"What kind of favor?" Zach asked.

"Santa Claus and Mrs. Claus are supposed to be here tonight to give presents to the children," Jerome said, wiping his hands on his apron.

"Christmas was yesterday," Zach replied, puzzled.

"Most of the parents worked on Christmas Day," Jerome explained. "I thought it was better to do the gifts the day after Christmas. The couple who were playing Santa Claus and Mrs. Claus both have the flu, so I wonder if you'd do it."

"Why don't you be Santa Claus?" Zach wondered.

"I'm going to handle the food," Jerome said. "I already have a replacement for Mrs. Claus. Rebecca said she'd do it."

Rebecca! Zach wondered why she hadn't mentioned it while they were filming.

"When did you talk to Rebecca?" Zach asked in surprise.

"She stopped by yesterday afternoon," Jerome said. "She brought ham sandwiches and gingerbread cookies for the kids."

"And you asked her to be Mrs. Claus?"

"She gave me her cell number, I just called her." Jerome nodded. "I was going to call you next."

Zach didn't have any plans for the evening. And it was a great way to help children at Christmas.

"All right, why not," Zach agreed.

"Excellent." Jerome beamed. "I'll see you in a couple of hours."

Zach spent an hour getting shots of the kitchen. Then he walked back to Christmas Cove Lodge. The skating rink was filled with skaters and there was a line of people in front of the petting zoo.

The best part about Christmas was seeing children smile. That was the only reason he agreed to play Santa Claus.

He almost believed it.

Chapter Nine

When Zach arrived at the suite, Meredith was sitting in the living room reading a magazine with Buttons curled in her lap.

"Zach, it's nice to see you," Meredith said, looking up.

Meredith had just returned from cross-country skiing. The paths around the lake led deep into the forest.

"It's so different from downhill skiing, the trails through the forest are so peaceful." Meredith rubbed Buttons's nose. "Buttons loved it, especially the squirrels."

She noticed Zach's anxious, pained expression.

"How was the filming?" she asked. "You don't look happy."

"It was great, actually." Zach sank onto a chair. "Rebecca was perfect on camera."

Zach told Meredith about Rebecca's appendicitis and that Ben rented an apartment without telling her.

"It was so long ago, and it's none of my business," Zach finished. "But I can't stop thinking about it."

"I told you I think there's something odd about their relationship. I still think it's very strange that Ben isn't here on their honeymoon. Your reaction is normal. All good directors get close to the story," Meredith reflected. "I've seen directors go through two boxes of Kleenex, watching a film they've already seen a dozen times in the editing suite."

"I suppose you're right," Zach agreed.

He couldn't put into words why Rebecca's revelations had bothered him.

"Why don't you shoot another segment with me," Meredith suggested. "I'm just sitting here. I don't want to move until Buttons wakes up."

Zach didn't have to be at the community kitchen for two hours. And he always felt better when he was working.

He framed Meredith settled on the sofa. A fire crackled in the fireplace and there was a vase of white roses on the coffee table.

"I didn't hear from Phillippe for a month. I almost forgot about him. I got asked out often, though the relationships never lasted. Either the guys were my age and couldn't afford a second date, or they were lawyers and bankers in their late twenties. I didn't have the glamorous wardrobe for fancy dinner parties and weekends in the Hamptons.

"Phillippe showed up at the restaurant where I was working one evening in early September. It was the best time of year in New York. The summer tourists were gone and the stagnant feeling in the air had been replaced by a sense of anticipation.

"'I see you haven't been fired,' Phillippe said.

"His hair was a little shorter. He wore khaki shorts and a navy T-shirt with something written in French.

"'Why would I be fired?' I asked.

"'For begging people to come inside.'

"'We were taught to give out menus,' I said briskly. 'No one but you ever complained. We've been very busy; I have to turn people away.'

"Phillippe shrugged his shoulders. I remembered how he made me feel. Unsettled and not quite myself.

"'I hope at least you get a day off,' he continued. 'We're going on a date.'

"'In America, men ask women if they want to go out,' I remarked. 'They don't make the decision for them.'

"'In France, we believe in enjoying life,' he said. His brown eyes found mine. 'I wouldn't insist, if I didn't think you'd have a good time.'

"I was about to say no. Then I saw one of the waitresses admiring him, as if he was some kind of French film star.

"'I'm off tomorrow,' I conceded.

"'Excellent. It will be a surprise.' He smiled. 'In France, we also appreciate a little mystery.'

"I didn't want to give him my address, so we met in front of the restaurant. I wore jeans and sneakers. The first thing he did was comment on my shoes.

"'Thank goodness you're wearing sensible shoes. We're going on a walking tour of New York.'

"I almost laughed. I only owned two pairs of shoes and they were both sneakers. I'd kill for a pair of Christian Louboutins like Sarah Jessica Parker wore in *Sex and the City*, but I couldn't even afford knockoffs.

"'Shouldn't I be showing *you* New York?' I asked. 'I'm the one who lives here, you just arrived.'

"'This is a special tour," he said as he took my arm. 'I'm going to show you the best places to eat in Manhattan.'

"I experienced a moment of panic. Maybe Phillippe thought I

was one of those wealthy young women whose parents gave them an allowance. I didn't mind paying for myself. But I could barely afford a slice of pizza, let alone dinner in a nice restaurant. I was saving any extra money I earned to go back to school and get a degree in social work.

"The first place we went was Union Market in the East Village. At first, I was puzzled; it was like any supermarket. Phillippe walked straight up to the cheese counter and asked for two samples of Camembert. The cheese was delicious—sweet and tangy, with a golden rind. He did the same thing at the meat counter and the deli. I was embarrassed until I noticed other customers doing the same thing. Apparently, Union Market is known for its free samples: roasted macadamia nuts and freshly baked cookies and thimbles of pumpkin soup.

"Next, we visited a bakery in Chelsea Market that gave out chocolate brownies, and PJ Wines on Broadway, where they served paper cups of a French chardonnay.

"We walked for hours and I'd never had so much fun. By then it was evening and we were hungry again. It was a Sunday, and most of the cafés were closed. On top of that, it had started raining.

"I was about to suggest we split a pizza, when Phillippe stopped in front of a restaurant.

"'It's closed,' I said, pointing to the sign.

"'The light is on inside.' He tapped on the door. A moment later he returned to where I was standing.

"'The waiter said we can come in and have a bowl of soup.'

"It was the kind of restaurant that is nondescript from the outside, but inside is sleek and elegant. There were hardwood floors and padded gray booths. Framed reviews hung on the walls and there were a few photos of celebrities.

"I told myself that a bowl of soup couldn't cost a fortune. But as soon as we finished the French onion soup, the waiter set down plates of lamb chops and sautéed spinach. There was a loaf of sourdough bread and olive oil.

"Everything was delicious, but I was too anxious to enjoy it. Finally, when he brought the dessert—chocolate mousse with hazelnut shavings—I had to say something.

"'You have to send the dessert back.'

"Phillippe glanced at me as if I told him to send his own mother back to France.

"'Do you know how long it takes the chef to prepare chocolate mousse? First, he has to beat the eggs until the whites are foamy. The chocolate is cut into small pieces and mixed with butter for at least twenty minutes,' he said as the waiter glowered at me. 'A good chef only uses a hand mixer, none of those electric contraptions.'

"'I can't afford the mousse,' I blurted out. 'And I refuse to let you pay for it.'

"Phillippe picked up his fork and ate a bite of the mousse.

"'I told you, we're not paying for anything.'

"'Then, I don't understand.'

"'Maxime's is one of the hottest French restaurants in New York. I'm the new assistant sous-chef,' he said triumphantly. 'I traded a week's salary for use of the kitchen.'

"'You cooked the whole meal?' I gasped.

"'Everything but the sourdough bread. I started in the kitchen at five a.m.' He nodded. 'Even the top restaurants in Paris have their bread delivered.'

"I could never give up a week's salary, I wouldn't be able to pay my rent. I didn't want Phillippe to see how flattered I was.

"'You thought of everything.' I took a bite of the mousse. 'Did you order the rain too so I had to come inside?'

"'That was luck. The most important thing about luck is to recognize it when it happens,' he said and looked at me seriously. 'Like when you walk down the street and see a beautiful girl standing outside a restaurant holding a menu.'

"'How is that lucky?' I asked. It was hard to swallow and I told myself it was because the mousse was so thick.

"He touched my hand. 'It's the moment when everything in your life changes.'"

Zach turned off the camera. He was getting better footage than he dreamed of.

"That was fantastic, but I have to go."

He told Meredith about playing Santa Claus at the community kitchen.

"You're spending a lot of time with Rebecca." Meredith raised her eyebrows. "Shouldn't you tell her the truth?"

Zach hated lying to Rebecca, but it was too late now. If he told her the truth, he'd lose her as a friend.

"I can't," he said as he shook his head. "She'd never trust me again."

"Sometimes people will surprise you." Meredith ran her fingernails over Buttons's collar. "You just have to give them a chance."

Rebecca was already at the community kitchen when Zach arrived. He almost didn't recognize her. Her hair was hidden under a white wig and she wore a full-length red velvet gown.

"Zach," she greeted him. "Jerome said you'd be here."

"I've never played Santa Claus before," Zach admitted. "I hope I look authentic."

"Ben and I used to dress up as Santa Claus and Mrs. Claus for Big Brothers Big Sisters." Rebecca smiled. "Hold your stomach and say, 'ho, ho, ho.' You'll do fine."

Everything went perfectly. The children sat on Zach's knee and Rebecca handed out presents. Jerome moved around the room, distributing reindeer-shaped sandwiches and cupcakes with Santa hats made of strawberries.

It was only when Zach and Rebecca changed back into their clothes and joined the children for hot chocolate that Zach ran into trouble.

"Santa Claus isn't real," a boy of about ten said to Zach.

Zach glanced around to see if the other children were listening.

"Of course he's real," Zach replied. "You saw him, he was just here."

"If Santa Claus was real, he'd give equal presents to everyone," the boy said stubbornly. "My mother cleans houses and sometimes she takes me with her. Johnny Price got a football signed by Tom Brady, he's one of the most famous football players in the world. All I got was a set of Legos."

"Do you like football?" Zach inquired.

The boy shook his head. "Football is boring, I like soccer."

"Do you like Legos?"

"I like to build things," the boy said, nodding. "When I grow up, I want to be an architect."

"It seems that Santa Claus gives each child exactly what he wants," Zach said knowingly.

The boy's eyes brightened and he took a long gulp of his hot chocolate.

"So, next year, if I want a turtle, I'll get one?" he asked eagerly.

Zach smiled to himself. He'd had a turtle when he was a child.

"As long as you take care of the turtle yourself," he answered. "Santa Claus knows how busy parents are, he doesn't want to create more work."

Zach and Rebecca walked back to Christmas Cove Lodge together. It had started snowing and snowflakes covered the pavement. Christmas lights twinkled in the shop windows and the giant oak tree was decorated with a red bow.

"You were very good with that little boy," Rebecca commented.

"My family owns a sports camp, and I helped out every summer." Zach grinned. "I'm used to kids thinking they're smarter than adults."

Zach told Rebecca how his father had offered Zach a position to join him and his older brother at the sports camp after college, but Zach wanted to be a filmmaker.

"I'm surprised you still shoot your own footage," Rebecca reflected. "I would have thought by now you'd have a huge team. The closest you'd come to your movies is when you pitch the idea to the studios."

"My favorite place is still behind the camera and in the editing suite," Zach said honestly. "That hasn't changed since college."

"I envy you." Rebecca pulled her scarf around her neck. She wore a red-and-green snowflake sweater and red ski pants. A beanie was pushed over her hair and she wore brown Uggs.

"My favorite time at Dealbreakers was before we got our office space, when we ran the whole thing from Ben's apartment. Even after the company moved into our offices it was still fun. As long as we made rent and payroll, we could do whatever we liked. We once spent a week choosing the colors for the logo, and we rearranged the office furniture for days.

"Now everything that happens affects one hundred employees. Last year, the site crashed for twenty-four hours. Our lead programmer, Kimi, refused to leave until it was fixed, even though she was eight months pregnant," Rebecca recalled. "She's my best friend and I still couldn't convince her. I finally threatened to cancel her baby shower unless she went home and put her feet up."

They strolled past the teddy bear shop with a family of teddy bears wearing Santa hats in the window.

Rebecca stuck her hands in her pockets and kept talking.

"That's one of the reasons I picked Christmas Cove for our honeymoon. If we were in Europe and there was a serious problem, the whole office could screech to a stop."

"Except Ben isn't here," Zach pointed out.

As soon as the words left his mouth, he wished he hadn't said them. It wasn't any of his business.

Rebecca waited a moment as if she was thinking what to say.

"He's terribly disappointed. Something came up about the public offering and he's the only one who can solve it. It's not the kind of thing he could fix on his computer or by Zoom."

"It's none of my business, I shouldn't have said anything." Zach's cheeks reddened. "I don't want to ruin your holiday."

"You haven't done that at all," Rebecca assured him. She gave a small smile. "It's not how Ben or I expected to spend our honeymoon. At least he only had to drive a few hours, instead of getting on a plane to come and join me," she finished. "And Christmas Cove has everything we wanted. We promised to put away our laptops and sit in the Jacuzzi and go sledding and ice-skating."

"Would you like to go ice-skating now?" Zach asked.

Zach didn't know what he was thinking. Rebecca would wonder why he wasn't in a hurry to get back to Meredith. And she probably had plans. But the ice-skating rink looked so festive. Christmas music played over the loudspeaker and the lights turned the ice different colors.

"You want to go ice-skating now?" Rebecca repeated.

"We can do it another time," he said hastily.

Rebecca shook her head.

"I'd love to go ice-skating." She walked toward the rink. "I have to warn you, I'm quite good. My father and I used to ice-skate in Union Square every Christmas."

"I'm good too." He hurried to catch up with her. "When I lived in Prague, I ice-skated on the frozen river."

Chapter Ten

Rebecca sat in the living room of her suite and went over her notes for Howard's party. She was meeting the caterer in an hour and she had so much to share. The first piece of advice a caterer gave her when Rebecca had been planning her wedding was to always provide toothpicks with the finger food. Women often got their nails done before a party. They didn't want to ruin their new manicures by picking up a polenta bite or a turnover stuffed with ricotta cheese.

And never let guests get too hungry. At Rebecca and Ben's wedding reception, waiters would have been scattered around the space, holding trays of tea sandwiches shaped like snowflakes. Rebecca wondered what the chef at the Four Seasons had done with six dozen tiny sourdough buns spread with honey mustard and filled with roast beef.

She had to stop thinking about Ben and the wedding. The last two days had been better than she had hoped. Ice-skating with Zach had been so much fun. They raced each other around the rink like children. Afterward she took a long bath and then she stayed up reading and drinking hot cocoa with a splash of brandy.

For a little while, the future seemed bright and easy. A pleasant outing with a good friend, followed by a quiet evening alone in front of the fireplace. Surely, she wouldn't need more than that when she returned to San Francisco.

But this morning when she woke up, she remembered how wonderful it had been to wake up next to Ben. Their bed had been huge; a king-size mattress and a tall, quilted headboard piled with pillows. Ben would pull her close and whisper in her ear: he couldn't wait to start their day or he had a surprise to tell her about at breakfast. Even the hardest days—when one of their programmers quit because her mother was ill and she had to move home to take care of her, when the marketing firm they hired folded and they had to find a new one—were manageable.

Rebecca had been in love with Ben; it was impossible to simply turn those feelings off.

But now, she found herself thinking about Zach. Zach was good-looking and warm and so easy to be around. She had expected to be shy and nervous for the camera, but he immediately put her at ease. And he had been so kind to the little boy at the community kitchen.

She wanted to tell Zach the truth, but she couldn't bear him feeling sorry for her. She told herself that wasn't important. Everyone at Dealbreakers would feel sorry for her the minute she returned to the office and Ben and Natalie appeared with matching suntans.

But somehow telling Zach was different. Zach believed she was happy and successful. If she told him the truth, everything that happened with Ben would become more real. The cocoon of being in Christmas Cove—the warm luxury of her suite, the festive feeling of strolling down Main Street—would all unravel and she'd be left with a lump in her throat as painful as laryngitis during an important tech conference.

Howard wasn't at the cabin when she arrived. It looked even more like a storybook cottage than it had the previous day. The overnight flurries left a thick layer of snow on the peaked roof and footprints of tiny animals dotted the snow-covered path to the boathouse.

Just as she went inside, her phone rang.

"Rebecca, it's Howard. I wanted to make sure you got into the cabin all right."

"I just arrived. I'm meeting Sylvia, the caterer," Rebecca said, dusting snow from her jacket.

"I can't tell you how relieved I am, knowing you're handling everything," he enthused over the phone.

"You don't know that yet." Rebecca laughed. "I haven't done anything."

"I trust my instincts," Howard replied. "I just wanted to call and say please let me know if you need anything."

"I will, and I appreciate you giving me the chance. I won't disappoint you."

Rebecca hung up as a woman opened the gate. Sylvia was in her mid-forties with blond hair, pulled into a bun. Rebecca could tell right away that they'd get along. Sylvia listened to Rebecca's suggestions for a western-themed menu: honey-glazed ham and potato casserole and homemade biscuits. And she added a few ideas of her own: cowboy boots filled with Christmas greenery as centerpieces and a bar that served hot drinks—white hot chocolate, coffee eggnog, and a hot mulled wine.

Rebecca felt a new sense of excitement. After dinner, they could have a roping contest and the winner would receive a Christmas cake. Instead of only western-style desserts, there would be desserts from the places in Howard's postcards. Dutch windmill cookies from the Netherlands, the traditional chocolate Yule log served in Belgium.

By the time Sylvia left, it was lunchtime and Rebecca was starving. She walked to the diner on Main Street and ordered a bowl of vegetable soup. Then she unbundled the packet of postcards and spread them on the table.

The next postcard was from Denmark. There was a photo of a bronze statue of a man wearing a cape and holding a book. Underneath were the words *Statue of Hans Christian Andersen in Rosenborg Castle Gardens, Copenhagen.* Her eyes went to the journal entry below the postcard.

December 1990, Copenhagen, Denmark

This is my third day in Copenhagen. The city is stunning. Tivoli Gardens is the second-oldest amusement park in the world. In December, it's decorated with lights and ornaments, and they even build a Christmas village. I took a tour of the Viking boats at the museum, and an hour outside of the city there are castles with moats and drawbridges.

The only issue is that I'm supposed to be in sunny Greece. Three days of visiting the Acropolis and celebrating the feast of St. Nicholas, followed by Mykonos where they welcome the Christmas season by decorating the fishing boats and drinking shots of ouzo until one has to be carried back to their hostel.

It's my fault. I made the classic mistake of keeping my

money and emergency credit card in the same place and was robbed. Luckily, the American girl, Kat, came to my rescue.

"That's a completely rookie move," Kat said. "You always keep one credit card separate from the others."

We were sitting in a café in Amsterdam. It had been snowing for three days and I was beginning to think I'd never see a blade of grass again.

"I kept all my credit cards in an envelope under my pillow," I admitted, grudgingly. "I have no idea how the thieves took them while I was asleep."

"Thieves in Amsterdam have more skillful fingers than the best pianists." Kat stirred cream into her coffee. She was treating me; I didn't even have enough money for a pastry.

"I see that now," I said glumly. "I was supposed to meet friends in Greece, but I can't afford it. I already have my return ticket so I'll have to change the date and fly home."

"Can't your parents send money?"

"They're away, they can't get to an American Express office until next week. After I pay the hostel, I barely have enough money to get to the airport."

Kat drank her coffee thoughtfully.

"I'll lend you the money."

"How would I pay you back?"

Kat was leaving too. She was going to Denmark and Sweden. And she wasn't receiving money from home. She had saved up for the trip by working all summer.

"You can come with me to Copenhagen," she suggested.

"Your parents can send money to the American Express office there. Then you can go to Greece."

Copenhagen was even colder than Amsterdam. But it would only be a few days, then I'd be lying in the sun on a Greek island.

"Are you sure you don't mind?" I asked.

She was wearing so many layers—a turtleneck and sweater and scarf—that I could barely see her face. But her eyes held so much expression: warmth and humor and an appreciation of life. It was infectious.

"Quite sure," she said impishly. "I need to take turns with someone sleeping on the train, in case thieves try to steal my backpack."

We're staying in a hostel near King's Square, which is the most famous spot in the city, with statues and majestic buildings and a Christmas tree as tall as a skyscraper. We've done all the tourist things. We bought woolen mittens at the outdoor market and sat at a café in one of those narrow, painted buildings on the harbor. The traditional holiday drink is glogg—which sounds like cough syrup, but is mulled wine with spices and raisins and almonds. The Danish drink it with aebleskiver, apple pastry served with whipped cream.

We even took a "medicinal bath," which means jumping into the frozen canal. Afterward we treated ourselves to a sauna. It was the first time I've been properly warm in days.

This is our last afternoon. Denmark is lovely, and Kat is

a great travel companion, but I can't wait to soak my feet in the Aegean Sea.

"There's one more place we have to visit," Kat said, folding her map of Copenhagen.

We were sitting in a café facing a canal. There was an open brick oven where they baked pizza and I was in no hurry to leave.

"Can't we sit here all afternoon," I pleaded. "I'm just beginning to feel my fingertips."

Kat shook her head. She looked particularly lovely in a green wool sweater that brought out the color of her eyes.

"I've been wanting to go to Castle Rosenborg all week, but it was closed for renovations."

I slipped my book in my backpack and stood up. If it wasn't for Kat, I'd be back in Philadelphia. I didn't want to disappoint her.

When we reached Castle Rosenborg, the sign said renovations would last another week.

Kat folded her arms. Her mouth wobbled and tears came to her eyes.

"What's so important about this castle?" I wondered. "Copenhagen is full of castles."

"Castle Rosenborg is the whole reason for my trip! We have to find a way to get in."

I felt like a character in a classic 1970s heist movie, but Kat wouldn't give up. We finally discovered a section of the wall that was lower than the rest of the wall. I hoisted Kat on my shoulders and she climbed over it, then she opened the gate and let me in.

"Now what do we do?" I asked, glancing around nervously for a guard with a big, ferocious dog.

Kat didn't answer. Instead, she walked through the frozen gardens to a courtyard. There was a bench and a bronze statue of a man holding a book.

Tears were streaming down Kat's cheeks.

"It's a statue of Hans Christian Andersen." She gulped, accepting the handkerchief I gave her.

She told me the whole story. Last summer her father had been diagnosed with cancer and given a year to live. He was a children's book illustrator, and Hans Christian Andersen was his inspiration. Kat and her father decided to spend December in Europe. It would be their last Christmas together, and she wanted to take him to all the places he longed to go.

Except the prognosis was wrong. He died in October. Kat's mother is an emergency room nurse and wanted to stay home, so Kat went by herself. The statue of Hans Christian Andersen was at the top of her list; she couldn't leave Copenhagen without seeing it.

"Tomorrow I go to Stockholm," she said, fiercely wiping her eyes. Kat wasn't the type of girl who liked people to see her cry. "My father wanted to see a St. Lucia concert. They have them all over Stockholm, the carolers carry candles on their heads. After that, Stuttgart and Brussels."

"I'm going with you," I announced.

"But your friends are expecting you in Greece."

All those places sounded impossibly cold, but I couldn't let Kat go alone.

"Who wants sunshine and beaches at Christmastime?" I shrugged. "And my friends will be too drunk to miss me.

I'd much rather eat smoked salmon and go sledding in the Hagaparken."

Kat reached up and kissed me on the cheek.

"You won't be sorry. But we should probably buy more scarfs and mittens. The temperature in Stockholm is supposed to be minus fifty Fahrenheit."

Rebecca came to the end of the journal entry. Poor Kat! She couldn't imagine losing a parent at such a young age. Suddenly she felt grateful for everything she had: Kimi, and Howard's party to plan, and a new puppy, Oliver, waiting for her to bring him home.

She took out her phone and typed out a list.

This afternoon, she'd call Sylvia the caterer and ask her to add glogg and apple pastries to the dessert buffet.

She'd tell the florist about the cowboy boot centerpieces, and glance through her favorite websites for ideas before she met the lighting designer.

Her finger paused on the screen.

And she'd stop picturing Ben and Natalie frolicking on a white sand beach.

The phone buzzed, and Kimi's face appeared. Her eyes were red and her usually smooth, dark hair was tousled.

"Are you all right? You look like you haven't slept in weeks," Rebecca asked.

"I must look terrible. I haven't slept properly since Leila was born, and you never commented on how I look before." Kimi groaned.

"Is Leila teething again?"

"It has nothing to do with Leila, it's my mother," Kimi replied. "Yesterday, I took Leila for a drive after all the relatives left. Leila was so wound up from the attention, it was the only way to get her to fall asleep.

"I drove for an hour, listening to the soundtrack from the *Alvin and the Chipmunks* movie. Leila loves Alvin so much.

"When I got home my mother was in the living room." Kimi's voice rose. "With six suitcases and the tea set that has been sitting on her counter for thirty-five years."

"I don't understand," Rebecca responded, puzzled.

"My parents got into a fight. Instead of giving each other time to cool off, my mother decided to move in with us for a while. Andy let her! Andy said she could have the second bedroom that he uses as an office, but she refused. Instead, she set up the air mattress we sometimes use for overnight guests in the living room."

Kimi's parents had been married for thirty-five years. They met on a blind date set up by relatives and they barely knew each other when they got married. After all these years, they still sometimes got on each other's nerves. But they had three wonderful children who now all had families of their own.

"Andy couldn't turn her away. She is his mother-in-law," Rebecca said reasonably.

"Of course he could!" Kimi stormed on. "If he sent her home, this would have blown over. Instead, we're rooming with a sixty-year-old woman who has more pairs of shoes than the shoe department at Macy's."

When Kimi's parents came to America, her mother took a job. Even though eventually her father earned enough to support the family and her mother no longer needed to work, she liked having something of her own. She bought shoes with the money she earned.

"She brought all her shoes?" Rebecca asked.

"Of course not! That would take up our whole apartment,"

Kimi moaned. "That's not the point. In South Korea most couples don't divorce, they don't even separate."

They talked until Kimi had calmed down. Perhaps Kimi's mother just needed a few days to herself. Kimi would invite her father to dinner on New Year's Eve and everything would be all right.

Rebecca hung up and gazed out the diner window. Christmas was supposed to be about being with the person you loved most in the world. Sometimes that seemed as much of a fairy tale as the stories by Hans Christian Andersen.

Chapter Eleven

A few hours later, Rebecca stepped into the ski gondola. They had scheduled another interview for Zach's film. It was Zach's idea to hold it on the observation deck at the top of the mountain. It was a crisp, sunny afternoon, and the fresh, white powder, with people skiing down the slopes in their colorful skiwear, would make a perfect backdrop.

Rebecca was surprised how much she was looking forward to speaking on camera. Having someone listen, without making comments or criticisms, was almost like seeing a therapist. And it was nice to relive the early days. For a long time, she had been so happy with Ben.

And she was looking forward to spending time with Zach. Being with him opened something inside her. He was interested in what she said, and she felt a small spark, like the tail of a firecracker on July Fourth, when they were together.

The observation deck's restaurant had a wraparound deck with views of the whole valley. Skis and poles were lined up against the wall and people clomped around in ski boots. Rebecca had never seen so many people! They sat, laughing and talking, at outdoor tables. The air smelled of hot dogs and burgers and sunscreen.

"There you are," Zach said, warmly greeting her. He wore a blue ribbed sweater and brown ski pants.

"Ben and I used to go skiing, but it was never like this." Rebecca watched a group of young people pass around plates of tacos and salsa. "We just piled into the car, skied all day, and drove back to San Francisco."

"I would have thought this was the kind of thing the tech crowd did all the time," Zach offered.

"Dealbreakers only started making money a short while ago," Rebecca said honestly. "For ages, every cent we made went back into the company."

Rebecca let out a little laugh. She already sounded as if she was on camera, and Zach hadn't started filming.

"Do you want something to eat before we start?" Zach asked, as if he could tell what she was thinking.

Rebecca shook her head. "I had a bowl of soup for lunch."

They moved to the far side of the deck. It was quieter, and the view was breathtaking. Miles of white trails, dotted with pine trees. The lake far below, and the clouds above it, white and fat as marshmallows.

"Tell me when you first knew that Dealbreakers was going to be successful," Zach suggested.

Rebecca thought about it for a moment.

"In the beginning, it was a bit like skiing. In skiing, the first time you ski to the bottom of a bunny slope you think you're ready for the Olympics," Rebecca began. "Every step—when we hit ten thousand subscribers, when we had our first write-up in *Fast Company* magazine—felt incredible. But the moment when I really knew the company would be a success and we wouldn't have to get new jobs occurred during the second summer that we were in the office space.

"It was during a summer heat wave." Rebecca paused, remembering. "Heat waves in San Francisco are as rare as finding a parking space on the weekends. I was in the kitchen in our apartment, making a salad for dinner, when Ben burst through the door. He wore slacks and a white button-down shirt.

"'You can put away the salad dressing, we're going out to eat.'

"He had bicycled home from the office in ninety-five-degree heat, but he still looked perfectly composed. He was always like that. Even when we didn't have money, Ben sent his shirts to the laundry. Wearing a crisp, white shirt to the office was an investment, like serving potential investors fancy sparkling water even though we couldn't afford it.

"'We can't eat out again,' I protested. 'We've already blown our dining-out budget.'

"'Budgets are made to be adjusted,' Ben said as he took my arm. 'We're celebrating. We're this close to landing our first venture capitalist.'

"Ben took us to a burger place across from the baseball park. It wasn't fancy, but it had air-conditioning and was cold as an igloo. I wanted to sit there forever.

"'What are we celebrating?' I asked, loading my burger with lettuce and tomatoes and mayonnaise.

"'We've been invited to a cocktail party at the home of James Park on Saturday night,' Ben said, eating a handful of fries. 'Gordon Massey is going to be there.'

"James Park was the founder of Fitbit, he had one of those cool lofts South of Market. And Gordon Massey was a venture capitalist. Gordon was based in Seattle. He was known for investing in young, hungry start-ups.

"But I had tickets to a fund-raiser for the Save the Elephants foundation. I've always been passionate about elephants. It's impossible to imagine hunters killing such majestic and peaceful animals for a bit of ivory.

"'We can't go,' I said, and reminded him of the tickets.

"'Gordon will only be in San Francisco for twenty-four hours.' Ben took a bite of his burger. 'You go to the fund-raiser; I'll attend the dinner alone.'

"I couldn't believe Ben suggested it. We did everything for Dealbreakers together. We even shopped at Costco for office supplies together, because Ben believed that stopped either of us from making impulse purchases. You know, when you go to Costco for a packet of pens and come out with peanut butter protein bars for the whole office, and an ergonomically designed office chair.

"'Do you really mean it?' I asked for the second time.

"'I know how important this is to you. Or we wouldn't have a whole shelf of books about elephants in our living room.' He leaned forward and kissed me.

"Ben's kiss tasted like mayonnaise. I didn't argue, I'd been looking forward to the fund-raiser for ages.

"Ben was so sweet, he surprised me with a new dress. I told him we couldn't afford it, but he said I could wear it to all the parties we'd be invited to once we got our funding.

"The fund-raiser was in the Fairmont Hotel's ballroom. Save the Elephants works in forty countries to stop the trafficking of ivory. The keynote speaker had just returned from tracking elephants in Kenya, and his speech was followed by a film depicting the lives of a herd of elephants in Tanzania.

"By the time I arrived home, I was filled with adrenaline.

"Ben was sitting in the living room with two glasses and a bottle of chilled champagne.

"'This is for you,' he said and handed me a glass.

"The champagne was delicious; icy cold and not too sweet.

"Ben told me about the cocktail party. It was terribly crowded; he only spoke to Gordon Massey for a few minutes. But Gordon was taking us to lunch the next day before he flew back to Seattle.

"'How did you arrange that?' I gaped at him.

"'I apologized that you weren't there, then I mentioned you were at a fund-raiser for Save the Elephants.' Ben sipped his champagne. 'I read in an article that Gordon is a huge supporter of the Elephant Foundation. He wished he could have been there himself, but it conflicted with the cocktail party. He was so impressed that you attended, he asked if we could have lunch.'

"'Is that why you suggested I go to the fund-raiser?' I said in shock.

"'Of course not, I would have told you to go anyway,' Ben assured me. 'But it worked out perfectly. I know we'll get the funding, he as good as wrote the check.'

"I believed him. That's what is unique about Ben. He fiddles with our lives and the company as if it's a jigsaw puzzle and he isn't satisfied until everything falls into place."

"Did you get the funding?" Zach asked.

Rebecca had forgotten about the camera. Instead, she was remembering the smile on Ben's face when he told her the news, and how his kisses had tasted of champagne bubbles.

"Gordon gave us a check at the end of lunch," Rebecca recalled.

Zach turned off the camera and gathered his gear.

"That was great." He unzipped the camera case. "I'm starving. Can I buy you a burger?"

"Don't you have to get back to Meredith?" Rebecca asked.

"Meredith knows I have to work on the film," Zach replied.

Rebecca was in no hurry to go back to the lodge. And the burgers smelled delicious.

"All right," she said, nodding. "But I'll pay for the drinks. The website said not to miss their Pink Lady apple cider."

They sat at an outdoor table and ate cheeseburgers and onion rings. The apple cider contained just the right amount of whiskey to make Rebecca feel relaxed and happy.

"I've done nothing but talk all afternoon," she said between bites of her burger. "I don't know anything about you since college. What was it like making your first film?"

"My first film?" Zach repeated.

"You received a grant to go to France," Rebecca prompted.

Zach sipped his apple cider.

"I arrived in Paris and rented the cheapest room I could find." Zach smiled and Rebecca noticed that his teeth were very white. "Then I spent a few days mapping locations. The film was going to be about culture in Paris.

"The first morning, I filmed in the Luxembourg Gardens. A girl was sitting on a bench in a wedding dress and she was crying.

"Her name was Anouk and she was getting married that afternoon. Her mother lived a few hours from Paris in Honfleur. Her mother was supposed to be at the wedding, but she broke her leg and couldn't come.

"That was before everyone had a decent camera on their phones, so I offered to film the wedding," Zach continued. "Anouk and her husband were leaving right after the wedding for their honeymoon, so I said I'd deliver the film to her mother. It was only two hours by train and it would give me a chance to see the countryside.

"The ceremony was beside the lake, followed by a picnic in the statue garden. Anouk and the groom left on a rowboat and I headed straight for the train station.

"Anouk's mother asked me to stay and shoot an interview of her congratulating the bride and groom. The only problem was I was supposed to show the grant review board a draft of my film the following morning. I figured I'd be back in Paris by evening. I'd have enough time to film the footage I needed before the meeting.

"Except the train was delayed. By the time I returned to Paris, all the places I needed to film were closed. I decided to edit the wedding footage and Anouk's mother's interview instead. The grant review board might hate it, but I didn't have any other ideas.

"The next morning, I sat across from the review board. I was so nervous. They watched the film twice and then the grant director turned to me.

"He said that Americans perceive the French to only be concerned with great art and food. My film showed a different side of French culture; a mother who couldn't bear being apart from her daughter on her wedding day, a young bride who couldn't afford a fancy wedding dress or a church wedding.

"The director leaned forward to congratulate me. I was shaking so badly, I laughed and pretended it was from all the café au laits I had been drinking."

"What a wonderful story," Rebecca said when he finished.

Zach looked at Rebecca thoughtfully.

"Those are still my favorite films, just people talking into the camera," Zach reflected.

They finished their burgers and Zach gathered their plates.

"That's the best burger I've had since the Burger Shack at Berkeley," Rebecca said, handing him her plate. "Do you remember that place? It was the only decent burger place near campus. That's actually where Ben and I met. I was . . ."

She noticed a spot of mayonnaise on her sweater. She stopped to rub it off and a peculiar expression came over Zach's face.

Suddenly, a little boy carrying a plate of French fries bumped into their table. The French fries scattered all over the ground.

"Are you all right?" Zach bent down and asked the boy.

"I was waiting in line for ages, now I won't be able to get more fries."

"C'mon, we'll get you a plate of fries." Zach led him inside. He turned to Rebecca and grinned. "We have an emergency; I'll be right back."

A while later Rebecca sat in the living room of her suite. She had so much to do. Sylvia had sent a sample menu, and the lighting designer e-mailed with questions about the electrical outlets.

But she couldn't concentrate. She was still thinking about her afternoon with Zach. It wasn't only that he was easy to be around, or that he was handsome. Lots of men were good-looking, it hardly meant anything. This was something else.

She was attracted to him. She wanted to get to know him better.

That was ridiculous. Two days ago, she was supposed to get married. It was too early to think about men. And Zach was in Christmas Cove with Meredith.

She had been about to say that she had been waiting for Zach at the Burger Shack when she met Ben, and stopped herself just in time. Then the little boy ran into Zach. She wondered again why Zach had an odd expression on his face. It had probably been nothing.

Rebecca and Zach were just two old college acquaintances who happened to meet on vacation.

Chapter Twelve

Zach entered the gift shop on Main Street and examined the shelves. There was a display of Christmas china, and boxes of postcards, and a coffee mug shaped like a reindeer.

He wanted to get Rebecca a small gift for everything she'd done: helping out at the community kitchen, agreeing to be in his film, and paying for the drinks at lunch.

The last few days had been the best Zach could remember. He told himself it was the thrill of working on a new film. That was part of it. He couldn't wait to hear what happened next between Meredith and Phillippe. Meredith was so glamorous and sophisticated. But when he turned on the camera, she was a sensitive, eager young woman in love for the first time.

And Rebecca's segments pulled at his heart. Every time she mentioned something Ben had done, a steely feeling rose up inside him. Like when he was watching a television show and could see everything that was about to happen and wanted to stop the main character from getting hurt.

Ben obviously loved Rebecca. But Zach wondered if he loved Dealbreakers and himself more.

It was none of his business, Ben would be back soon. Rebecca and Ben would disappear into their suite, and Zach would only see Rebecca when they passed in the lobby. Perhaps Rebecca would introduce Zach to Ben, and Ben might suggest the four of them have dinner together. Zach would have to sit through three courses of watching Ben squeeze Rebecca's hand, while wondering how he was going to pay for his share of the meal.

It was time to admit to himself he had feelings for Rebecca and put those feelings behind him. Then why was he picking out a gift for her?

He was about to walk out when the salesgirl stopped him.

"Can I help you?" she asked.

"I was looking for a present. Something small but memorable of Christmas Cove."

The salesgirl walked to a table in the corner.

She handed him a snow globe. Inside was a scene of Main Street. There was the oak tree with the red bow, and the ice-skating rink and the pergola strung with lights.

He may as well buy a small gift. He could always decide not to give it to Rebecca.

"It's perfect." He handed it back. "Do you mind wrapping it with a bow?"

Zach left the gift shop and walked the few blocks to the community kitchen. Jerome was sitting at the table, going over some papers.

"Hey, it's good to see you," Jerome said as he looked up. "You were a terrific Santa Claus. I hope the children weren't too hard on you."

"It was fun." Zach grinned, remembering the little boy who wanted a turtle for Christmas. "I came to shoot a little footage."

"There's not much going on," Jerome said. His eyes brightened. "Maybe you could do me a favor tomorrow and film me proposing to my girlfriend."

Zach had known Jerome for a month and Jerome hadn't mentioned a girlfriend.

"You're getting married?" Zach asked.

Jerome pulled a box from his pocket. Inside was a small diamond ring.

"If Alesha says yes." Jerome showed him the diamond. "We haven't seen each other in four years."

Jerome hadn't returned to Trinidad since he and his family joined Jerome's father in America. Jerome had finally saved enough money for Alesha's airfare and a small apartment for both of them.

"Alesha is going to get her credential and teach elementary school. Every kid in class will have a crush on her. She's got a smile that could light up Rockefeller Center at Christmas."

"How do you know you still have feelings for her?" Zach asked.

Jerome took a photo from his wallet. Alesha had wavy auburn hair and a bright smile.

"True love doesn't change over time, even if you've been apart." Jerome tucked the photo back in his wallet. "That's how you know it's really love in the first place."

Zach strolled along Main Street toward Christmas Cove Lodge. The sun had set and the stars on the lake shimmered like a thousand fireflies. For a moment, he wished he had someone to share it with.

God, he was getting maudlin. It was talking with Jerome, and seeing the light in his eyes when he described Alesha. Zach had to stay focused. Even if Rebecca wasn't married and on her honeymoon, Zach didn't have time for love. If he didn't finish the film for the contest, he'd have a lot more to worry about than toasting s'mores with Rebecca in front of a firepit.

He was about to turn toward the lodge when he noticed Rebecca standing inside a shop. It was a men's clothing store. A stack of Christmas sweaters was arranged in the window.

"Rebecca, what are you doing here?" he asked, entering the store.

Rebecca had changed from the parka and ski pants she wore that afternoon. She wore a pink angora sweater with jeans and après-ski boots.

"Zach! This *is* a small town. We can't go a few hours without bumping into each other." She held up the cowboy boots she had been admiring. "What do you think of these?"

"Are those for Ben? Is he in Christmas Cove?" Zach asked, trying to keep his voice neutral.

Rebecca set the boots hastily on the counter.

"Ben isn't back yet. There's a glitch in our sales data for the last few months. Ben has to scour through the records and figure it out. The public offering will be delayed and some of the investors might get cold feet if it isn't fixed right away," she answered. "We didn't get a chance to exchange Christmas presents before the wedding. I thought he might like them when he returns."

"The cowboy boots would make a great Christmas present. He'll be thrilled."

"I'm glad you like them." She pointed to his bag. "It looks like you've been doing post-Christmas shopping. Something for Meredith?"

This wasn't the time or place to give Rebecca the snow globe. Rebecca was buying a present for Ben.

"Just something I picked up in the gift shop," he said, nodding.

Rebecca paid for the boots and they walked onto the sidewalk. There was something different about Rebecca. Her step wasn't as brisk and her smile was a little muted. Zach had been so wrapped up in his film, and examining his feelings for Rebecca, he hadn't thought about how lonely she must be without Ben.

"Meredith and I are having dinner at a brewery tonight; would you like to join us?" Zach asked.

"You want me to join you for dinner?" She turned to him.

They were standing in front of the lodge. Snow was piled high on the sidewalk and, through the window, Zach could see the colored lights on the Christmas tree.

"Meredith enjoyed meeting you," he went on, ignoring the voice in his head warning him that this was a bad idea. "And I've never been to a brewery. Isn't it the sort of thing people our age are supposed to do?"

Rebecca let out a small laugh. Her shoulders relaxed and her eyes were brighter.

"According to every Instagram I follow, it's a popular activity." She nodded. "Up there with vlogging and hosting game nights for friends."

"Should we meet in the lobby in an hour?" Zach asked.

Rebecca clutched her shopping bag to her chest.

"Yes, I'd like that. I'll see you then."

* * *

An hour later, Zach stood nervously in the lobby, waiting for Rebecca to appear. The minute he had gone to his suite he regretted inviting her. What good could possibly come of spending time with Rebecca and Meredith together? It was as if he was still in high school and purposely sent himself to the principal's office.

But Rebecca had seemed so lonely. And whenever he was near her, it was as if he was being drawn to her by a magnet. He wanted to stay and talk to her forever.

Meredith had been happy to have dinner with Rebecca. But Meredith's approval didn't make him feel better. Meredith's play-acting was how he got himself into this mess in the first place.

"Zach," Rebecca said, interrupting his thoughts. Zach turned around; his mouth dropped open.

Rebecca had never looked so beautiful. She wore a red velvet cocktail dress with a heart-shaped neckline. Her hair had been released from its ponytail and fell in light brown waves to her shoulders. Small diamond earrings glittered in her ears and she wore a gold bracelet.

"Wow," Zach said, without thinking. "You look amazing."

"I probably should have worn jeans. I can go and change," Rebecca said, embarrassed.

"Nonsense, you look perfect," Meredith said, joining them. Meredith was dressed in a cowl-necked sweater and suede pants. Gold earrings dangled from her ears and she wore high-heeled suede boots.

Meredith held out her hand and gave Rebecca her most radiant smile. "I'm glad you could join us."

"It's nice to have company for dinner," Rebecca said honestly. "But if you'd rather be alone . . ."

Meredith took Rebecca's arm. Her eyes twinkled merrily. "I love being in Christmas Cove with Zach, but I always like meeting new people. It's the best part of being on vacation."

They were about to go out onto the street when a man entered the lobby. He was about sixty with salt-and-pepper hair.

"Rebecca! I was coming to see you," the man said as he gently stopped her.

"Zach, Meredith, this is Howard Brewster."

"It's a pleasure to meet you." Howard nodded. He turned back to Rebecca. "I brought you the guest list for the New Year's Night party. Should I leave it with the front desk?"

Rebecca's cheeks turned slightly red. "That's a great idea."

"I won't keep you," Howard said briefly. He turned to Zach and Meredith. "It was nice meeting you."

The brewery was perched on the lake, nestled between a line of fir trees. A large pizza oven stood in the corner, and the walls were lined with photos of copper distilling tanks. There was an oak bar with dozens of different beer bottles.

"When I was in my twenties, craft breweries barely existed," Meredith said when they were seated at a window table. "You were served your beer in a mug and didn't ask where it came from. Now you can take tours of breweries the same as you do of wineries."

Zach hoped the waiter would take their order soon. Meredith was doing a wonderful job of keeping the conversation going, but he needed a beer to help him relax.

They ordered truffle Parmesan fries and a deep-dish pizza to share. There were so many beer options, Zach laughed that it was like being in a lecture hall and they should be taking notes. The waiter suggested a Mr. Toad's Wild Rye—an amber ale with a touch of rye and herbs—and Meredith and Rebecca ordered Stillwater Stout, which was black ale with chocolate and caramel malt.

"Tell me about Dealbreakers," Meredith said to Rebecca, when they were eating their pizza.

Zach was halfway through his beer and finally feeling less agitated. Outside the window, the moon reflected on the lake and the firepits let off a warm glow. A few boats were moored along the shore, and the mountains were large and dormant in the moonlight.

"I've been talking about Dealbreakers nonstop on camera," Rebecca said, smiling at Zach.

"I've never used a dating app," Meredith continued, sipping her beer. "You must have wonderful stories."

Rebecca told them about the couple who met through the app and lived in Chicago. They both hated the snow and rain, but were too worried about money to take vacations. They pooled their resources and went to one of those all-inclusive resorts in the Bahamas. Now they were married, and every year they traveled somewhere warm at Christmas.

"It's wonderful if it works," Meredith acknowledged. "But dating online just seems backward."

"Backward?" Zach and Rebecca repeated at the same time.

Meredith ran her long, pink fingernails over her glass.

"With online dating, first you learn the facts about a potential partner, but it's only later that you find out if there's any chemistry.

My first husband, Phillippe, was French. We didn't know a thing about each other when we met," she reflected. "It was all about being attracted to each other. Everything else came later."

"Why did you fall out of love?" Rebecca asked.

"Fall out of love?" Meredith turned to her.

"You're divorced, so I thought . . ."

"When you're really in love, you can't fall out of love even if you want to." Meredith looked out at the lake. Her eyes glimmered under the lights. "On the contrary, we divorced because I loved Phillippe too much. I'd rather talk about weddings than divorces." Meredith changed the subject. She turned to Rebecca. "Zach hasn't told me anything about your wedding. Where was the ceremony and reception?"

Rebecca seemed surprised by Meredith's question. She took a long gulp of her ale before she answered.

"I always wanted to get married at Grace Cathedral, I've been listening to the San Francisco Boys Chorus sing Christmas carols there since I was a child." Rebecca nursed her glass. "And it was Ben's idea to hold the reception at the penthouse suite of the Four Seasons. I didn't want a big ballroom wedding, the penthouse was much more intimate."

Zach pictured Rebecca and Ben greeting their guests in a plush suite high above the San Francisco skyline. Rebecca would have looked stunning in a white gown, and Ben would have been slick and sophisticated in his tuxedo beside her.

"Do you have any photos on your phone?" Meredith asked. "I love looking at bridal gowns."

"On my phone?" Rebecca repeated. She fiddled with her glass. "We wanted to make sure the wedding stayed private so we asked everyone not to bring their phones. The photographer will send me some soon."

After dinner, they walked back to the lodge and Meredith suggested they have after-dinner drinks in the lobby. A fire crackled in the fireplace and the bar was filled with couples in evening clothes. The waiter set down three eggnog martinis and a plate of gingerbread cookies.

"Excuse me, I have to take this call," Meredith said, glancing at her phone.

Zach wondered whether Meredith made up the call so that he and Rebecca could be alone. Meredith believed something odd was going on between Ben and Rebecca, and that Ben should be here on his honeymoon.

But Meredith hadn't seen Rebecca on camera, or at the men's clothing store, buying those expensive cowboy boots. Rebecca was clearly in love with Ben; Meredith was probably imagining things.

Zach gulped his eggnog martini and told himself he should really go to his suite. It was all very well to interview Rebecca for his film and help out together at the community kitchen. It was even acceptable to share a burger on the observation deck, surrounded by people. But Zach shouldn't be sitting in the dimly lit lobby with a pianist playing Christmas music while Rebecca sat across from him in that red dress with her hair curling over her shoulders.

"I had a lovely time," Rebecca said, interrupting his thoughts. "You know, when I first saw you and Meredith together, I thought it was a bit odd," she admitted. "I still saw you as the guy I knew in college and she seems so sophisticated. But now I see how much you have in common."

"You do?" Zach said curiously.

"Meredith has traveled everywhere and you lived all over Europe. She understands people and you do too."

"How do you know I understand people?"

"You couldn't make your films if you didn't," Rebecca replied.

Zach took another sip of his martini. He wanted to tell Rebecca everything. That he barely saw Paris or Berlin because he was locked in the editing suite, trying to meet a deadline. That he spent all his time worrying his funding would run out. And even when he received a new grant, he was afraid his next film wouldn't be good enough.

He wanted to say that he had never worked in Hollywood, he was making the film for a contest. If he didn't win, he'd spend his life teaching twelve-year-olds how to kick a soccer ball. That he was frightened working in the sports camp would change him, and he'd never feel like himself again.

More than anything, he wanted to tell her that the biggest mistake of his life, the only thing he really regretted, was being late for their meeting at the Burger Shack.

"I don't know anyone who has been more successful since college than you." Zach held his glass tightly. "You own a Fortune 500 company, and an apartment, and now you're married to your college sweetheart."

"You forgot Oliver."

"I was saving the best for last." Zach grinned, lightening the mood. "You're about to become parents of a Bernadoodle."

Rebecca smoothed her dress. She took a sip of her cocktail and smiled.

"You're right, you and I are both lucky. We're barely thirty and we've both realized our dreams."

Chapter Thirteen

It was 10:00 a.m. the next morning and Zach was already on his third cup of coffee.

He made himself stay in bed until 7:00 a.m., then he brewed coffee in the suite's coffee maker and pulled out his laptop. He was always this way when he edited a film. Often, he lay awake all night, and had to count sheep to stop from turning on his computer. It was impossible to think clearly without sleep, and he ended up re-editing the footage the next morning.

Dinner with Meredith and Rebecca last night had felt so easy. Then sitting with Rebecca in the lobby, talking about themselves, made him realize something he hadn't felt before. He was proud of what he had accomplished since college. His name might not be in the credits of a major motion picture, and he may not live in some swanky apartment, but he had experienced different cultures and he made films that meant something.

Without meaning to, Rebecca made him believe in himself. He was more determined than ever to win the contest.

The door opened and Meredith entered. Buttons jumped from her arms and she dusted snow from her parka.

"I woke up early, it must be the mountain air." Meredith set a cardboard tray on the coffee table. "We brought you cranberry muffins and coffee from the bakery."

"Thank you, but this is my third cup." Zach pointed to his mug. "I can take my laptop and work in my room."

"I don't mind," Meredith said, taking the lid off her coffee. "I thought we could film another interview. Buttons and I are taking the holiday train around the lake this afternoon. Would you like to join us?"

Zach shook his head. He told Meredith about promising to film Jerome's proposal.

"That sounds so romantic." Meredith sighed as she tapped her fingernails on the table. "It's interesting that last night Rebecca didn't go on about her wedding. Even after I asked her about it, she hardly said anything at all."

"What do you mean?" Zach picked up his coffee cup.

"She's only been married a few days. Usually, the bride bores you with details. The expression on the groom's face when he saw her in her wedding gown, the best man getting drunk at the reception and forgetting his toast. How she can't decide which was the best moment: the first dance that they practiced forever and that went off perfectly, or when the groom sang to her as a surprise at the reception. Rebecca didn't mention anything. If she wasn't wearing a wedding ring, I wouldn't know she was married."

"She was being polite," Zach said, though he had to admit Meredith was right. Rebecca didn't seem keen on answering Meredith's questions about the wedding. But Rebecca had said it was very private. Maybe she and Ben promised each other not to divulge any details.

"And who was that man, Howard? Rebecca didn't say anything about him."

"That's because it's none of our business," Zach returned.

"I googled him; he owns a travel company."

"Why did you google him?" Zach asked.

"I'm always curious about people." Meredith smiled coyly. "Why was he giving her a guest list?"

It was a bit odd. Rebecca hadn't mentioned a New Year's Night party. But she and Ben were a high-profile couple. Perhaps Ben wanted to approve the guest list.

"I don't know why I invited Rebecca to dinner in the first place," Zach said, trying to change the subject. "The minute I did, I regretted it."

"Because you have feelings for her," Meredith said matter-of-factly. "It's as obvious as the snow on the windowsill. It might not be obvious to Rebecca, but it is to me."

Zach took in everything Meredith said. Rebecca had never shown any interest in him, except as a friend. The rest was all in his head.

"Not all marriages work out. I thought Phillippe and I would be together forever."

"Even if you're right about Rebecca and Ben, Rebecca and I are in such different places in our lives. She's so successful and I'm an unemployed filmmaker. And I lied to her," he reminded Meredith.

"Sometimes people lie for a good reason," Meredith said. "I told Phillippe the biggest lie in the world."

"You did?" Zach asked curiously.

Meredith nodded. "Why don't I tell you about it on camera? It's the best part of the story."

* * *

"It was the following February and Phillippe and I had been seeing each other for six months," Meredith began when Zach had framed her in front of the Christmas tree.

"I was still working two jobs and Phillippe was working longer hours at the restaurant than was probably legal. But when we were together, it was magic. Except for a short time in Paris, Phillippe had never lived in a city before and he adored New York. He was happiest when we were lying in bed, listening to the sound of traffic. He said it was like a drum, encouraging him to work harder and achieve his dreams. And I saw New York through his eyes. At Christmas, we took a carriage ride through Central Park, and ate Christmas dinner at the restaurant where he worked. Phillippe got up on a table and sang Christmas carols in French and everyone joined in.

"Phillippe's roommate, James, spent most of his time at his girlfriend's apartment, so I often stayed over. I became quite domestic; we did the shopping and cooking together." She smiled softly. "It was almost like being married."

"Then one day, I knocked on the door and his roommate answered it."

"'Phillippe isn't here. He's at the airline office.'

"'The airline office?' I repeated, puzzled.

"James looked at me with a guilty expression.

"'Never mind, forget I said anything.' He walked to the kitchen.

"'Why is Phillippe at the airline office?' I followed him. 'He didn't say anything about his family visiting.'

"James turned around and sighed. He knew I wasn't going to leave him alone until he told me.

"'The plane ticket is for himself. He's going back to France.'

"'For how long?'

"James put the dishes in the sink before he answered.

"'Forever.'

"Phillippe's work visa had run out. His restaurant was going to sponsor him, but it was having financial problems and Phillippe had been laid off. He couldn't find another job without a visa, and he was running out of money.

"'I can lend him money,' I said quickly, calculating how much I had in my bank account. The money was supposed to go toward returning to school to get my degree in social work. But that could wait.

"'Phillippe is too proud to take money from anyone,' James said. 'He won't let me pay for a loaf of bread without promising to pay me back.' He showed me a piece of paper. 'Who writes an IOU for half a loaf of sandwich bread from Grand Union?'

"James was right. If I showed Phillippe my bank account balance, he'd get one of his dark, brooding expressions and make me promise to never mention lending him money again.

"'There has to be some way he can stay!'

"'The only way to get his green card and stay permanently is if he gets married.' James shrugged.

"James said it lightly, but I couldn't stop thinking about it. Even if Phillippe loved me, he'd never propose. We were so young and we couldn't even afford our own apartment. I considered proposing to him. But Phillippe would know I was proposing because he needed a green card and wouldn't accept.

"Then the strangest thing happened. One day, after work I stopped at the pharmacy and bought a pregnancy test. I'd been feeling slightly sick lately and wanted to make sure. I took one test and it was negative. I must have left the bag with the second test on the bathroom counter because the next day Phillippe confronted me.

"I should have known how Phillippe would react. He was raised as a strict Catholic.

"'What's this and when were you going to tell me?' he demanded.

"'Tell you what?' I asked.

"I was standing in the kitchen, making a cup of tea.

"'That you were pregnant!' he exclaimed, brandishing the package.

"I looked up from the teapot. He was holding the pregnancy kit. Before I could answer that I took a test and it was negative, he kept talking.

"'We'll get married, of course,' he said. 'We'll go to city hall and get a marriage license this week.'

"I was about to tell him that he got it all wrong, but the words wouldn't come. I wasn't lying exactly, I just wasn't correcting him. This was the solution to my fears that Phillippe would give up his dreams to open a restaurant in New York. That he'd return to France and I'd never see him again. I couldn't tell him the truth. It was fate, answering my prayers.

"Instead, I decided to give him a way out.

"'I have some money saved, I'll take care of it,' I said bravely.

"'What do you mean, you'll 'take care of it'?" His head snapped up.

"'We're too young to get married and have a baby. And we can't afford it. I'm going to get another degree; you're going to open a restaurant.'

"He paced around the kitchen.

"'Since when is listening to other people's problems as a therapist more important than being there for your child? And people start businesses and have babies all the time. When you're busy, I can put the baby in a carrier and take him to work. He'll grow up loving the smell of olive oil and spices.'

"Phillippe looked so impassioned; I was sorry that I wasn't actually pregnant. He would make a wonderful father.

"'We're too young to get married,' I said stubbornly.

"'My parents were younger when they married,' he replied. 'Are you worried that I'll run off and leave you when times are hard?'

"'Of course not.' I shook my head. 'It's just that . . .'

"Phillippe's eyes narrowed. He gazed at me intently.

"'You don't love me enough,' he said fiercely.

"My eyes filled with tears. For the first time that day, my answer was completely honest.

"'I love you more than I ever imagined I could love someone,' I whispered.

"Phillippe kissed me. Then he strode to the entry and took something from his jacket pocket. He returned with a small box.

"For a moment I was speechless. Was there a ring inside? Had Phillippe been planning to propose?

"'New York has always been the city of my dreams. But, when I arrived, I didn't know it would also be the place where I discovered the woman I love.' He opened the box. 'Meredith, will you marry me?'

"Inside was a pair of turquoise earrings.

"'I was going to give them to you for your birthday,' Phillippe explained. 'We'll exchange them for a ring.'

"I fastened them in my ears and kissed him.

"'We'll do nothing of the sort. We have the rest of our lives to buy an engagement ring. But I'll never again have the present you bought me for my twenty-fifth birthday.'"

"The wedding was planned for the following Saturday. The ceremony would be at the city clerk's office, and afterward James and his girlfriend were taking us to lunch. I was going to wear a party dress I owned since college, and I splurged on a pair of pumps.

"But I started to feel guilty, I couldn't eat or sleep. The morning of the wedding I realized that I couldn't trap Phillippe into marrying me. Even if he went back to Paris and I never saw him again, even if his dreams of owning a restaurant in New York were ruined. I couldn't go through with it.

"I hurried to his apartment. He was standing in front of the bathroom mirror. He wore navy slacks and the new tie he'd bought for the wedding.

"'You're not dressed for the wedding,' he said, turning around.

"'I've been to the doctor. Sometimes those home pregnancy tests are unreliable. It was a false alarm, something to do with my hormones.' I kept my eyes on the ground. 'I'm not pregnant, we don't have to get married.'

"It wasn't the whole truth, but it was enough to allow him to break our engagement.

"He stopped brushing his hair. He looked at me for so long, I couldn't bear it.

"Finally, he said, 'That doesn't explain why you're not dressed.'

"'It doesn't?' I asked in surprise.

"'Our appointment at the clerk's office is at noon. James booked a table at Le Soufflé for the wedding lunch.'

"'You still want to get married?' I nearly gasped.

"'It's you that I'm marrying. A baby will come in time,' he answered. 'We just have to be patient. Like we have to be patient for all the good things that are waiting for us.'

"'Since when are you ever patient?' I laughed.

"Phillippe gazed at me and his brown eyes danced.

"'You're right, I'm not. Get dressed and hurry. Le Soufflé gets crowded, and I refuse to sit at a table next to the kitchen at our wedding lunch.'"

An hour later, Zach hurried down Main Street toward the Christmas Cove community kitchen. A light snow was falling and he lugged his camera bag.

There was a bounce to his step. He felt lighter, and he hummed "Jingle Bells" under his breath. He even smiled when a little girl carrying a cup of hot chocolate bumped into him and almost spilled it on his shoes.

His personal life might be a mess, he may not have any money, but he loved shooting the film. After they recorded the segment, Meredith went to her room, saying she had to get dressed for the holiday train. Zach sensed that she had become so emotional, she needed time alone. And he felt the same. There was something magical about watching Meredith, beautifully framed in front of the Christmas tree, speaking so honestly to the camera.

The sleepless nights, the hard feeling in his stomach because he was living on caffeine, would be worth it when the film was finished. He even came up with a title: *Happy Beginnings: Stories of First Love.* It was a play on the fact that romantic movies always had happy endings.

Perhaps Jerome and Alesha would allow him to use the proposal in the film. There was a reason that the best moment in any romantic movie was the final frame, when the couple kisses and the camera sweeps around them. Every time it happened, even in the corniest movie when Zach saw it coming, his eyes turned wet with tears.

Jerome was fastening a star to the top of the Christmas tree when Zach arrived. Zach almost didn't recognize the space. The wood floor was littered with red and white rose petals. A vase of Christmas chrysanthemums sat on the table. Candles flickered on the counter and there was a sign with WELCOME HOME, ALESHA in red letters.

"Do you like it?" Jerome turned around.

Zach took in the Christmas stockings taped to the fridge. The bowl of oranges, and the small stack of wrapped presents standing next to a fruitcake.

"I wanted it to be special." Jerome wiped his hands on his apron. "Alesha and I haven't celebrated Christmas together in four years."

Jerome had cooked a Christmas feast with traditional Caribbean holiday dishes: beef pastelles, which were served in almost every home in Trinidad; pigeon peas, which were peas cooked with pumpkin and coconut milk; and a juicy ham. To drink there was ponche de créme—a creamy alcoholic drink like eggnog made with condensed milk—and for dessert the fruitcake and a sweet bread with a slightly burnt crust the way Jerome's grandmother used to make it.

"It didn't matter how much money we had, the relatives always came together and served Christmas dinner," Jerome said, adding canned pineapple to the ham. "You'll have to join us after the proposal, we couldn't possibly finish everything."

Alesha was at Jerome's apartment, changing out of her traveling clothes.

"I told her we'd grab something to eat, then I'd give her a tour of Christmas Cove." Jerome grinned. "She's never seen snow before. We had to stop and buy a pair of boots on the way back from the airport."

Zach set his camera up in the pantry. He hid behind the door and wiped a trickle of sweat from his forehead. He was as nervous as if he was going to propose himself.

There were footsteps, and Alesha entered. She was even prettier than in her photo, with brown eyes and long, wavy hair. She wore a yellow sweater and jeans; a striped scarf was wrapped around her neck.

"What's all this?" she gasped, twirling around.

Jerome had taken off his apron. He wore a red sweater with a snowflake pattern and tan pants.

"I wanted our first Christmas in America together to be special. Even if it's a few days late."

Alesha leaned forward to smell the chrysanthemums. She picked up the plate of fruitcake.

"It was worth the wait," she said and kissed him. "I never want to be apart at Christmas again."

They sat at the table and exchanged presents. Alesha gave Jerome a set of serving plates with a tropical design and a briefcase for his first year of law school. She opened Jerome's gifts: wool gloves and a pair of silver earrings.

The last present was a long box tied with a red bow. Inside was a pencil box. Jerome had drawn a heart that read: *Jerome Loves Alesha.*

The pencil box slid open. Nestled on red velvet was a small diamond ring.

"Alesha, the first time we met, we were twelve years old and I asked to borrow a pencil at school." Jerome took out the ring. "You told me to choose any pencil in your pencil box and I immediately fell in love. In all the years since, my feelings for you have only grown stronger. I want to spend the rest of my life proving that lending me that pencil was the smartest thing you ever did. Will you marry me?"

Alesha held out her left hand.

"Of course I'll marry you."

Jerome slipped the ring on her finger and kissed her. He poured two glasses of ponche de créme and they clinked their glasses together.

Zach gave them time to finish their drinks, then he stepped into the kitchen. Jerome introduced them and they all sat at the table.

"We're going to have the wedding tomorrow evening," Jerome said, passing Zach the bowl of peas. "I wanted to know if you'll be the best man."

"You're getting married tomorrow?" Zach said, surprised.

"There's no reason to wait." Jerome shrugged. "Alesha's family is in Trinidad, and my parents can't afford to come. We'll have the ceremony on the lakefront and then go out to dinner."

"I'd be honored to be part of it." Zach nodded.

"Excellent." Jerome beamed. "Alesha is going to ask Rebecca to be her matron of honor."

"Rebecca?" Zach repeated.

"It was my idea. Alesha doesn't know anyone in Christmas

Cove." Jerome squeezed Alesha's hand. "They haven't met yet, but I'm sure they'll get along."

Zach pictured standing across from Rebecca at the ceremony. The lights would be twinkling on the lake and it would be so romantic. It didn't seem to matter what he did, he and Rebecca kept getting thrown together.

"That's a great idea," he said, hiding the anxiety in his voice. "I'm sure Rebecca would love to be Alesha's matron of honor."

After, Zach packed up his gear and walked down Main Street. There was an odd feeling in his stomach, as if the ponche de créme was stronger than he thought. But he knew it was something else. It was seeing Jerome and Alesha so happy together. The way they finished each other's sentences and couldn't stop touching each other.

How hard was it to find love, and when would he have that for himself?

Rebecca was walking on the other side of the street. She was carrying the shopping bag with the cowboy boots. He thought she was going to enter the men's clothing store. He was about to call out, but she kept walking.

Zach watched her turn the corner. Then he put up his coat collar and hurried back to Christmas Cove Lodge.

Chapter Fourteen

Rebecca pulled her jacket around her and walked the last few blocks to Howard's boathouse. It was early afternoon and she was meeting the lighting designer.

Her morning had been so busy, she'd barely had time to think about last night's dinner with Zach and Meredith. First, she went running. She breathed in the fresh, clean air, and listened to one of her favorite podcasts, and didn't let her mind focus on anything except how beautiful the winter sun looked sparkling on the lake.

Then she returned to her suite and worked on finding pieces for the New Year's Night party.

She ordered a giant corkboard, which was perfect for hanging the postcards, and a map of the Pony Express. On Etsy, she found a wheat-colored rug, and a Christmas-themed mural for the wall. There were cowboy figurines for the table, and ornaments shaped like Stetson hats and barns for the Christmas tree.

It was only now, walking to the boathouse, that she allowed herself to think about the previous evening. It had started off awkwardly when they ran into Howard. At least Howard didn't stay to talk or mention Ben, but Zach and Meredith still must have thought it was odd.

Dinner itself had been lovely. Meredith was glamorous and sophisticated, but there was something about her that put Rebecca at ease. The only part of the dinner that made her uncomfortable was when Meredith asked about the wedding. Rebecca tried not to lie. She had been looking forward to getting married at Grace Cathedral, and Ben had picked the location for the reception. And she couldn't blame Meredith for being interested. Rebecca loved looking at photos of people's weddings; it was one of the things she enjoyed most on Instagram. But she still felt guilty. Twisting the facts wasn't the kind of thing she liked to do.

Then after dinner, sitting in the lodge's lobby and drinking eggnog martinis with Zach had been so enjoyable. Unlike Ben, he wasn't always checking his phone or peppering conversation with descriptions of the best gyms and trendy restaurants.

She had longed to tell Zach the truth about her and Ben. Then he remarked how she and Ben must be so happy, and had even mentioned Oliver, and she'd lost her nerve. At the end of Christmas week, they'd never see each other again. There was no point in admitting that Ben had left her and she had lied about everything.

The lighting designer was a tall woman named Claire. Her dark hair was cut in a geometric wedge and she wore wide, navy slacks and a matching quilted jacket.

Claire and Rebecca bounced around ideas: spotlight lighting above the boathouse door so when guests entered, they felt like movie stars. Bright lighting behind the bar, because the quicker people held drinks in their hands, the sooner they relaxed and enjoyed themselves. And no garish strobe light bouncing off the walls at midnight. Instead, the lights would turn off and all you would see is the twinkling lights on the Christmas tree, and the fireworks exploding over the lake.

Rebecca stood in the middle of the boathouse and recalled meeting with the lighting designer for her wedding reception. The spotlights above each table would be the same colors as the center-pieces. And Rebecca spent an entire day choosing the lighting for their first dance, so it seemed like they were dancing on a bed of diamonds.

Her mind went fleetingly to Ben and Natalie. Had Ben can-celed with the lighting designer too? None of it mattered now, she had to stop thinking about it.

After the meeting, Rebecca sat at a café on Main Street and pulled out the stack of postcards.

Her phone buzzed. It was Howard.

"I wanted to make sure you received the guest list." His voice crackled over the line. "I'm sorry I haven't been around. I had to drive to Sacramento to see a contractor."

"Everything is going wonderfully." Rebecca told him about the meetings with the caterer and florist and lighting designer. "I'm reading through the postcards. Are you sure you don't mind?"

"I said you can use anything you find," Howard replied. "I'm glad all those boxes aren't just gathering dust."

Rebecca said goodbye and hung up.

She ordered pumpkin soup and took out the next postcard. It was of a picturesque snow-covered village. Thatched cottages bor-dered a cobblestone street and, in the background, bubble-shaped gondolas climbed up a mountain. The caption underneath: *St. Anton in the Tyrolean Alps.* Rebecca read the journal entry below the postcard.

December 1990, St. Anton, Austria

When I started this trip, I never thought I'd end up at a ski resort in the Tyrolean Alps. Not just any ski resort. St. Anton is the birthplace of skiing. It's produced innumerable ski champions for a reason. The slopes, that look so pristine and innocent from the chalet window where I'm writing, are practically vertical drops and the most terrifying things I've ever encountered.

The only thing more frightening than the slopes was the train ride to St. Anton. St. Anton is only six hours from Vienna, and I thought the trip would be relaxing. Trains in Europe are so comfortable compared to America, and the scenery is spectacular. I didn't account for train tracks that seemed as sturdy as the toy train tracks I built as a kid. And I wasn't prepared for the train to have engine problems and stop for an hour on top of an icy precipice.

If it hadn't been for Kat sitting next to me, reading out loud from a gossip magazine and feeding me marzipan balls she bought at the train station, I would have fainted in my seat.

Kat, apparently, isn't afraid of anything.

Vienna was terrific. We took photos in front of Belvedere Palace, where they have a Christmas tree made entirely of sleds. We ate roasted chestnuts at the outdoor markets and drank Weihnachtspunsch—hot Christmas punch made with mulled wine and fruit. The punch is so popular, the markets have "punch stalls" and you pay a deposit for a mug. Half the tourists forget to return the mug, and the stalls make a healthy profit.

We saw an Advent concert, where the musicians performed Strauss and Mozart, which Kat loved, and we joined a group of young people we met for a traditional Austrian dinner of schnitzel and apple strudel.

It's because of that dinner that we're in St. Anton.

After dinner, we went back to the hostel and started packing. We were leaving the next day for Munich.

Kat came in and flopped on my bed.

"Don't pack your boots," she said, watching me. "Do you have a parka? If not, we can buy one at one of those used ski stores."

"Why would I need a parka in Munich?" I asked. "My winter coat works just fine."

Kat looked very pretty. She had treated herself to a new sweater and paired it with slim slacks and calf-length boots.

"We're not going to Munich; we're going to St. Anton."

I stopped packing and waited for her to explain. Kat loved doing things impulsively. She booked a bus tour of Vienna and made us hop off halfway through the tour, because exploring the Rathauspark—the square in front of city hall where the Christmas tree is full of lighted hearts—was more interesting.

"We bought train tickets to Munich," I reminded her.

"They weren't expensive." She waved her hand dismissively.

"Anyway, we'll save tons of money. For a whole week, we're going to stay for free in St. Anton."

Kat met a girl named Emma at dinner who was a "chalet girl" in St. Anton. The girls arrive at the chalets at 7:00 a.m. and cook breakfast for the guests. After the guests leave for the slopes, they clean the rooms and prepare sandwiches for lunch. They're free to ski all day and they return in the evenings to serve dinner and turn down the beds.

For that, they get free room and board in a house in the center of the village and free ski passes.

"One of the chalet girls ran off and eloped with a ski instructor," Kat explained. "I'm going to fill in for a week until the new girl arrives."

I was a good skier in high school, but I haven't skied since. Skiing is too expensive and ski resorts are so crowded.

"What will I do? I can't afford to ski, and I don't want to sit around all day."

"A pub in the village is hiring bartenders. You can work there," Kat said. She rolled onto her stomach and rested her chin on her hands.

"We have to go! I've always wanted to go skiing and I never have. And St. Anton looks exactly like an illustration in a fairy tale."

Kat was always so upbeat, but I knew she still missed her father.

"Where would I stay? I doubt there's a hostel, and I can't afford a room in a ski lodge."

"I told Emma that I can only take the job if I have a private room for me and my boyfriend."

"You don't have a boyfriend," I blurted out.

Kat still hadn't told me if there was someone waiting for her at home. But she never wrote to anyone besides her mother.

She smiled like a kitten with a warm bowl of milk.

"We'll pretend you're my boyfriend." Her eyes danced. "Think of it! Six nights in a ski resort in the Tyrolean Alps. By the time we leave, we'll be Olympic champions."

I couldn't say no. Six free nights and meals was too good to pass up.

"Or we'll both have broken legs and spend the rest of our trip hobbling around on crutches." I sighed, turning back to my packing.

She bounced from the bed and kissed me on the cheek.

"That's not going to happen. How hard can skiing be?"

It's our fifth day in St. Anton. The village is very special; it's as if we've turned the clock back a hundred years. No cars are allowed and the sidewalks are made of cobblestones.

Kat and I stroll through the village at night, and it's like the outside world doesn't exist. She tells funny stories about the chalet guests and I share things I heard at the pub, and we watch the night skiers glide down the mountain.

Sometimes, when we're walking I smell her perfume and see her smile under the streetlamps, and I don't want to leave.

There have been terrifying moments. Like yesterday, when we went skiing together. I've taken Kat on easy runs and she's quite good. But we got separated at the top of the gondola. I spent a nerve-wracking hour scouring the slopes and finally skied down and waited at the bottom.

"What happened to you? I've been looking for you everywhere," I demanded when she finally appeared. I had visions of her lying bleeding on a rock, or stranded at the top of a glacier.

"I skied the Albonabahn," she said, naming one of the black diamond runs.

"You must have been terrified! How did you end up there?"

"I didn't end up there, I skied it on purpose." She pushed her goggles to her forehead. "I was tired of the easy runs."

I wouldn't ski the Albonabahn. It was completely vertical.

"You're crazy!" I exclaimed. "You could have been killed."

"I've never felt so exhilarated, I can't wait to go again."

I don't know why I was so upset. Kat had been traveling all over Europe. She could take care of herself.

She touched my arm, as if she could sense my discomfort.

"Let's ski it together," she suggested. "It will be so much fun."

Luckily, it was late and the gondolas had stopped for the day.

"Maybe tomorrow," I grumbled. "I've been standing here for ages; all I want is a hot shower."

Later we were walking through the village. It was snowing and fat, wet flakes stuck to Kat's parka.

"How can you not be afraid? You've only been skiing for three days," I asked.

I had calmed down, but I was still puzzled. I'd never met anyone who skied black diamond runs so quickly.

"Reading fairy tales taught me not to be afraid of anything." Kat lugged her skis. "Fairy tales are full of dragons and goblins. Little Red Riding Hood had to fight off the big bad wolf, and the witch in 'Sleeping Beauty' put her to sleep forever. Children love fairy tales because they show that life is about having adventures, and there's always a happy ending."

I was going to say that we're adults now, and there are plenty of things to be afraid of, just read a newspaper. But Kat really was brave. She traveled to Europe alone while she was still grieving for her father.

Instead, I did the one thing I hadn't been able to stop thinking about. I leaned forward and kissed her.

For a moment she kissed me back, then she pulled away.

"Why did you do that?" she asked.

"I've been wanting to kiss you for ages, but I've been afraid of ruining our friendship," I admitted.

She thought about it and then she reached up and kissed me again.

"Then you shouldn't have waited. You wasted three days of kissing me."

Rebecca peeled off the tape on the postcard and tucked it in her purse. What happened between Howard and Kat? Had they kept in touch?

She made a note to get ornaments shaped like skis for the Christmas tree and to add Austrian apple strudel and marzipan balls to the dessert table. Then she closed the journal and walked back to Christmas Cove Lodge.

Rebecca's phone buzzed as she entered her suite. Kimi appeared on the screen. She was dressed in a blue dress, and she wore lipstick and eyeshadow.

"Where's Leila and why are you all dressed up? I haven't seen you wear makeup since before she was born." Rebecca settled on the sofa.

"Leila is in the other room. Andy is putting on her new dress," Kimi replied. "Anyone who designed a baby's dress with buttons should be fired. It's impossible to do the buttons up without Leila wriggling out of the dress at the same time."

Kimi slipped something into her purse.

"I might be out of range for a couple of days, we're going on a cruise."

"A cruise!"

Kimi and Andy hadn't taken Leila anywhere. It was hard enough packing Leila's supplies for an afternoon at Kimi's parents' house. Between toys and diapers and extra clothes in case Leila spit up, it made traveling impossible.

"It's a five-day holiday cruise to Mexico," Kimi said. "We're going with my parents."

"I thought your parents weren't speaking to each other."

"They weren't. Even Andy was growing tired of having my mother here. The final straw was when he tried to give Leila a bath and he almost tripped over my mother's shoes, which took up the hallway. So we staged an intervention."

Kimi's father wouldn't come over while his wife was there, so Kimi lied and said Leila kept crying because she wanted him to pretend to be an elephant like he had at Christmas.

"Who knew that my sixty-year-old father, who only paid attention to his children when they won awards at school, could be influenced by a nine-month-old wanting him to impersonate a zoo animal," Kimi said cheerfully.

"The minute he arrived, we locked him and my mother in a room until they worked it out. They each made a list of changes they wanted in the marriage. My mother wants my father to do more exercise. She wouldn't admit it at first, but she's worried he's too sedentary and he'll have a heart attack. My father wants my mother to stop wearing her favorite brand of face cream at night. It makes him sneeze when they're in bed."

Kimi ticked off the items on her finger.

"Then my mother insisted they go on a cruise. Apparently, before they moved to America, my father brought home brochures of cruises. My mother thought all Americans took cruises, so she started planning her cruise wardrobe. It's been thirty-five years and they've never been on a cruise. She said if he doesn't take her now, she's going to go by herself and run off with the Elvis impersonator."

Rebecca stifled a laugh.

"And you and Andy and Leila are going too?"

"My mother insisted," she said, her voice softening. "She wants to show us how far they've come from being two frightened young immigrants. She really is proud of my father; she just doesn't show it."

They talked for a while, and then Rebecca pressed End.

She poured a glass of water and thought about her and Ben. If Ben had loved her, he should have come to her months ago and suggested changes in their relationship. Would Rebecca have listened? Would she have been willing to live in a penthouse apartment, or drive a car that was so low to the ground that it made her queasy?

Her heart turned over a little. She put her hand to her chest, as if she was brushing the feeling away.

In an hour, she was meeting Zach to film another interview, and she had to order favors for Howard's New Year's Night party.

There wasn't time to think about love.

Chapter Fifteen

An hour later, Rebecca headed out of the lodge, away from Christmas Cove. She was meeting Zach at Vikingsholm Castle, an actual castle on the lake. It was built one hundred years ago by a wealthy stockbroker to resemble a Scandinavian castle. It had turrets and a drawbridge and outdoor benches carved from stone. The castle was open to the public and during the summer there were tours of the gardens.

Rebecca was feeling much better. Jerome had called and asked her to be Alesha's matron of honor at their wedding, and Meredith sent a box of chocolates with a note saying it was wonderful to have a new friend. Howard texted that the lighting designer was impressed with Rebecca's ideas and that he was lucky to have found her. Then Rebecca was browsing online and discovered the perfect gifts for the guests: boxes of Christmas cookies wrapped in cashmere scarves.

And she was looking forward to the interview. She really enjoyed spending time with Zach. He was so excited about the film, and being around him made her happy.

"There you are!" Zach was waiting for her when she arrived.

"Can you believe this place?" His hand swept over the view. "It's like we stepped into another country."

The castle was three stories with rounded windows and ivy climbing the walls. The slate roof was covered with snow and it had great wooden beams. Above them was a frozen waterfall and below, the lake was almost hidden by a thick forest of pine trees.

A separate garage held a few antique cars, and a large kitchen had wooden counters and an icebox from the 1930s. There was a living room with a huge fireplace and upright piano. And a mudroom with old-fashioned skis and snowshoes.

Zach suggested he set up the camera in the library. It would be quieter if there were other tourists, and there was a writing desk and bookshelves filled with dusty old books.

They talked about Jerome and Alesha's engagement, while Zach fiddled with the lighting.

"What should I talk about?" Rebecca asked. She wore her pink angora sweater and her hair was scooped into a ponytail.

Zach stepped from behind the camera.

"Anything you like. Tell me how Ben proposed. And tell me more about the wedding. I remember my brother Cory's wedding. They served an amazing chocolate wedding cake. I wanted two servings but there was only enough for each guest to have one slice."

Rebecca didn't want to talk about Ben's proposal. It was so recent, and she had been so thrilled. From the moment Ben slipped the diamond ring on her finger, she had pictured returning to Lake Tahoe at Christmas for their honeymoon. They would toast s'mores in front of a firepit and drink hot toddies in an outdoor Jacuzzi.

And she didn't want to tell any more lies about the wedding. She had to think of something else to talk about instead.

"I could talk about the time I thought Ben was going to propose, but didn't," she suggested.

"You thought he was going to propose?" Zach repeated, surprised.

Rebecca smiled, the sequence of events coming back to her.

"You know what it's like when a couple has been together for a long time," she said. "We were happy and I didn't think about getting engaged very often. But Kimi wouldn't let it go."

"It had been last December, the week before Christmas. I was looking forward to a week of being home with Ben. We were going to look for a new puppy, and try out a Thai takeout place near our apartment.

"'I'm thinking about creating an office pool, but you can't be part of it,' Kimi had said, entering my office.

"'What kind of pool?' I asked.

"Kimi sat on a chair. She was five months pregnant and wore a black blazer over a white shirt and slacks.

"'Taking bets on whether you and Ben will be engaged when we return from the holidays. The only thing is it might not be fair; I have insider information.'

"For the last few months, Kimi had been wondering when Ben would propose. She and Andy had only been seeing each other for a year when he asked her to marry him. It had been a complete surprise. Kimi thought they were going to hang wallpaper in his apartment. When she arrived, the walls were papered with love notes, and there was a trail of Post-its leading to a velvet box. Andy had hired a photographer, so their engagement photos were of Andy in a collared shirt and Kimi wearing her oldest T-shirt and ripped jeans.

"She didn't want the same thing to happen to me. It was better to have an idea when Ben would propose, so I could be prepared.

"'What kind of information?' I asked suspiciously.

"Kimi had been in Tiffany's looking for a baby shower gift for a friend, and saw Ben at the diamond ring counter.

"'We're paying you too much if you're shopping for shower gifts at Tiffany's,' I said, smiling.

"'She works at Google,' Kimi said, shrugging.

"'Ben was probably browsing. It is almost Christmas, lots of people go to Tiffany's at Christmas.'

"Ben had been acting oddly lately. He wanted to know the name of my favorite restaurant, even though we usually ate takeout unless we were with a client, and he made comments about how I had such slender fingers. Once, I even caught him rifling through my jewelry box. He said he was looking for a safety pin, and thought it was my sewing kit instead.

"'I saw him point to an engagement ring,' Kimi replied. 'A few minutes later he left, carrying a Tiffany's bag and the biggest smile I'd ever seen.'

"'Did you see the salesgirl ring it up at the cash register?'

"'Not exactly; a woman stepped in front of me on the escalator,' Kimi admitted. 'But it had to be a diamond ring. He didn't have time to go to another counter.'

"I tried to hide my excitement. We had been together for eight years, and we were still so in love. It would be wonderful to get married, to buy a house and plan a family.

"I didn't say anything to Ben, but I returned the blazer I'd bought him for Christmas and bought a watch for his watch collection instead. If he was going to give me a diamond ring, I wanted him to have something special.

"Ben's parents were in town, so we celebrated Christmas with them. Then we went back to our apartment to open presents.

"I loved to fill stockings for both of us and we opened them first. They were silly things: oranges, packets of mints, thick socks because our bedroom floor was freezing in the mornings. Then I gave Ben the watch.

"He opened it and his eyes flew to mine.

"'This is amazing,' he said and held it up, kissing me. It was some foreign brand recommended by the salesman. It could be worn underwater and told the time in six time zones.

"Ben walked to the back of the Christmas tree and took out a bag.

"I gulped; it was a turquoise Tiffany's bag.

"'This is for you,' he said and handed it to me. 'Because you make me so happy.'

"My fingers fumbled with the bow and Ben reached forward.

"'Here, let me help you.'

"He untied the bow and opened the box.

"Inside was a gold bracelet with tiny ruby butterflies. It was beautiful, but it wasn't an engagement ring.

"'I love it,' I said uncertainly.

"Ben slipped it around my wrist.

"'I knew you would.' His eyes were bright.

"It was perfect—not too extravagant, just right to wear to the office. Ben would propose eventually, and the point of Christmas was being together.

"A few days later, the clasp on the bracelet came loose and I went to Tiffany's to have it repaired.

"The saleswoman looked puzzled when she saw me.

"'I remember you. You and your fiancé came in one day. Don't tell me you didn't like the ring.'

"Ben and I had gone into Tiffany's during Thanksgiving. But we hadn't stayed long.

"'He's not my fiancé, and it's not a ring.' I showed her the bracelet and explained about the clasp.

"'But he did buy a ring, I helped him pick it out,' the saleswoman insisted. 'He was going to pay for it the next day, after it was polished.'

"I shrugged and said she must have confused him with someone else. The rest of our holiday was perfect. We watched cheesy Christmas movies, and went ice-skating and saw the giant gingerbread house at the Fairmont Hotel.

"The only person who was upset was Kimi. She'd bet twenty dollars in the office pool and lost."

Zach hit Pause on the camera. "That's a wonderful story. I'd love to shoot the bracelet for the film."

"It's in my jewelry box, I'll bring it by." Rebecca nodded.

"Ben did make up for it," Zach commented. "Your engagement ring is fantastic."

Rebecca glanced down at her hand. She felt awkward that she was still wearing it. But Zach would think it was strange if she took it off.

Zach packed up the gear, and Rebecca waited in the castle's entry.

There was something bothering her. At first, she couldn't put her finger on it.

Had Ben bought an engagement ring and then returned it? That would mean he had doubts about their relationship a year ago. Before Natalie started working for the company. Maybe Ben had never loved Rebecca enough. He loved being a couple, he loved their successes, but he didn't love Rebecca for herself.

"Are you all right?" Zach glanced at her curiously.

Rebecca pulled her thoughts back to the present. Her hands were cold and her whole body felt chilled.

"I'm fine, it's just a little cold in here."

"You're right, I got wrapped up in the story," Zach apologized. "Why don't we go back to the lodge and have hot chocolates?"

They sat in the lobby and drank hot chocolates with whipped cream and nutmeg. Rebecca wished she could add a shot of Kahlúa. She was still upset about her memories of last Christmas and the thoughts that wouldn't stop running through her head.

She tried to think of other times this past year when Ben seemed unclear about his feelings. There was the time before he proposed that she suggested they visit her father in Seattle at Christmas. Ben didn't answer, and she thought it was too early to plan the holidays. But maybe Ben wasn't sure if they were still going to be together in December.

And sometimes when they were both working on their laptops in the evenings, she'd catch him looking at her with an odd expression. She always thought that he was just going over sales projections in his head. But maybe he was wondering if there was someone else out there who would make him want to dash home at night, weighted down with flowers or boxes of chocolate. Someone he couldn't stop thinking about, and who gave him that clammy feeling in his chest.

Then Natalie came along, with her long legs and impressive degrees, and Ben immediately fell in love. Could it have happened so quickly if he had really loved Rebecca?

She had to stop thinking about it.

She and Zach talked about their favorite romantic Christmas movies: *Last Christmas* and *The Holiday*.

"Our film professor would be horrified if he heard us," Rebecca said, smiling. "According to him, films are only worthwhile if they're three hours long and filmed in black and white."

"One has to study the great directors to learn the craft," Zach said earnestly. "But to me the best story line is always boy meets girl, something separates them, and eventually they end up together."

"Then in the last frame they kiss, and the music comes up and the screen fades to black," Rebecca finished for him, recalling the dozens of romantic movies she'd watched on Netflix.

Zach glanced at her in surprise.

"That's what I'm trying to capture in this film. Especially when it's about the boy and girl falling in love for the first time. There's nothing like first love; it changes you forever."

They sipped their hot chocolates and the pressure in Rebecca's chest went away. The lobby really was lovely. Candles flickered on the fireplace mantel and the air was scented with pine needles. Outside the window, a steamship glided along the lake, and a family of squirrels scurried along the snow-covered ground.

Rebecca let herself relax. Zach looked so handsome. His dark hair was slightly messy from being outside, and a green scarf was wrapped around his neck.

Zach placed his glass on the coffee table.

"Rebecca, there's something I've wanted to tell you . . ."

Suddenly, there was a barking sound and a small dog leapt into Zach's lap.

Meredith appeared. She wore a quilted down jacket and long, wool gloves.

"Zach, Rebecca," she greeted them. "I'm sorry about Buttons, I need to teach him better manners. It's freezing outside. Those hot chocolates look delicious."

While Zach patted Buttons's head, he seemed oddly deflated. "We were just talking about our old film class, why don't you join us?"

Chapter Sixteen

The next morning, Zach set the camera up in the suite's living room and filmed the Christmas tree and the view from the window.

He couldn't sit still long enough to edit, and he had already taken Buttons for a walk and bought muffins at the bakery. He even stopped at the pet shop and picked out gifts for Buttons—a squeaky toy reindeer and a gingerbread-flavored dog bone. He was very grateful to him. If Buttons hadn't jumped into his lap when he and Rebecca were drinking hot chocolates, Zach would have admitted that he had been late to the Burger Shack all those years ago. That he had seen Rebecca and Ben through the window and decided not to interrupt.

It seemed a perfectly logical thing to say at the time, since they had been talking about their old film class. But what would Zach have said next? That he had a crush on Rebecca and was hoping their meeting would lead to a first date? That he hadn't felt the same about anyone since, and that the last few days he'd felt . . .

He wasn't even sure what he felt. Every time he was with Rebecca he wanted to talk to her forever. She was pretty and effervescent and asked interesting questions. But Zach would never interfere with her marriage, or any marriage. Yet Ben had been gone a long time. Maybe Meredith was right, something was going on between them.

But admitting his old crush was still the wrong thing to do. Zach couldn't ask Rebecca about Ben; it was up to her to confide in him.

The door opened and Meredith entered.

"You must have been up early," Meredith said as Buttons jumped into her arms. "I went to the gym, and you and Buttons were already gone."

"I needed to get out," Zach sighed. "People think filmmaking is so glamorous; traveling to exotic locations and attending red-carpet openings. It's mainly about sitting in an editing suite for so long, you forget what it's like to see sunshine. Right now, I can't concentrate on anything."

Zach told her about almost admitting his feelings to Rebecca, and Buttons jumping into his lap.

"I don't know what I'd do without Buttons," Meredith said, stroking the dog's nose. She looked at Zach thoughtfully. "Have you ever thought there might be a reason you and Rebecca ran into each other in Christmas Cove?"

"What do you mean?"

"You haven't seen each other in almost a decade. Suddenly, you're floundering in your career, and Rebecca appears on her honeymoon, but without a husband. On Christmas." She let Buttons jump down. "Maybe you were meant to find each other."

"I don't believe in fate."

"Do you believe in Santa Claus?"

"Of course not." Zach grinned. "That myth was dispelled by my older brother when I was seven years old."

"You should believe in him." Meredith held up her phone. "It's easier to believe in a cheery man with a white beard and a sack full of presents than believe that everything we need in life is stored in this piece of metal. And you make movies!" She pointed at the camera. "How can a tiny microchip hold scenes of people and places that are then blown up on a huge movie screen?"

"That's different," Zach said stubbornly. "That's science and technology."

"Fate is a different kind of science," Meredith reflected. "Sometimes you have to believe good things will happen. Phillippe taught me that." She sat on the sofa. "Why don't you turn on the camera, and I'll tell you the story."

"Phillippe and I had been married for two years and we were terribly happy. We had the usual New York problems. Our apartment was tiny. It was called a one bedroom, but it was really a studio with a door separating a window alcove. And the oven didn't work all the time. I begged the owner for a new one, but it would mean rewiring the whole apartment.

"I was sharing an office with another therapist, and Phillippe was ready to open his own restaurant. It was hard to find a space. Even though we could afford it, the landlords would see Phillippe's youth and lack of business experience, and rent to someone else.

"It was September and Phillippe's parents were visiting from France. Phillippe had invited them to dinner at our apartment. I was nervous; there was barely enough room for four chairs at the dining table. But Phillippe was proud of our flat, and he had boasted to his mother I was a wonderful homemaker. That afternoon, the oven stopped working and the profiteroles I was baking for dessert collapsed.

"Phillippe came in while I was standing in front of the oven. I'd been to the bakery, and there was a bag with a loaf of bread on the table.

"'You must never leave bread facing down. It's bad luck.' Phillippe turned the loaf over.

"One thing I had learned was how superstitious Phillippe was. I had no idea that the French had so many superstitions.

"When we moved into the apartment, the dining table had to be brought in first for good luck. He never gave me chrysanthemums because they brought bad luck, and whenever he made pancakes he held a gold coin in his left hand, because that was supposed to make us rich.

"'I've already had enough bad luck for one day.' I sighed, poking the gooey profiterole.

"I shouldn't have tried to make a French dessert in the first place. But I wanted to impress his mother and profiteroles are delicious: pastry balls filled with custard, and covered with chocolate and spun sugar. 'The oven stopped working and I stepped in a dog's mess on the way home.'

"'Did you step on it with your right shoe or left shoe?' Phillippe asked.

"I tried to remember.

"'With my left shoe. Why does it matter? I still ruined my shoe.'

"'It matters greatly,' he said, his voice serious. 'Stepping on it with your right foot brings bad luck, but stepping on it with your left foot guarantees good fortune.'

"Before I could comment, Phillippe strode to our bedroom. He returned holding up the polka-dot dress he'd bought me the previous Christmas.

"'Wearing a polka-dot dress brings good luck. Put this on and go to the bakery and buy profiteroles.' He handed it to me. He smiled that wide, white smile that made me believe in anything. 'I promise, you'll have the best luck.'

"The bakery was a few blocks from our apartment. It resembled a French patisserie with an espresso machine and little tables next to the window. In the summer, Phillippe and I sat there for ages, drinking café au laits and talking about our plans for the future.

"While I was waiting, I overheard the owner, Pascal, talking. His father had just died. He was moving back to Paris, and needed someone to take over his lease.

"I got so excited. The bakery could easily be turned into a restaurant. It already had a kitchen, and if the pastry cases were removed, there would be room for more tables.

"Pascal recognized me, and I told him Phillippe's plans to open a French restaurant. He promised not to show it to anyone until Phillippe and I talked.

"I went home and told Phillippe all about it. His parents were arriving for dinner in an hour. We had just enough time to run back to the bakery. Phillippe took one quick look around the kitchen, and wrote a deposit check on the spot.

"Just as exciting, Pascal had an apartment above the bakery. It had a proper bedroom and new appliances and a window overlooking the street. In New York, you're often staring out the window at your neighbor, but here there were trees and stone stoops. We decided to take the apartment too.

"We arrived back at our place as his parents arrived. Dinner went off perfectly, and everyone loved the profiteroles.

"After they left, we did the washing up together. I was flushed from happiness and from the champagne Phillippe bought to celebrate.

"'I never thought we'd find a space for the restaurant,' I said, handing him a dish towel.

"'I knew it the moment you left this afternoon,' he declared.

"'How could you? We've been turned down by every commercial landlord in the East Village.'

"'Because you ruined your shoe stepping in a dog's mess, and you were wearing a polka-dot dress.'

"I let my hands soak in the soap bubbles.

"'You can't really believe those superstitions.'

"'Of course I do,' he insisted. 'Do you think French people would never give each other knives as presents because it brings bad luck, if it wasn't true? Or that my mother would refuse to iron my father's underwear, even though she irons his shirts and his socks? To iron a husband's underwear brings bad luck to the whole household.'

"I tried to imagine Phillippe's sophisticated mother abiding by ridiculous superstitions and burst out laughing.

"'Americans are so literal,' he said as he kissed me. His mouth tasted like champagne and profiteroles. 'Americans forget to look for the magic in life. One has to believe in luck, or there's no point in living.'"

After finishing up with Meredith, Zach zipped up his parka and strode through the lobby to the sidewalk. He wasn't getting any editing done, so he decided to go sledding.

Meredith's story made great footage, but it didn't solve anything in his own life. Even if he did believe in fate, Rebecca already had her happy ending. It was only Zach who was hanging on to his dreams.

Christmas might be magical, but it only came once a year. In January, he had to face up to reality.

Rebecca was walking a few steps ahead of him. She turned and noticed him.

"Zach!" she greeted him. "It's such a gorgeous day. What are you doing?"

The fog that blanketed the lake when he walked Buttons had lifted, and the sky was a bright blue. It had snowed during the night and the paths were now covered with fresh, white snow.

"I seem to have a filmmaker's version of writer's block," Zach admitted. "I'm going sledding to clear my head." He shielded his eyes from the sun. "Would you like to come?"

Rebecca seemed surprised by his invitation. Zach inwardly berated himself. He had to stop saying things without thinking them through.

"It's more fun with two people," he added. "But if you're busy, that's okay."

"I'm not. I had a meeting, but it got postponed."

"A meeting?" Zach repeated, puzzled.

"A Zoom meeting with a software supplier," Rebecca corrected hurriedly. "I haven't been on a sled in ages. I'd love to come."

They rented a wooden sled from the kiosk at the foot of the mountain. A magic carpet took them to the top, where the view was breathtaking. Pine trees were heavy with icicles, and trails had thick blankets of soft powder. The lake spread out below, and children sailed past on sleds and rubber snow tubes.

They made four trips up and down the mountain, stopping to

watch a deer standing in the forest and a rabbit whose tail was the same white as the snow.

After they returned the sled, they sat at the outdoor restaurant and ordered grilled cheese sandwiches.

"San Diego was a great place to grow up, but it never snowed." Zach bit into his sandwich. "My parents took us to Disneyland at Christmas because they made fake snow. But the minute you left the parade on Main Street and walked back to your car, it was seventy degrees."

"I never saw snow until my father moved to Seattle," Rebecca replied. "That's why I always dreamed of a white Christmas. Someday I want a chalet on the lake. Nothing fancy, but with one of those big kitchens where everyone does the cooking together. After the presents are opened and dinner is finished, there'd be snowball fights and sledding." She smiled. "At midnight, we'd attend Christmas services and it would be just like a postcard."

Rebecca looked so lovely. Her cheeks were radiant from the cold, and she had a light tan. It took all Zach's willpower not to say everything he was thinking. Where was Ben and why had he missed half his honeymoon? Did Rebecca ever guess that Zach had a crush on her all those years ago? Would it have made a difference?

Instead, he put down his sandwich and grinned.

"You forgot about Oliver," he reminded her. "There's nothing better than a big, furry dog. They keep your feet warm, just like a blanket."

They finished their sandwiches and talked about Jerome and Alesha's wedding later that day, and Zach's film.

"I have a confession to make," Rebecca said, sipping a cup of hot apple cider. "The day I was supposed to assist you in college, I almost didn't come."

Zach glanced at her in surprise. "What do you mean?"

"We were going to film at Fisherman's Wharf, and I hate going to amusement parks. I got stuck on a Ferris wheel when I was a little girl. Now I'm afraid of all of it, even the merry-go-round."

"Why didn't you tell me? We could have filmed somewhere else."

"You had every scene planned out; it was too late to change it. I was going to say that I came down with the flu or had food poisoning, and that you should find someone else."

"What made you change your mind?" Zach questioned.

"I stayed awake all night. I kept telling myself it would be fine, but I was terrified," Rebecca recalled. "In the morning, you sent me a text reminding me to bring a sweater because it was always freezing beside the bay," Rebecca said thoughtfully. "I knew you wouldn't let anything bad happen to me."

Zach put down his cup. There was a lump in his throat, but he told himself it was from the hot apple cider.

"You're right, I would have made sure that you were safe."

Chapter Seventeen

Zach adjusted his tie in front of the bathroom mirror. Then he untied it and tied it again.

Jerome and Alesha's wedding was in an hour and he was running late. He had meant to spend the afternoon writing his best man's speech, but when he'd returned from sledding with Rebecca, he sat down at his laptop and started editing the film.

It was either the fun of careening down the slopes or the camaraderie of being with Rebecca, but suddenly editing the footage felt as easy as sipping his first cup of morning coffee.

He only dragged himself away from his laptop when Jerome called to make sure Zach knew what time the ceremony started. They only had the officiant for half an hour.

He slipped on his jacket and grabbed the hastily written speech from the counter. Then he dashed through the lobby and walked briskly to the community kitchen.

When he arrived, Jerome was standing in front of the oven. An apron was tied around his waist, and he held a spatula.

"Hey, Zach." Jerome looked up and grinned. "You're all dressed up, you look like you're going to a wedding."

"I'm going to *your* wedding." Zach frowned. "But you're not dressed."

He hadn't known Jerome long, and he couldn't help being nervous. It was the biggest day in Jerome and Alesha's lives and he wanted it to be perfect.

"I'm making brownies for Alesha," Jerome replied. "The restaurant is providing a wedding cake, but brownies are Alesha's favorite dessert."

"You're making brownies on your wedding day!" Zach exclaimed.

"They're almost done, then I'll get dressed. Alesha's at the apartment getting ready. She had a great idea. She's going to use the community kitchen to offer free children's cooking classes." He peered into the oven. "This afternoon, we went around to the shops to get donations."

"I don't know how you can be so calm." Zach tugged at his tie. "In an hour, your life is going to change. From now on, you'll wake up next to the same person, and see her every evening across the dinner table. Your entire future: where you'll take a job, when to go on vacation, even what color towels to hang in the bathroom, will be discussed with her first. And when you get in a fight, you won't be able to think straight until you work it out."

"You make it sound like a prison sentence, but you've got it wrong," Jerome said with a smile. "You marry someone because from then on, you don't have to make those decisions by yourself. There's someone to talk to, someone who cares about the outcome as much as you do. And there's nothing wrong with the occasional disagreement." He chuckled. "Making up can be the best part of a relationship."

"But how do you know you're marrying the right person?"

Jerome shrugged. He took the brownie pan out of the oven.

"Some things you just know. Like I know that mixing butter and eggs and cocoa powder makes the best brownies."

Zach went ahead to the restaurant, while Jerome got dressed.

Rebecca was waiting on the patio. He had never seen her look so lovely. She wore an oyster-colored dress, the color of the lights reflecting on the lake. Her shoulders were covered by a cashmere cape, and her hair fell softly around her shoulders.

"You look stunning in that dress," he blurted out.

Rebecca smiled appreciatively.

"Even tech people don't wear jeans every day. It's fun to dress up, especially for a wedding."

"I forgot you just got married. I haven't been to a wedding in ages." Zach groaned. "I'm more nervous than the groom."

"I saw Alesha, she's completely relaxed," Rebecca replied. "As long as you have the rings, we'll be fine."

Zach put his hands to his pockets. Suddenly he froze. At the last minute he had changed jackets. The wedding rings and his room key were in his other jacket.

"I don't have the rings, or the room key. If I run back to the lodge, I might not be able to get in the room."

Meredith was out. By the time the front desk made him a new key it might be too late. The officiant would have to go on to his next wedding.

Rebecca thought quickly. She strode into the restaurant. She approached a couple sitting at a window table and told them the story.

"If we could borrow your wedding rings for an hour, we'll return them," she said, opening her purse. "I'll write you a check as a deposit."

The woman shook her head.

"I'm sorry, but I haven't taken off my wedding ring in thirty years."

The couples at the second and third tables said the same thing.

Zach and Rebecca were about to head back to the terrace when Zach noticed an older woman walking toward them.

"I heard you talking to another couple," the woman said to Rebecca. She pulled a gold band off her finger. "You can borrow mine, and here's my husband's. You don't need to write a check. Anyone who does such a nice thing for a friend can be trusted."

Rebecca handed the rings to Zach and they dashed to the patio. Jerome and Alesha arrived together. Jerome wore a navy blazer over a white shirt and tie. Alesha was beautiful in a two-piece cream-colored suit. Her hair was festooned with flowers, and she carried a small bouquet of roses.

The ceremony went off perfectly. Afterward they popped a bottle of champagne and went inside to their table.

"Nice wedding rings," Jerome said, grinning, when they were all seated.

Zach explained what had happened. After dinner, he'd go back to the lodge and get their rings.

"I would have offered my ring, but my finger is very slender. It might not have fit," Rebecca explained.

"Don't worry about it. Everything was perfect," Alesha said happily. "Now we have a story to tell our children."

The restaurant had prepared a winter wedding menu of macaroni and cheese bites as appetizers, followed by baked salmon and root vegetables for the main course. To drink there was hot chocolate with beer and whipped cream, and the wedding cake was a traditional sugar cake from Trinidad, made with coconut and sugar and pink food coloring.

After they cut the cake, Zach stood up and took out his speech.

"I wish I was as calm as everyone else at the table," he began, unfolding the paper. "To be honest, weddings have always scared me. They're like a final exam at college. You can't afford to fail, because it can affect your whole future." He looked from Jerome to Alesha. "At least weddings did frighten me until tonight. Listening to Jerome and Alesha recite their vows, I realized when you marry the right person, there's nothing to be afraid of. Getting married means you found someone to help you celebrate your achievements, someone to help you shrug off your failures. Most importantly, you found someone to count on."

Jerome and Alesha kissed and the waiter passed around the desserts. They talked about Jerome and Alesha's plans, and Zach's film.

"The film is about first love and happy endings," Zach said. He addressed Jerome and Alesha. "How did you know you were in love?"

"Jerome always answers it was love at first sight, but it took me much longer," Alesha recalled, smiling. "We met in sixth grade, but I was twelve and only interested in the pop stars on the radio. When we were sixteen, there was a dance. I was quite popular, and a few boys invited me," she continued. "I told them to run a race, and the winner could escort me to the dance."

"You made them run a race?" Zach repeated incredulously.

"One of the boys was on the track team," Jerome cut in. "Alesha wanted him to win."

"I did not, I thought it would be fun." Alesha laughed.

The other boys ran as fast as they could, only Jerome lagged behind. After the race was over, Alesha was upset. She and Jerome had gone on a few dates. She liked him and thought he felt the same.

"Alesha wouldn't talk to me, she thought I lost the race on purpose," Jerome said, picking up the story. "I brought her a plate of brownies, and explained that love wasn't about being faster than the other guys, it was about finding the perfect fit. I knew that Alesha and I belonged together. I didn't have to prove it."

"Jerome was right, and he does make the best brownies," Alesha finished, her eyes twinkling. "Why do you think I came all the way to America? I haven't eaten his brownies in four years."

"It was a beautiful wedding," Rebecca reflected, unwrapping her cape and setting it on the side table in the lobby.

Jerome and Alesha had gone on a night cruise. Zach and Rebecca were sitting in the lobby at Christmas Cove Lodge. He had offered to buy Rebecca a hot toddy and she accepted.

"There wouldn't have been a wedding without you," Zach said ruefully.

After dinner, Zach retrieved the wedding rings. He still felt terrible about almost ruining the ceremony.

"It was almost worth it to see the expression on those couples' faces." Rebecca smiled. "As if I was asking them to strip to their underwear, instead of lending us their wedding rings."

"It was an unusual request," Zach pointed out. "I can see why you're so successful in business."

"What do you mean?" Rebecca asked, sipping her drink.

"You went into action. As if you encounter impossible problems every day, and never let them stop you."

"That's what building a company is about," Rebecca said thoughtfully. "You achieve one goal, and go on to the next. Until they stack up behind you like branches on a tree."

"What happens when you reach the top?" Zach asked curiously.

Rebecca seemed to think about it.

"Ben believes that isn't possible; there's always a higher tree to climb."

"If it was me, I'd stop to admire the view," Zach said without thinking.

He didn't mean to say anything bad about Ben. He didn't even know Ben. All he knew was that Rebecca was the best person he'd ever met. And somehow tonight, even though she was wearing that gorgeous dress that must have cost a fortune, and they had eaten one of the best pieces of salmon Zach had ever tasted, she didn't seem truly happy.

During dinner she had been quiet. And when they reached Christmas Cove Lodge, she had been in no hurry to go to her suite.

"Tell me more about your wedding," he prodded. "Was it everything you dreamed of?"

Rebecca stopped, surprised by his question.

"I planned it myself, I wanted it to be perfect," she said slowly. "It was my idea to have the wedding on Christmas Day. Christmas is the only day of the year when everything stops and the only thing that's important is celebrating with the people you love. Christmas is magical and your wedding should be the same. Taking the time to do it right shows how much you care for each other."

Zach gulped his drink.

He didn't know if it was the hot toddy after the hot chocolate and beer he'd drunk at dinner, or the beauty and emotions of Jerome and Alesha's wedding, but he didn't want to keep lying to

Rebecca. Even if she never spoke to him again, she had to know everything. That when he noticed her and Ben through the window at Burger Shack all those years ago, he was so disappointed. That he wasn't a successful filmmaker, he was at a crossroads in his career. That he wasn't in a relationship with Meredith.

He was sorry that he'd lied to her, and he wanted to be there for her, if she needed him.

He set his glass on the table.

"Rebecca, there's something I've been trying to tell you . . ."

A male voice called out Rebecca's name. Rebecca jumped up as a familiar-looking man walked toward them.

"Rebecca, I found you," he said as he approached them.

Zach hadn't seen Ben in eight years, but he recognized him immediately. His hair was shorter and he wore an expensive-looking sweater instead of a college sweatshirt, but otherwise he looked the same.

"Ben!"

Rebecca's eyes opened wide. She glanced down at her phone.

"What are you doing here? You didn't call or text."

"I wanted to surprise you." Ben leaned forward and kissed her cheek. He turned to Zach, waiting for Rebecca to introduce them.

Rebecca's eyes were glittery and Zach noticed a catch in her voice.

"This is Zach Mason; we were in a film class together at Berkeley. He's staying at Christmas Cove Lodge."

Ben shook Zach's hand. He had the kind of firm, confident handshake one would expect from a CEO.

"It's nice to meet you," Ben offered. "I'm glad Rebecca found someone in Christmas Cove to keep her company."

Rebecca glanced at Ben hesitantly. "Are you staying . . . ?"

"Of course I'm staying. I just drove for six hours," Ben replied. "Traffic was terrible."

Zach jumped up. He felt the way he did when Ben and Rebecca were sitting in the booth at the Burger Shack. Like he didn't belong, and needed to get away as fast as possible.

"It was nice meeting you," he said to Ben and turned to Rebecca. "Rebecca, I'll see you later."

Then he crossed the lobby without looking back.

Chapter Eighteen

Rebecca sat in the living room of her suite, sipping Kahlúa with coffee. She shouldn't be drinking it. The coffee would keep her up all night and she'd already had too much to drink. But Ben ordered it before they came to the suite, and she was too stunned to refuse.

Now Ben was giving his car to the valet. Rebecca had come up ahead of him. She couldn't sit at the lobby bar while her thoughts whirled inside her head.

What was Ben doing in Christmas Cove when he was supposed to be in St. Barts with Natalie?

Her first instinct was to tell him to leave. He had walked out of the bridal suite six hours before their wedding. Rebecca didn't want to talk to him.

Yet, when he kissed her cheek, there was the familiar fluttering in her chest. She told herself it was a gut reaction; she was used to his kiss. But she couldn't ignore the way just seeing those bright blue eyes, the light brown hair, made all the familiar feelings return.

And he had driven six hours to be with her. She would hear what he had to say.

The door opened and Ben entered.

"It's freezing out there," Ben said, picking up his glass. "Do you remember when we discovered Kahlúa and coffee? It was when we were working twelve-hour days and couldn't stay awake. The Kahlúa was left over from some fraternity party. It was just what we needed to keep working."

"You didn't come here to discuss the company's beginnings," Rebecca said. "Where's Natalie and why are you here?"

Ben sank onto the sofa.

"Our flight to St. Barts was canceled. By the time it was re-scheduled, I decided not to go. Natalie is at her apartment."

"*You* decided not to go?" she repeated, wondering if Ben had actually left Natalie.

"Natalie wasn't happy about my decision." Ben flinched.

"Most women don't appreciate having their plans changed at the last minute," Rebecca retorted.

"I know you're furious with me for everything." Ben rubbed his forehead. "You don't know how hard it was sitting in stopped traffic, knowing how angry you'd be when I arrived. But I had to come." He looked up at her. "I made a mistake, Rebecca. I'm still in love with you."

Rebecca glanced down at her hands. Ben almost never admitted to mistakes. He simply brushed them off as learning experiences.

"I don't know why you're telling me this." Rebecca's voice was shaky. "You walked out six hours before our wedding."

"The last few months have been a blur." Ben's brow creased. "It didn't have anything to do with you. It just got too . . . easy."

"Easy?" Rebecca repeated.

"Everything was too easy." He stood up and paced around the room. "Investors coming to us instead of us having to grovel at their door. Interviews in magazines and speaking at those conferences, where attendees wanted to shake our hands as if they were covered in gold dust." He turned to Rebecca. "I didn't even have to check our bank balances anymore. The zeros kept multiplying by themselves."

"You needed a challenge, so you had an affair? That's the oldest excuse in the book," Rebecca scoffed. "You're ten years early—most men wait until middle age and *after* they actually marry."

"It was the dumbest thing I've ever done," Ben acknowledged. "I came to make it right." He strode back to the sofa and took her hands. "I love you, Rebecca. I want to be together."

Rebecca wrenched her hand away. She stood up.

"It's too much for me, I think you'd better go."

"I haven't eaten all day and I'm starving. Have dinner with me," he pleaded. "If you still feel that way, I'll leave."

"I guess we can order room service." She shrugged.

"Not here," Ben said. "Let's go to Pine Tree Inn."

"How do you know about Pine Tree Inn?" Rebecca asked in surprise.

The Pine Tree Inn wasn't the kind of restaurant Ben preferred, with extensive wine lists and an elaborate menu. It was housed in a stone building, with ivy-covered walls and white shutters.

"On the drive up, I asked Siri for the name of restaurants in Christmas Cove."

The Ben she knew—the Ben with the soccer star smile and irresistible charm—stood before her. "I wanted to go somewhere you liked." He grinned. "I knew I wouldn't get much time to change your mind."

* * *

"I made a spreadsheet." Ben pulled out his phone.

They were sitting at a window table at Pine Tree Inn. Inside, it was furnished like a New England cottage. Round dining tables were scattered around the front parlor, and there were more tables in the library. The kitchen was across the hallway, and there was a garden strung with colored lights.

Rebecca wasn't hungry, but Ben convinced her to have a bowl of soup.

"A spreadsheet?" she repeated, puzzled.

"Of things we need to change." He scrolled down the screen. "We'll move out of San Francisco and buy a house in Woodside. The house will have a big kitchen, and we'll learn to cook." His voice was eager. "We'll have proper weekends, no laptops or business calls allowed."

"What about the public offering?" Rebecca questioned. She didn't know why she was listening to Ben. He had broken her heart and ruined her trust. But it was easy to fall into their old routines, to look at a problem and try to solve it.

"We'll write all that into the prospectus." Ben nodded. "These days, unplugging on the weekends is encouraged. It makes one more productive when one returns to the office."

Rebecca set down her soup spoon. She couldn't let Ben sweep her up with his enthusiasm.

"Did you buy me an engagement ring last Christmas and return it?"

Ben stopped scrolling through his phone. He glanced at her in surprise.

"What are you talking about?"

Rebecca told him how Kimi had seen him at Tiffany's. About

Rebecca's conversation with the salesgirl when she went in with the bracelet.

"It's not what you think." Ben toyed with his soup. "On the way home with the diamond ring, I happened to listen to a podcast of a competing dating site. A few of the women's pet peeves were men who proposed on their birthdays or special occasions: Valentine's Day or Christmas. From then on, they had to celebrate the two events together. It made sense, so I returned the ring. I knew I was going to propose eventually."

"You didn't mind having our wedding on Christmas Day," Rebecca reminded him.

Ben shrugged. "That's what you wanted. I was happy; I was marrying the woman I loved."

Rebecca wanted to believe him. And he had a point. Leila was born on Kimi's birthday. Kimi often groaned that from then on, instead of being treated to a nice birthday dinner, she'd be surrounded by little boys and girls with birthday cake frosting on their noses.

"You don't know what the last forty-eight hours have been like," Ben said, interrupting her thoughts. "I couldn't eat or sleep. I kept wanting to retrace my steps, and replay our wedding day again. But with me putting on my tuxedo and driving to the church. I wasn't thinking clearly. You have to give me another chance."

Rebecca had said the same thing. That she wanted to restart the day and end up in her wedding dress at the altar. But Ben was the one who had left her.

She wondered if people really made mistakes. At least they hadn't been married when Ben left her. Ben had the sense to call it off first.

Ben seemed to sense what she was thinking.

"Let me stay in the suite tonight. I'll sleep in the living room, you can have the bedroom," he begged. "We'll have twenty-four hours to get to know each other again. If you still want me to leave, I won't argue."

It was already late, she couldn't make him drive back to San Francisco. And there were no other available rooms in Christmas Cove.

"All right, you can stay tonight," she agreed reluctantly.

Ben ate his plate of pork chops and roasted potatoes, while Rebecca finished her soup.

"Who was that guy, Zach?" Ben asked curiously. "You looked pretty relaxed together. And you were wearing that gorgeous dress."

Rebecca glanced up in surprise. Ben sounded jealous.

She told him about running into Zach and Meredith the first night she was in Christmas Cove, and about Jerome and Alesha's wedding.

"Zach thinks we're married," she admitted. "I was too embarrassed to say the wedding had been canceled."

"That's good." Ben's voice was low. He reached forward and touched her hand. "Because I can't wait to be married to you."

After dinner, Ben drove back to Christmas Cove Lodge. The lake looked so beautiful. There was a full moon, and stars shone down on snow-covered fir trees.

Ben had rented an SUV with supple leather upholstery. He had been waiting for years to do the things he dreamed of and buy the things they could never afford: season tickets for baseball games, eating at the hottest new restaurants. If she took Ben back, her life would be like this all the time. Staying in fine hotels, eating and drinking whatever they liked. They would have stresses at the office, but there would be someone to come home to, someone to build a life with.

How could Ben say he loved her when he had lied to her? She tried to imagine doing anything like that to him. There was the time last year, when Kimi was pregnant and Rebecca covered for her.

Kimi hadn't finished a coding program for a crucial client meeting. Rebecca found her in the bathroom, throwing up. She insisted that Kimi go home, and then secretly found another coder to finish the program. The coder wasn't as experienced as Kimi, and Ben would have been furious if he knew. But Kimi was Rebecca's best friend. She couldn't let her sit in her cubicle when she should be in bed with her feet up and a cold compress on her forehead.

And there had been the Christmas party four years ago, at the home of a venture capitalist. It was the only time in their eight years together that Rebecca had paid attention to another man. Even remembering it now made her feel guilty.

The party was held in one of those ridiculously large Pacific Heights mansions, with views of the San Francisco Bay. There was a grand living room with silk sofas, and the dining room had a long oak table, and glass cabinets filled with priceless artifacts. The Christmas tree in the foyer was as ornate as the Christmas tree at Macy's, and everywhere there were crystal vases of flowers.

A man was playing Christmas carols on the piano. After he finished playing "Have Yourself a Merry Little Christmas," he came and sat beside her.

"You look like you're not enjoying my playing," he said. He was in his early thirties and good-looking, with brown eyes and blond hair.

"It's not that, you play wonderfully," Rebecca replied. "I haven't eaten all day and I'm starving. All there is to eat is caviar on melba toast, and platters of julienned vegetables. I can't sit here in front of all these people, munching carrots and shoveling fish eggs into my mouth."

It was the third Christmas party she and Ben had attended that week. Rebecca didn't usually mind going to parties. It was fun to get dressed up and see San Francisco's most beautiful homes. But there had been an office crisis, and she'd missed lunch. Dinner wouldn't be served for an hour, and her stomach was turning over.

"Wait here," the man said. He returned with a plate of sourdough bread and roast beef and three kinds of cheeses.

"Where did you get this?" she asked.

"From the kitchen. The hostess, Jane, thinks serving filling hors d'oeuvres will ruin the guests' appetite for dinner." He sat in front of her on the window seat. "I'll hide you. You can make a sandwich and no one will see you."

The man's name was Lucas and he was an old family friend of the hostess. He was the only person at the party who wasn't in the tech world. He played piano with the San Francisco Symphony and gave piano lessons on the side.

"I don't know anyone who plays the piano for a living," Rebecca said, devouring her sandwich.

"It doesn't pay very well. I'm never going to be able to buy fine art or designer furniture like this family's"—he swept his hands around the room—"but I love what I do, and it makes people happy."

They talked about music and Christmas concerts.

"My boyfriend and I are thinking of getting an electronic piano for Christmas," Rebecca said, popping the last bite of sandwich into her mouth.

Lucas reached into his pocket and drew out a card.

"Here's my card, if you want lessons." He handed it to her and smiled. "I give discounts to hungry girls I meet at Christmas parties. I wouldn't want you to skimp on your groceries."

Rebecca kept Lucas's card for a week before she threw it out. It wasn't that she didn't trust herself. It had been fun to chat with a handsome man, someone who was interested in things besides website analytics and stock evaluations.

But Rebecca had never done anything about it. Ben and Natalie had been having an affair for six months.

Now Ben reached for her hand, but she placed it firmly in her lap. A rented luxury SUV, or the guilt of a slight attraction four years ago, wasn't going to change her mind. She needed time to think.

She had twenty-four hours to make her decision.

Chapter Nineteen

The next morning, Rebecca woke up early and e-mailed the florist and caterer and lighting designer. Luckily, Howard's party was under control. She wanted to read the rest of Howard's journal entries and have follow-up meetings with the vendors, but she wouldn't miss anything by spending the day with Ben.

For a moment, Rebecca's mind drifted to Zach. She had promised to lend him the butterfly bracelet for the film. And he had been about to tell her something when Ben appeared in the lobby. She'd go see and him this evening.

Ben was sitting on the sofa in the suite's living room when she appeared. She was surprised, as he usually started the day with a run.

"I decided to take the week off from running," Ben said, putting down his phone.

Ben hadn't missed his morning run in years. Even when it rained, he put on waterproof pants and a hooded jacket and ran his usual six miles.

"It's such a beautiful day, I thought we'd go out to breakfast," he said, standing up.

"Let me guess, you asked Siri where are the best places to have breakfast in Christmas Cove?" Rebecca couldn't help but smile.

Ben took her arm. "She suggested Heidi's Pancake House; there's a fireplace and views of the lake."

At Heidi's Pancake House, they both ordered a short stack of buttermilk pancakes with warm fruit. Rebecca didn't know anyone besides Ben who liked warm fruit on their pancakes. Stewed pears on golden brown pancakes was one of her favorite things.

"How did you know I was in Christmas Cove?" Rebecca asked, stirring her coffee.

"I called your father." Ben handed her a packet of sugar.

Rebecca had talked to both her parents when she arrived in Lake Tahoe. She told them the wedding was called off, but she didn't say anything about Ben and Natalie.

"I called your mother too," Ben said. "I told her we might go to Argentina in February. It's summertime there, the weather would be perfect."

Rebecca had been suggesting they go to Argentina together for years. She had only been a few times since college, and she loved everything about the vibrant cities and green countryside. But flights were expensive and it was far away. She and Ben couldn't both be gone from the office for so long, so she had traveled by herself.

Rebecca looked at him questioningly. "You want to go to Argentina?"

"I don't want to spend the day talking about business," Ben replied. He wore a blue wool sweater that brought out the color of his eyes, and a pair of sunglasses was perched on his forehead.

"But that's the beauty of going public. We won't be carrying the weight of the company by ourselves. We can take time off and travel. We could even go to Antarctica and take pictures of the penguins for Leila," he said.

Rebecca stifled a laugh. In the last month, Leila had become obsessed with penguins. Rebecca had bought Leila a giant stuffed penguin for Christmas.

"You called my parents without asking me?" Rebecca questioned.

"I hope you don't mind." Ben cut his pancake. He changed the subject. "This morning, I was looking at real estate online. If we live in Woodside, Oliver would have a huge garden to run in, and we could even get a horse."

"I don't expect every day to be like Christmas," Rebecca said abruptly. "I don't need to travel to Argentina and Antarctica or own a horse to be happy."

"We've worked so hard, we deserve nice things," Ben answered. "And we'll teach the same thing to our kids. That when they find the right person, and share the same goals, they can have everything they want."

Rebecca's thoughts were too mixed up to answer. She changed the topic and they talked about the lodge and Christmas Cove.

"There's something I've never told you. It's about when we met at the Burger Shack." Ben sipped his coffee. "I was walking by that day and noticed you through the window. I'd seen you around campus, and wanted to talk to you. So I went in and pretended we were standing at the counter at the same time by accident."

"I don't understand." Rebecca frowned. "What about the steak fries and mayonnaise?"

"That part was real." Ben nodded. "I couldn't believe we both hated ketchup on fries. But I would have found a way to ask you to eat with me."

Ben had been the soccer star and belonged to a fraternity. She'd always felt lucky that they met and fell in love. But Ben had noticed her, and he wanted to get to know *her*.

"Why are you telling me now?"

Ben shrugged as if he was thinking about it.

"I thought it was something you should know." He finished his pancakes and took out his phone. "What shall we do next? Apparently, we shouldn't miss the steamship ride around the lake. Or we could go snowshoeing. The rental place even packs a picnic."

They took a cruise around the lake, which stopped in Emerald Bay, with its hidden inlets and chalets built on the waterfront. Then they went snowshoeing, which was even lovelier than Rebecca expected. The forest was completely still, and there were no sounds except the slip-sliding of their snowshoes on the fresh powder.

Afterward, they strolled down Main Street and watched a puppet show in the village square. They finished the afternoon with tea and scones at a teahouse that was built a hundred years ago.

Now it was evening and Ben had gone to take a Jacuzzi at the lodge's spa. Rebecca was getting dressed. Ben had convinced her to have dinner together, before she made her decision.

She wished she could talk to Kimi. But Kimi was on the cruise and her phone went straight to voicemail.

Rebecca decided to go see Zach. She picked up the butterfly bracelet and crossed the lobby to his suite.

"Rebecca." Meredith answered the door. "What a nice surprise."

"I was looking for Zach," Rebecca replied, holding up the bracelet. "He wanted to shoot this for the film."

"Please, come in. Zach isn't here." Meredith ushered her inside. She removed a squeaky dog toy from the sofa. "I was watching some of the footage. Would you like to see it?"

Ben wouldn't be back for an hour, and it would keep her mind occupied.

"I'd love to."

Rebecca settled on the sofa, and Meredith clicked Play on the laptop. Rebecca's face came on the screen and she saw herself talking about her appendicitis and Ben finding an apartment. Rebecca watched each segment and there was a funny feeling in her stomach. Her throat closed up and it was hard to swallow. Finally, the final scene at Vikingsholm Castle faded to black.

Rebecca jumped up.

"Please tell Zach the film is wonderful," she said to Meredith. "I have to go."

"What about your bracelet?" Meredith asked.

"I'll come back for it later," Rebecca said. She felt lighter than she had all day. "There's something important I have to do."

Rebecca paced around the living room of her suite. Zach had said that the camera told the truth, and he was right. Every story she related was about Ben, or about Ben and Rebecca. None of them were about Rebecca herself.

Ben was the star in their relationship. At best, Rebecca had a supporting part.

The film made it obvious, but she had never seen it clearly before. Everything that Ben did for Rebecca, everything in their relationship, started with something he wanted for himself. Most of the time it had been easy, as she wanted the same things too. But in the future, even when they compromised, it would be Rebecca accepting a different version of one of Ben's ideas.

For the wedding, Ben had wanted a large ceremony at Grace Cathedral followed by a reception in the ballroom of the Four Seasons. Rebecca wanted a small wedding, so they'd compromised by holding the ceremony in the small chapel and the reception in the Four Seasons penthouse. Rebecca's dream wedding wouldn't have been in San Francisco. It would have been at a winery or in a chalet on the lake.

Ben wouldn't be happy owning any horse. He'd want a Thoroughbred, like he insisted on buying a Porsche. They wouldn't teach themselves how to cook from videos on YouTube. He'd hire an expensive chef to come and teach them. Rebecca didn't want to live like that, always buying new gadgets, going on trips to exotic places. She wanted to do normal things. Have a career she enjoyed and a loving husband and children.

Mostly, Ben didn't love Rebecca for the right reasons. He loved Rebecca because he could see in her eyes how much she loved him. He didn't love her for herself.

That afternoon, she felt flattered when he admitted he had noticed her through the window at Burger Shack. But that didn't mean anything. She had been different from the other girls Ben knew at Berkeley, and for a few moments she'd gotten his attention.

Ben would always need a challenge. He may not have another affair, and he might pull back at the company, but he would always be looking for something new. It would be Rebecca's role to listen to him talk about a new project.

Rebecca would never find the space to create her own dreams, and eventually she'd stop trying.

The door opened and Ben entered. A robe was knotted around his waist, and he carried a bottle of water.

"I forgot how relaxing it is to sit in a Jacuzzi." He beamed. "I'm going to shower and get dressed for dinner."

"You don't need to get dressed. We're not going to dinner."

"I don't mind ordering room service." Ben shrugged. "We can see what movies are on Netflix."

"We're not going to watch a movie either." She kept her voice steady. "I'm sorry, Ben, but you're leaving."

"What do you mean, I'm leaving?"

"It's not going to work." Rebecca gulped. She wished she had poured a shot of brandy from the minibar.

"Rebecca, we haven't talked about Natalie, but I can suggest to her that she leave the firm," Ben urged. "We don't have to wait until February to go to Argentina. We could get married here in Christmas Cove and continue on our honeymoon. By the time we get back, everything will feel different. We'll be Mr. and Mrs. Ben Cole."

"It isn't about Natalie, it's about us," Rebecca said, sitting against the cushions. "In a marriage, there needs to be space for two people to grow. We could buy the biggest house in Woodside, with room for a swimming pool and a tennis court. It still wouldn't help.

"I want a relationship where sometimes I come up with the ideas, and then we compromise. Or I don't run the ideas by my partner at all. I have something of my own, something I can be proud of." She took a deep breath. "You'll make someone a good husband, and you'll be a wonderful father. But neither of those things will happen with me."

* * *

Rebecca waited while Ben packed his bag and left. Then she pulled on her boots and walked briskly down to the lake. The sun slipped lower behind the mountains, and the sky and the lake turned the same milky white.

Chapter Twenty

The following day, Rebecca tried to sleep in and stay in bed.

The night before, she'd drunk two cups of Sleepytime tea and done an hour of yoga. When she woke in the middle of the night, and saw the outline of Ben's empty pillow, she turned to her other side and counted sheep. In the morning, she woke up much too early, even before the snow-grooming machines started up the slopes, and played the meditation app on her phone. She breathed deeply, imagining herself on a mountaintop in Tibet, or sitting in a field of poppies in the South of France.

None of it helped. The mountains surrounding the lake outside her window were as majestic as any mountain range in Tibet. And breathing in the scent of pine trees was every bit as soothing as inhaling the perfume of fragrant flowers.

Christmas Cove was exactly where she wanted to be, but she still couldn't relax.

It wasn't that she worried that she'd made the wrong decision. She had never been more sure of anything in her life. Seeing Ben walk out the door, his jacket thrown over his shoulders, his expression set in a wounded frown, had been strangely freeing. She would miss him, but he had lied and betrayed her trust.

It was more that she spent her entire twenties certain that she was in love. Now she was thirty and had to start all over again. What if she never found the person she wanted to spend the rest of her life with? Someone who wanted a home and a family as much as she did.

Having a satisfying career was important, but love and marriage were everything.

And what would she do for a career? For now, she'd have to work at Dealbreakers. But sitting across from Ben and Natalie at a conference room table would be so awkward. And it was more than that. In the beginning, she had loved that Dealbreakers made a difference in people's lives. But now there were so many dating apps. Couples had hundreds of ways of meeting each other.

She wanted to do something that really helped people, like the community kitchen. Jerome and Alesha weren't simply making things easier for busy young professionals, they were providing families with essentials. Children couldn't learn on empty stomachs. And their parents couldn't work long hours if there wasn't a healthy dinner waiting when they arrived home.

Finally, Rebecca jumped out of bed and switched on her laptop. She confirmed her meetings at the boathouse, and quickly scoured after-Christmas sales for a jacket with teddy bear ears for Leila. Then she poured a cup of coffee and settled down with Howard's postcards.

The next postcard was a photo of the Eiffel Tower strung with rows of silver lights. The caption read: *Paris: The City of Love at Christmas*. She read the journal entry.

December 1990, Paris, France

Kat and I have been traveling together for almost two weeks. We have explored the outdoor markets in Strasbourg, France, and eaten bredele—Alsatian Christmas cookies— and drunk vin chaud—hot mulled wine with cognac and cinnamon sticks. In Dresden, Germany, we visited the Royal Palace, where people dress in clothing from the Middle Ages and shoppers are serenaded by strolling minstrels.

We spent two days in Stuttgart, Germany. I hoped there wouldn't be so many tourists—it is in the middle of the Black Forest. But apparently it has the oldest and biggest Christmas market in Germany, with an entire section devoted to children. Kat convinced me to take the train ride through a miniature Christmas village, even though my legs are too long and bumped up against the seat in front of us, and the children on the train kept shouting in my ear.

I've learned a few things about Kat, and about myself. Firstly, we're complete opposites. Kat likes to do everything on the spur of the moment. At the mittelaltermarkt (the medieval street market) in Stuttgart, we were about to sit down to a proper meal—grilled sausages and sauerkraut and their famous chocolate-dipped fruits molded to look like St. Nicholas—when she announced we had to ride the Ferris wheel before it closed. I managed to stuff a sausage in my pocket, but it was cold and soggy by the time I ate it.

And in Strasbourg, we saved our money to take a night

river cruise. Seventy minutes in a heated boat while you drift past the twinkling lights of Strasbourg's famous bridges. At the last minute, Kat decided we should see the outdoor Christmas concert in Place Kleber. The concert was uplifting, and the Christmas tree in Place Kleber was breathtaking— eighty feet tall and decorated with letters to Santa Claus. But it was freezing cold, and there were so many people, someone kept stepping on my feet.

We're different in other ways too. Kat likes to start each day with a short excursion, while I prefer to hang around the hostel, enjoying a pastry. And she insists on doing her laundry almost daily, so we're constantly looking for the closest laundromat and exchanging our money for local coins.

The most important thing I've learned, the thing that makes our differences so inconvenient, is that we've fallen in love.

I'm not sure when it happened. I assumed our kiss in St. Anton wouldn't lead to anything more than a night or two spent in bed before we decided to just be friends. Instead, that night we walked around the ski village for hours, and then went back to our separate rooms. We still haven't made love, but in every other way, we couldn't be closer. We hold hands walking down the street, and feed each other foods at the outdoor markets, and buy silly little gifts when the other person isn't looking.

I tell myself that Kat is only reacting to the grief of losing her father. Or that we're two Americans in a foreign place; of course we'd ended up together. On our last day, we'll wave goodbye at the airport terminal or the train station, and by the time our flight is called or the train moves off, each of us will notice a cute guy or pretty girl and go on to something new.

But it isn't like that. It feels as if I know everything about Kat, even though she's hardly told me anything, and she feels the same. She knew that I'd get choked up when we visited the cathedral in Strasbourg—even though I'd never mentioned the article I'd read about the years of backbreaking labor it took to build those ancient cathedrals.

And I knew that she'd love the Wilhelma Zoo in Stuttgart, even though we'd never talked about her love of animals. Kat travels with a stuffed elephant toy, how could she not love seeing black bears and elephants?

The problem is that we view love and the future in different ways.

It all came to a head yesterday when we went to the American Express office to collect our mail.

I had a couple of letters from my parents. Kat had a letter from her mother and a letter with a return address from someone named Stewart Green.

"Who's Stewart Green?" I asked.

We were sitting in a café on the Champs-Élysées. I realize that the Champs-Élysées is the most touristy spot in Paris. But we'd already visited the Christmas markets in Saint-Germain-des-Prés, and attended a Christmas concert at the Church of Saint-Eustache, and for once I didn't mind the overcrowded sidewalks. There is nowhere in Paris, nowhere in the world, as glorious and intoxicating as the Champs-Élysées at Christmas.

The whole boulevard is made for Christmas, and for

love. Over a million light bulbs are entwined in the trees. The Arc de Triomphe stands on one end, and on the other, the Luxor Obelisk is lit with blue lights and encircled by a forest of pine trees. Every store window has a Christmas display with lights and animation and music. At one children's clothing boutique, actors perform a scene from *Beauty and the Beast*, and at a jewelry store, each window displayed a different romantic location: an underwater grotto, the inside of an Egyptian pyramid filled with presents. For the first time, I wished I was rich. I'd love to buy Kat a cashmere sweater or a pair of knee-high boots.

And the cafés are made for romance. The tables are pressed together, and couples are constantly leaning close and sharing dishes: escargot dripping in butter and sauces, bûche de noël, which is sponge cake covered with chocolate ganache.

Kat and I were sitting in a café, sipping café au laits. She glanced at Stewart's name on the envelope.

"Just a guy from home," she replied.

It seemed odd that Kat had never mentioned him, and that he would write her a letter.

"Was he your boyfriend?" I wondered.

Kat shrugged her shoulders. She wore a red wool sweater over a turtleneck. A striped scarf was wrapped around her neck.

"We dated on and off." She concentrated on the foam on her coffee. "Until Stewart proposed. Then I called the whole thing off."

"He proposed!"

"Our parents were best friends before his family moved to London. I didn't see him for years, now he's in his last year of medical school," she said. "I told him he was being silly. I'm too young to get married, if I get married at all."

"Were you in love with him?"

"Of course not," she declared. She leaned forward and kissed me. "Let's talk about something else. I've decided we should spend the day at Versailles. There's a new exhibit called 'The King and His Animals.'"

Versailles at Christmas would be more crowded than Disneyland. But I could tell by the way Kat pursed her lips that I couldn't dissuade her.

The trip to Versailles started well enough. The Grand Trianon—the large palace—was magnificent. It's hard to imagine people lived like that. Being serenaded by musicians during meals, and having their own shooting galleries and concert halls. King Louis XVI even had his own set of apartments consisting of a bedchamber, a clothes cabinet, and a dog's room hidden away from palace courtiers. He built a smaller palace for Marie Antoinette, which he only entered with her permission. Kat laughed that no wonder they never tired of each other. They each had their own space and when they wanted to be together, they were served candlelit dinners by footmen.

The exhibit we came to see was across the gardens and the ground was wet and muddy. After the guide talked about the king's companion animals—King Louis XVI loved cats and dogs and exotic birds—he described the king's passion for hunting. Apparently, Louis XVI became so obsessed with the sport, he neglected his governmental duties. Kat got so upset about all the poor rabbits and deer that were killed, she fled across the gardens and burst into tears.

On the train back to Paris, she sat hunched in the corner and wouldn't talk to me. It was only when we arrived back at the hostel that I discovered what was really bothering her.

We were eating bowls of soup in the hostel's kitchen. Kat took out some writing paper and an envelope.

"Who are you writing to?" I asked.

"To Stewart. I've changed my mind, I'm going to marry him."

My soup spoon dropped on the floor. I reached down and picked it up.

"What are you saying?" I demanded.

"I love art, but there's no money in it as a career," Kat reflected. "I'll be much better off by marrying a doctor. My mother is still paying my father's medical bills, and I have student loans. I'll get a part-time job in an art gallery, until we have children. Then I'll do charity work."

"You can't marry Stewart! You're not in love with him."

"That's the beauty of it, it's almost like an arranged marriage. King Louis XVI was sixteen and Marie Antoinette was fourteen when they wed, and they never had anything in common. He liked to make clocks and she loved pretty dresses and chocolates. They didn't have children for the first seven years, because they were hopeless in the bed-room."

"What does that have to do with you?" I asked.

"If you go into marriage without love, it's impossible to get hurt," she said, and I noticed a glimmer in her eyes. "If you love someone and then you lose them, it's a lot worse."

It all fell into place. Kat was afraid of falling in love, because of what happened to her father.

"I'm young and healthy." I touched her hand. "I'm not going to die."

"Not now!" Her eyes blazed. "But perhaps in twenty-five years when our children are in college and we're about to enjoy our retirement. We'll have planned a silver anniversary cruise to Alaska and I'll have to go by myself. Or you'll die when I'm seventy, and can't remember what it's like to live alone."

I took out a handkerchief and wiped her eyes.

"Firstly, if I die in twenty-five years you can take a cruise made especially for older singles, it will be the perfect way to meet a handsome widower. And if I die when you're seventy, you'll be surrounded by so many grandchildren, you'll wish you had a moment to yourself."

She didn't say anything, so I kept talking.

"We're too young to think about marriage, I don't even know what I want to do as a career. But we're not too young to fall in love." I touched her cheek. "Some things you do drive me crazy. I haven't been warm and dry since the day we met. But the idea of not having you around is unthink-able. Somehow we'll work it out."

"I don't want to be in love with you," Kat said, as stubborn as a child refusing to be bought off with a slice of cake.

I had taken a course in the nineteenth-century novel in college. I put it to use now.

"We can't choose who we love, that's the whole foundation of literature," I said, smiling. "But we can choose how to act. Why don't we take an evening stroll down the Champs-Élysées? Then we'll come back to the hostel and drink cheap wine in my room."

"In your room?" Kat repeated.

"My roommate's left. I'm the only one there. We could . . ."

She didn't let me finish my sentence. She jumped up and tossed the writing paper in the garbage.

"You have the room to yourself and didn't tell me!" She took my hand. "The Champs-Élysées will always be there, you never know when you'll get another roommate. Why don't we go to your room first and then . . ."

This time, I stopped her. I put my arms around her and kissed her. Then I picked her up and carried her into my room, and closed the door behind us.

Rebecca finished the journal entry and peeled off the postcard to include with the others. Howard and Kat had seemed so in love. But Howard said he'd never been married. Maybe love never worked out. She wouldn't spend time thinking about that right now.

She made a note to include a chocolate Arc de Triomphe and

a bûche de noël on the dessert table at Howard's party. Then she grabbed her parka and walked briskly through the village to the boathouse.

The meetings with the vendors went wonderfully. Rebecca confirmed with the florist the cowboy boots they would use as centerpieces, and they agreed to hang mistletoe near the Christmas tree. The florist suggested adding succulents to the table decor and placing horseshoe-shaped wreaths on the walls.

Rebecca met with Claire, the lighting designer, next, and grew even more excited. Claire suggested changing the color of the lighting with each dinner course: a warm orange glow during the soup and salad, turning to a golden bronze for the glazed ham and vegetables, and then a riot of neon colors when they brought out dessert.

After Claire left, Rebecca took some measurements and walked back to the storage room. The vintage wedding dress was still hanging in the closet, and the snow globe was perched on a box.

Howard said the snow globe didn't have a scene in it because you were supposed to shake it and make a wish and then a scene would magically appear. Rebecca didn't even know what she'd wish for. She was about to pack it in the box when her phone buzzed.

Kimi's face appeared on the screen.

"I tried to call you," Rebecca said. "I was afraid you'd fallen into the Pacific Ocean."

"I wish I had, a lifeboat would be more relaxing." Kimi groaned. "I thought cruises were about lying on a deck chair and reading. When you board, you download an app that tells you what's going on in different parts of the ship. Every time I open my book, there's a ding alerting me to dance classes or pancake making, or an escape room. And don't get me started on the children's activities. Leila is ten months old and her schedule is more full than a debutante's." Kimi's brow wrinkled. "One should never let magicians near babies. The magician pulled a rabbit out of a hat and Leila started crying. Now she's terrified of her pink stuffed bunny."

Rebecca smiled. It felt good to put aside her own problems and talk to Kimi.

"The cruise is for your parents," Rebecca reminded her.

"And they're having a wonderful time," Kimi admitted. "The ship docked in Mexico and they bought sunglasses and huge straw hats. My mother thinks she looks like a movie star or an international spy. They even started calling each other yeobo; that's Korean for honey.

"The best part is I asked one of my aunties to pack up my mother's clothes while we're gone. When we get home, Leila can take a bath without my mother's shoes in the bathtub."

"I'm glad, they deserve to be happy," Rebecca said.

"Tell me about Christmas Cove. What have I missed?"

Rebecca told Kimi about Ben appearing at the lodge. He wanted to get back together, but Rebecca watched herself on camera and realized it would never work.

"You've been hanging out with an old college crush for four days and never mentioned him."

"Zach wasn't a crush, he's a friend," Rebecca replied. "And we're not talking about Zach. We're discussing Ben."

"You've spent enough time on Ben," Kimi said firmly. "I want to hear more about Zach. Is he cute?"

Rebecca thought about Zach's dark good looks. His easy smile and the way he really listened when she talked.

"I don't want to talk about men," Rebecca said. "I'm much happier finishing up the details of the New Year's Night party."

"You're right, you're lucky. On the cruise tonight, there's a huge fiesta. I'm going to watch my parents make goo-goo eyes at each other over fish tacos."

They talked a little more and then Rebecca hung up, wishing each other a happy new year. Her phone buzzed again and she answered it without looking at the screen. Kimi must have forgot to say something.

"Hi, Rebecca, this is Natalie." A female voice came over the line.

Rebecca gripped the phone tightly. "Natalie. This is a surprise."

"I shouldn't have waited so long. I've been wanting to call you for days."

"You mean you shouldn't have waited until Ben broke up with you too," Rebecca said before she could stop herself. It wouldn't help to take her hurt and anger out on Natalie.

"You have every reason to be furious at me," Natalie acknowledged. "I called to apologize."

"To apologize?" Rebecca repeated.

"You're a terrific boss and I thanked you by running off with your fiancé. It was a terrible thing to do and I'm ashamed of myself."

Rebecca tried to think of a reply. Natalie had done a terrible thing, but it wouldn't have happened if Ben truly loved Rebecca.

"It's not all your fault. Ben was part of it too."

"To be honest, I'm relieved that Ben broke up with me. It never would have worked. I would have always felt guilty," Natalie admitted. "I'll never do anything like that again."

Rebecca appreciated Natalie's apology, but she didn't feel like talking to her.

Chapter Twenty-one

Zach read the e-mail for the third time since it had arrived that morning. He already knew what it said. The contest deadline was in six days. It went on to list the opportunities for the winner—twenty thousand dollars, a chance to have the film produced by Sofia Coppola's production company, worldwide distribution, and future joint projects.

He knew he should feel excited, he was getting so close. A few more interviews of Meredith and Rebecca and it would be finished. But ever since Ben had shown up two nights ago, all of Zach's old feelings of insecurity had returned. What if the film wasn't any good? What if he lost?

With Ben in Christmas Cove, Rebecca might not have time to record another segment. She and Ben would be busy skiing and taking romantic drives around the lake.

He had relived the moment when Ben appeared in the lobby a dozen times. He had been about to admit the truth to Rebecca when Ben sauntered in as cocky and confident as he seemed in college. Zach couldn't get out of there fast enough and he hadn't seen Rebecca since.

Zach closed the laptop and entered the suite's living room. A brisk walk around the lake might clear his head.

Meredith was sitting on the sofa. Buttons was lying on her lap and they were watching a Christmas movie.

"There you are." Meredith turned off the television. "You haven't come out of your room all day. I was going to send Buttons in to make sure you were still breathing."

Zach had spent the last twenty-four hours staring at his laptop. He had only left the room to get a cup of hot soup and a sandwich. Even that he couldn't stomach. Half the sandwich was sitting on his desk.

"Two days ago I thought the film was brilliant and I was the next Peter Jackson. Now I think my six-year-old nephew creates better films on his iPad."

"All great directors feel that about their work," Meredith replied.

"It's not just the film," Zach admitted. He told Meredith about Ben appearing in the lobby as he was about to tell Rebecca that he had lied about being a waiter.

"I thought it was something like that. Just because Ben came back doesn't mean you know how Rebecca feels about him."

"They've just gotten married, I'm sure they're in love." Zach rubbed his brow. "The whole thing was in my head."

"Well, perhaps you can see for yourself." Meredith stood up and walked to the sideboard. "I forgot to give you this—Rebecca brought it over yesterday."

It was the butterfly bracelet that Ben had bought Rebecca at Tiffany's.

"Rebecca was here!" Zach exclaimed.

"She stopped by last night, while you were getting dinner."

Meredith stroked Buttons's fur. "I invited her to look at the footage while she waited. It was quite strange. Suddenly she jumped up and left. She said she'd come back for the bracelet later."

"They were probably late for dinner," Zach said gloomily. "Followed by a midnight Jacuzzi where they drank espresso martinis and fed each other pralines."

Meredith shook her head.

"She had the oddest expression, like she'd just discovered something. If I were you, I'd go and give her the bracelet. You never know what you'll learn."

"I know exactly what will happen," Zach groaned. "Ben will meet me at the door and punch me for having drinks with his wife in the hotel lobby."

Zach shot some footage of the bracelet, then placed it in its case. It was nice of Rebecca to lend it to him, but he couldn't let it sit there. He had to return it.

He crossed the lobby to Rebecca's suite and knocked. There was no answer so he took the jewelry case to the front desk.

"Could you please return this to Mr. and Mrs. Cole's suite?"

The man tapped on his computer screen.

"I'm sorry, we don't have any guests by that name."

"Ben and Rebecca Cole," Zach tried again. "It's the Santa Claus suite."

"Ahh, yes. The suite is under Rebecca Huntley's name. Mr. Cole isn't here. He left last night."

"What do you mean, he left?"

"He checked out. I asked the valet to bring around the car myself."

Zach felt a moment of panic. Rebecca couldn't have left without saying goodbye.

"And Mrs. Cole?" Zach asked.

"You mean Miss Huntley?" the man corrected. "She has the suite until New Year's Day. Would you like to send her a message?"

"No, thank you," Zach said, shaking his head. "I'll take care of it myself."

Rebecca probably kept her own name; lots of women did that these days. But why had Ben left already?

Zach was about to walk back to his suite when Rebecca walked through the doors. She wore a pink-and-white sweater and her hair was pulled into a ponytail.

"Zach! It's nice to see you," Rebecca greeted him.

"I just stopped by your suite but you weren't there."

"You came to my suite?" Rebecca repeated.

Rebecca had never looked so radiant. Her eyes were bright and her skin had a fresh glow.

Meredith was wrong, Rebecca was probably thrilled that Ben was there. They had a magical night and then he had to return to San Francisco on urgent business.

But why hadn't Rebecca gone with him?

"Would you like to come to my suite now?" Rebecca prompted.

"To your suite?"

He had to stop repeating what she said. He was acting like a schoolboy who could barely string a sentence together.

"Yes, it will only take a minute." He jumped up. "It's something to do with the film."

Zach followed Rebecca to her suite. The living room was warm and cozy. A Christmas tree stood by the window and there was a tray with sliced pumpkin bread on the sideboard.

"Would you like something to eat or a cup of coffee?" Rebecca asked, unwrapping her scarf.

"I've had so much coffee, I'll be awake until New Year's Day," Zach sighed. "I'm always like that when I'm finishing a film. At the coffee shop in Prague, they started cutting me off after four cups. I was rattling the saucer while I edited."

"I envy you," Rebecca mused. "It's wonderful to be passionate about your work."

"This is the point in the process that I go from writing my Oscar acceptance speech to wanting to throw my laptop in the garbage," Zach said ruefully.

He remembered the bracelet.

"I brought you this." He handed it to her. "Thank you for lending it to me."

Rebecca set the jewelry case on the coffee table. "You said you wanted to talk about the film?"

Zach didn't know why he was so nervous. He'd spent the last few days with Rebecca. But there was something different about her. She seemed more buoyant, as if she had been waiting for something wonderful to happen and it finally had.

"I'd love to shoot another interview." He pulled his mind back to the conversation.

Rebecca's face fell momentarily. She smoothed her sweater.

"I'm not sure I can."

"I understand, if you're going back to San Francisco . . ."

"Why would I do that?" Rebecca wondered.

"The desk clerk said Ben went back to the city and I thought you'd join him."

"Ben did leave, but I'm staying in Christmas Cove."

There was something about the way Rebecca said it that made

him want to ask more questions. But it was none of his business. If Rebecca wanted to tell him what was happening, it had to be her decision.

Rebecca's phone buzzed. "Excuse me, I have to take this," she answered. She talked for a few minutes and then stood up. "I'm sorry, I have an appointment. Can we continue this later?"

Meredith was still sitting on the sofa when Zach appeared. Her eyes were wet with tears.

"I watched the entire month of Christmas movies on Hallmark and Lifetime. The Hallmark movies end happily but on Lifetime, there's usually a character with some terrible disease who dies on Christmas Eve." She patted her eyes with a handkerchief and glanced at Zach. "You look like you've seen a ghost."

"Something even weirder," Zach said. He poured a cup of coffee from the coffee maker. It was too early for a drink, but he needed something to calm his nerves.

"I thought you said you'd had enough coffee," Meredith reminded him.

"Sometimes, when you drink so many cups, it starts acting in reverse." Zach took a sip. "I've just come from Rebecca's suite. You were right, Ben has gone back to San Francisco. Rebecca didn't say why."

Meredith stood up and walked to the minibar. She took out a tray of chocolate truffles.

She took a bite of a white chocolate truffle. "Sometimes I wish I was still a therapist. There's nothing more fascinating than couples' relationships."

"You're imagining things." Zach frowned. "Ben could have left for a dozen reasons. Perhaps there was another emergency at work."

Meredith ate her truffle thoughtfully.

"Two crises in the week between Christmas and New Year's? I doubt that. All week I've thought it was odd that Ben wasn't here on his own honeymoon." She raised her eyebrows. "Why didn't you ask her?"

"Because it's none of my business," he said hotly. "And besides, I have to finish editing this film."

"One thing I learned from being a therapist is the importance of communication," Meredith counseled. "Why don't you turn on the camera and I'll tell you a story? It's about the time when I thought Phillippe was miserable in our marriage. If only we had talked to each other, it would have saved us both so much anguish."

"We'd been married for four years, and for the most part, I considered us to be lucky. A few of my friends were already divorced. It was often for the smallest reasons: the husband wanted to go out with his friends on Thursday nights, or he didn't approve of his wife keeping in touch with an old boyfriend. Young people take everything so seriously.

"Once, Phillippe and I fell in love with an apartment in a co-op building. We put in an offer and I even started decorating the rooms in my head. I'd paint the kitchen yellow and put in bookshelves in the bedroom. We didn't pass the review board, and I thought I'd never be happy again. A month later we found another co-op that was less expensive and the other residents were nicer.

"It was the beginning of August and unbearably hot. They were doing some work on our building, and the air-conditioning in our apartment didn't work. Every day, I called someone to fix it, but they never came. Even the workmen had left New York; the city was an inferno and people couldn't wait to get out.

"Phillippe's restaurant usually closed in August and we stayed with friends in the Catskills. But someone told Phillippe the restaurant was going to be reviewed by *The New York Times,* so we had to stay in the city. Phillippe was miserable. When he wasn't working, he shuffled around the apartment, eating ice cream from the carton. Usually he wouldn't touch it; he said the carton made ice cream taste like cardboard.

"He talked about the chateau in Provence where he'd stayed when he was young. It had a swimming pool, and in the evenings his friend's parents entertained outside. He described it with such longing, I could almost taste the baguettes spread with thick layers of tapenade and the chilled glasses of Sémillon white wine.

"I was afraid he'd get so homesick he'd want to leave New York and move to France. So I came up with a plan. First, I begged his old roommate, James, to manage the restaurant in Phillippe's place. James usually joined his family in Woodstock, but he agreed to stay in New York City.

"Then I called a travel agent and rented a little cottage in Provence. It belonged to a large villa and we would have access to the swimming pool and gardens.

"The hardest part was affording it. We didn't have any savings in the bank. I got the idea from a French book of short stories that Phillippe kept on his bedside table. There was one by Guy de Maupassant called 'The Necklace.' It was sadder than anything I usually read, but at the same time it gave me an idea.

"I heard the front door open, and placed the book back where Phillippe had left it. Phillippe had tried to get me to read Guy de Maupassant's stories before. He was a famous nineteenth-century French author. But the stories were depressing. I'd rather read romance novels; they'd always been my guilty pleasure.

"In 'The Necklace,' Mathilde and her husband are invited to a ball. Her husband is only a clerk so they spend all his salary on her gown. She longs for jewelry to go with the dress, but they can't afford it. She borrows a necklace from a wealthy friend and loses it at the ball. Secretly, she buys her friend a replacement necklace and she and her husband spend ten years paying it off. He has to take two jobs and Mathilde becomes a charwoman and they give up their nice apartment. Years later, Mathilde runs into her old friend. Mathilde is so changed, her friend doesn't recognize her. Mathilde admits what she did and the friend is terribly upset. The necklace didn't have real gems; the diamonds and rubies were paste.

"'What are you doing home?' I asked Phillippe, walking quickly into the living room. 'The restaurant doesn't close until ten p.m.'

"The restaurant was only two subway stops from our new apartment but Phillippe's shirt was drenched in sweat.

"'We closed early, there weren't any customers.' He slumped on the sofa. 'No one is crazy enough to stay in New York. Even the dogs on the street look miserable. Their tails don't wag and their tongues hang out of their mouths.'

"'The heat has to break sometime,' I said nonchalantly. I couldn't let him know my plan, it would ruin the surprise. Instead, I simply wanted to sound sympathetic. 'Just think what a wonderful review you'll receive. The reviewer will flip over your Nicoise salad and chocolate soufflé.'

"'As long as the salad doesn't wilt in the time it takes to get from the kitchen to the table.' Phillippe's face took on a brooding expression. 'I bought peaches this morning. By the time I took them out of the bag they were rotten from the heat.'

"'Well, I have some good news,' I offered. 'We've been invited to a dinner party on Monday. One of my old college friends, Laura, and her husband. Their loft is air-conditioned and they're sending their driver to pick us up.'

"Phillippe studied me curiously.

"'You never mentioned them before.'

"'They were living in San Francisco. Laura's husband made a lot of money in software and now they're back in New York.'

"'You said Monday night?'

"'The restaurant is closed on Monday so I thought . . .'

"'Monday,' he said abstractly. 'Yes, I suppose that's fine.'

"I spent the next week putting my plan to work. We had a small emergency fund that we kept in an envelope behind a bookshelf. It would cover the plane tickets and cost of the cottage in Provence.

"Phillippe hardly ever checked it, so he wouldn't notice it was gone. When we returned from France, I would take my partner's therapy patients while she was on holiday, and pay it all back.

"I gathered our passports. I even packed our clothes. I had a momentary panic when I couldn't find our suitcases. So I bought new suitcases and hid them under the bed.

"On Monday night, the hired car would take us to the airport instead of the dinner party. I'd tell Phillippe everything while we were sipping ice-cold champagne in the United Airlines Club Lounge.

"Monday afternoon, I went out to get magazines to read on the plane. When I returned, Phillippe was standing with the head of the co-op board, Nolan, in our living room.

"'Don't tell me we have rats or a water leak, as well as the problem with the air-conditioning,' I said, noticing their troubled expressions.

"'Nothing like that; we've been robbed,' Phillippe replied. 'Nolan is going to call the police.'

"Phillippe showed Nolan the space behind the bookshelf where the emergency fund was kept. I knew the envelope was empty, of course. I didn't know why Phillippe checked it in the first place.

"I convinced Nolan not to call the police. After he left, I motioned Phillippe to sit down. It was only then that I noticed the missing suitcases standing in the foyer.

"'What are those doing there?' I asked.

"'It doesn't matter now,' Phillippe sighed, wiping the sweat from his forehead. 'The money is gone. We won't be able to use them.'

"'Use them to go where?' I said, puzzled.

"Phillippe couldn't have guessed the truth. He would have said something.

"He told me his whole story. I had looked so miserable the last few weeks, he'd decided we had to get out of New York. He'd used the emergency money to rent a house in the Hamptons. He was going to pay the money back by doing some catering business on the side. It meant he wouldn't have a day off, but it would be worth it to make me happy.

"'But what about the restaurant reviewer?' I said desperately, thinking about the car that was arriving in two hours, the cottage waiting for us in Provence.

"'I know someone at *The New York Times*,' Phillippe said. 'He begged the reviewer to come in September instead. Now the restaurant may as well stay open. I'll have to pay back the deposit on the house, as well as the month's rent.'

"'I took the money.'

"Phillippe looked at me as if I was crazy from the heat.

"'You took the money?'

"I told him everything. That he seemed so homesick, I was afraid he'd want to leave New York for good. That I'd rented a cottage in Provence, and James was going to cover for him at the restaurant. I was going to take on extra patients to pay the money back. I used my own money to buy the new suitcases and reserve the car to take us to the airport.

"'It's all because of Guy de Maupassant,' I said miserably.

"Phillippe didn't say anything.

"'You did all that without telling me?'

"'I had to. I've never seen you look so unhappy,' I said.

"'I was unhappy—I couldn't bear to see you so miserable.'

"I couldn't believe what we had done. Now we would both have to repay the money, plus what we had spent of our own savings.

"Phillippe went to the fridge and took out the ice cream. He handed me a spoon.

"'I'm not hungry,' I said.

"'We can't leave ice cream in the freezer for a whole month,' he said as he took a bite.

"'Where are we going?' I asked.

"'To France, of course'—he took another bite—'we'll stop by my parents' apartment in Paris. I have an old coin collection I've been meaning to sell. We can use that money to pay for the house in the Hamptons.'

"'You're not angry?' I asked.

"'How can I be angry when I did the same thing?' He smiled. 'We live in New York, so we can go to the Hamptons anytime. I can't wait to show you Provence.'

"We'd made a promise to always tell each other everything. Then I ran to the bedroom to get dressed. I reached for the Maupassant book of short stories, but I put it back. There was no point in reading anything depressing on vacation. I'd much rather read romance novels instead."

Meredith stopped talking and Zach turned off the camera.

"That makes wonderful footage, but it has nothing to do with me and Rebecca."

"If you want to know what happened between her and Ben, ask her," Meredith said, standing up and stretching. "It might save you both a lot of anguish."

"Even if something happened between them, it doesn't solve my situation." Zach polished the camera lens. "Remember, Rebecca thinks you and I are involved."

Meredith picked up her purse and wrapped her scarf around her neck.

"If you can watch Buttons, I have to do something."

"Where are you going?"

Meredith slipped on her jacket.

"I got you into this, I'm going to get you out of it."

Chapter Twenty-two

Rebecca rubbed her hands from the cold, and entered Christmas Cove Lodge. It was midafternoon and she'd just returned from meeting with the DJ for Howard's party. He was going to play Christmas music during cocktails, followed by dance music from every decade since Howard was young, and a medley of Frank Sinatra songs at midnight.

She had almost forgotten about the meeting. Luckily, the DJ called as she was talking to Zach in the lobby. She wouldn't have known what to say to Zach if he hadn't. She wasn't ready to admit that she and Ben weren't married. Zach would know she had lied, and it was more than just that. Even though Rebecca was the one who told Ben to leave, it was because of Ben's affair with Natalie, and because Ben had never put Rebecca first. If she tried to explain any of that to Zach, he would only feel sorry for her. She didn't think she could deal with that right now.

It didn't matter anyway. They'd have no reason to see each other again after New Year's.

But a small part of her wanted to see Zach again. He was warm and good-looking and when they were together she felt something between them. The attraction for him that had been growing all week was becoming impossible to ignore. It was still as gentle as a morning snow flurry, but it was there.

Then she reminded herself that Zach was in a relationship with Meredith. And it was too early for Rebecca to consider another man. She was just lonely; everywhere in Christmas Cove couples strolled down Main Street, and happy families browsed in shops. Once she got back to San Francisco and was busy at the company and looking after Oliver she wouldn't think about men.

"Rebecca!" a voice called.

Rebecca turned around. Meredith was sitting in a chair by the fireplace.

"How nice to see you." Meredith closed the book she was reading. "I was hoping to run into you."

"Were you?" Rebecca asked, joining her.

"I want to talk to you about something in private," Meredith continued. "I don't want to go to my suite, so perhaps we can grab a cup of coffee."

"We can go to my suite instead," Rebecca offered.

They sat in the suite's living room and Rebecca made some fresh coffee.

"Would you like something to eat?" she asked Meredith.

Meredith shook her head. "I already had a big breakfast and the maids always leave out the best pastries. I'm going to be very disappointed when I get home and there aren't fresh muffins waiting on my sideboard."

"I know what you mean. I haven't sat down to so many meals since we started the company." Rebecca added cream to her coffee. "Lunch is usually something wolfed down between meetings, and dinner isn't much better."

"Still, it's wonderful how much you've accomplished." Meredith stirred her coffee. "You should be very proud."

"In tech, it's often about having the right idea at the right time." Rebecca shrugged.

"I don't believe it," Meredith countered. "Women are so hard on themselves these days. Years ago, if a woman raised the children and balanced the household budget, she was content. Now she has to run a Fortune 500 company or win an academic prize to feel worthwhile."

"It's not that exactly," Rebecca said doubtfully. "I want to help people. I'm not sure that Dealbreakers does that anymore, there are so many dating sites."

"Well, that's what I want to talk about," Meredith said. "I wondered if you'd help me make a profile."

"You want to be on Dealbreakers?" Rebecca said, shocked. "I thought you and Zach were . . ."

"Involved?" Meredith prompted. "Zach and I broke up. He's still staying with me, but just as friends."

"You broke up!" Rebecca exclaimed. "Zach didn't say anything."

"It happened a little while ago. It was a mutual decision," Meredith answered. "Zach is wonderful, but he's young. He deserves to have a wife and a family.

"After my second divorce, I swore off men for a while," she continued. "There are so many ways to feel fulfilled. I can do charity work, or open a new therapy practice. But then I realized that I shouldn't give up on love when it's the best thing in life. It's like not celebrating Christmas because someone tells you Santa Claus isn't real. Christmas is just what you need to get over the disappointment."

"I never thought about it that way," Rebecca mused.

"I enjoy Zach's company, but I want someone who's at the same stage in life."

"You said that you don't believe in dating apps," Rebecca reminded her.

"It's difficult to meet men in Los Angeles. The men my age are either married or going through an ugly divorce." She shuddered. "I've seen too many friends put their time and energy into a new man. As soon as the ink is dry on his divorce papers, he stops needing a shoulder to cry on and starts dating twenty-five-year-olds."

"It's the same in San Francisco," Rebecca said with a smile. "The men buy new wardrobes from trendy wilderness companies and sign up for hikes around the Bay."

"At least with Dealbreakers, we'd begin by having something in common," Meredith said.

"We can set it up on my computer." Rebecca pulled out her laptop.

Rebecca clicked through her files. She created a username and entered the information that Meredith gave her.

"What do you want to put as the one thing that you hate that would stop you from dating someone?"

Meredith thought about it.

"I couldn't date anyone who didn't love dogs. Buttons is a big part of my life," she began. "What I hate most is people who aren't honest with themselves. We all make mistakes, but if we're not honest with ourselves, we never grow. I was madly in love with my first husband, Phillippe. When the marriage ended I thought I would never fall in love ever again. Then I met my second husband, Josh, at a gallery opening in Manhattan. He was good-looking and wealthy, and he was interested in me. We had a whirlwind courtship and got married in his Upper East Side brownstone.

"Then he wanted to move to Los Angeles to get into the movie business and it was like cutting off my right arm. I adored New York. It was where my first roommates and I lived in an apartment so small, we kept our silverware in the bathroom cabinet because there weren't enough drawers in the kitchen. It was where Phillippe and I ate leeks vinaigrette at every French restaurant, because he had to make sure no one else made it better. And it was where I spent every weekend after Phillippe and I broke up at the public library, looking for something to read that would help me forget him.

"When we got to Los Angeles it was even worse. We bought a house in Beverly Hills and I didn't know how to drive. Josh didn't want me to open a therapy practice so I spent all my time gardening, even though we had a full-time gardener.

"When we finally decided to divorce, I blamed myself. I should have known we weren't right for each other. But then I realized, ending a marriage doesn't mean you have failed. It means you know yourself well enough to realize when it's time to move on."

Rebecca looked up from the keyboard.

"Do you have a photo?"

"I'll text you some later," Meredith said thoughtfully. "Thank you for helping me set up an account. Sometimes I feel too old to try something new. Then I tell myself that life wouldn't be fun if we could see the road ahead of us."

Meredith left and Rebecca typed up some final notes for Howard's party. Then Kimi FaceTimed her. She wore a cotton caftan over a one-piece bathing suit. A pair of sunglasses were perched on her forehead.

"I almost didn't recognize you, I've never seen you in a bathing suit," Rebecca said.

"My mother bought it for me at the gift shop, she was embarrassed because I was the only one on the ship wearing T-shirts and shorts. Everyone either dresses like film stars or in resort wear, as if they spend their whole lives in Mexico and Hawaii."

"It suits you, and those sunglasses are fabulous."

Kimi dropped them over her eyes.

"The sunglasses are so I can hide when I'm with my parents," Kimi replied. "They've fallen madly in love with each other, it's embarrassing. When they're not together, they call and send each other texts. Every time my father calls, my mother's phone plays 'I Did It My Way.'

"Everybody on the ship seems to be having a great romance, except Andy and me," Kimi sighed. "I didn't put Leila in day care because I want to spend time with her, but that means Andy and I don't have any time alone. Leila's sleeping in our bed in the stateroom, so the most intimate thing Andy and I have done is brush our teeth together."

"It still sounds wonderful—you're celebrating the holidays with your family."

"It does have its moments," Kimi acknowledged. "I found my mother teaching Leila to say halmoni and halbogi; that's Korean for grandmother and grandfather. And she offered to take care of Leila once a week when we get home. Now that she and my father want to spend time together, they're going to take her to the park and the zoo."

"Your parents are lucky. At the rate I'm going, my parents may not have grandchildren."

"You're only thirty!" Kimi said. "You are getting a chance to start fresh with the right person. You get to look forward to a new romance with candlelit dinners and romantic weekends. The only thing is, if you do fall in love, in a few years you'll be right where I am. With a baby sleeping between you and your husband."

They talked a little more and Rebecca hung up.

Outside the window, a soft snow was falling on the lake. Rebecca stood up and poured a cup of coffee. Right now she'd give up the glorious stillness, the beautiful view, to be in the midst of a noisy family with an adoring husband and a baby bouncing on her knee.

Chapter Twenty-three

Zach was still sitting at his laptop when Meredith returned from talking to Rebecca.

She unwrapped her scarf and scooped Buttons into her arms.

"You're beginning to look like the Ghost of Christmas Past in Charles Dickens's *A Christmas Carol*," Meredith said. "You need to get some fresh air and eat a steak or at least a hamburger."

"The film won't edit itself." Zach pressed Pause on the keyboard.

"Well, I have some interesting news." Meredith stroked Buttons's fur.

She told Zach about her meeting with Rebecca.

"You set up a profile on a dating site!"

"I'll never use it, it doesn't even have my photo." Meredith shrugged. "I had to have a reason to confide in Rebecca. Now she knows you're single. It's up to you to do the rest."

"You forget that I lied about being a waiter," Zach sighed. "And we don't know what's going on with Ben. Maybe he'll show up tonight with some fabulous gift to apologize for leaving again."

"Not telling Rebecca that you were a waiter was a little white lie, she'll understand," Meredith said. "And I did a little sleuthing while I was in her suite."

"Sleuthing?" Zach repeated, uncomfortably.

"Didn't I tell you? I love mystery novels, almost as much as romances," she said mischievously. "Most of the time, the clues are so obvious, it's easy to overlook them. There were no thank-you cards."

"I'm not following," Zach said.

He reached for his coffee cup and put it down. He had to put something in his stomach besides caffeine and chocolate truffles or he'd get an ulcer.

"I've been married twice. The first thing a bride does after her wedding is write thank-you cards. If she doesn't start right away, the cards never get done. I searched the whole suite, I even used the bathroom so I could check the bedroom. There wasn't a thank-you card in sight. The only reason someone doesn't write thank-you cards is if they are going to send back the presents."

"That doesn't prove anything," Zach objected. "Rebecca could plan on writing them when she gets home."

"With her busy schedule?" Meredith raised her eyebrows. "And there were no mementos from the wedding. At my wedding to Josh, the wine bottles were inscribed with our names. We took a few bottles on our honeymoon. Trust me, I have an intuition about these things."

Zach closed his laptop and stood up.

"Where are you going?" Meredith asked.

"You're right, I need a walk and something to eat," he said. "I appreciate everything you're doing, but I still think you're wrong. Ben would be crazy to leave Rebecca."

* * *

Zach sat at a window table at Jake's on the Lake and ordered a double ranch burger and two sides of truffle fries. The waitress looked at him in disbelief when he followed it up with a slice of pumpkin pie and two scoops of vanilla ice cream.

It wasn't the fresh air that helped his appetite, it was what Meredith had said about Rebecca. Could he have a chance with her?

But it was already New Year's Eve. What if he didn't see her again? And how could he admit his feelings when she hadn't confided anything about her and Ben?

After he finished eating, he strolled down Main Street. He bought a red snowflake sweater at the pet store for Buttons. Then he went into a gift shop and bought coasters with pictures of Christmas Cove for Meredith and matching mugs for Jerome and Alesha.

He was about to turn back toward the lodge when he noticed Rebecca walking in the other direction. She was bundled in a long, red parka and carried two heavy bags.

"Rebecca," he said and ran to catch up with her.

"Zach!" She turned around. "I thought you were editing all day."

"I needed some lunch." He pointed to the bags. "You shouldn't carry those yourself, you might slip on the ice."

Rebecca seemed to think about it for a moment.

"All right." She handed him a bag. "Thank you, I appreciate it. I need to stop somewhere first, if that's all right."

"I'm not in a hurry." Zach took the bag. "And walking in the fresh air always helps me work."

They walked out of the village and down a road dotted with chalets. Rebecca stopped in front of a wooden cottage that resembled the gingerbread house in a fairy tale. There was a dock and a stone path that led to a boathouse.

A pit formed in Zach's stomach. Had Rebecca and Ben bought this lovely chalet? Meredith was wrong about everything.

Rebecca opened the door to the boathouse. Heaters were placed around the room. Sheepskin rugs covered the wood floor and a Christmas tree stood in the corner, next to a bag of ornaments.

"Where are we?" Zach asked, setting the bag on the floor.

"It belongs to someone I know; I'm helping him plan tomorrow night's New Year's party. He hosts a party every year on the night of New Year's Day."

Howard, the man at the lodge with the guest list. Zach pictured Rebecca and Ben arriving at the party. Ben would be wearing a tuxedo and Rebecca would look gorgeous in a shimmery evening gown with pearl earrings as delicate as snowflakes. The guests would all be tech CEOs and they'd eat blinis with caviar and drink champagne.

Zach felt as deflated as the balloons that would drop from the ceiling at midnight.

"That's very nice of you," he said stiffly. "I'm sure you and Ben will have a wonderful time."

Rebecca perched on one of the boxes. She motioned for Zach to do the same.

"Ben isn't coming back to Christmas Cove; our marriage didn't work out."

"What do you mean, it didn't work out!" Zach exclaimed. "You've only been married for a few days. Ben was here, you both looked so in love."

"I was in love with Ben for years." Rebecca gazed at the Christmas tree. "My mother left when I was ten. My parents never fought when I was a child. They got married when they were very young, and they were never right for each other. My mother wanted to be an artist and my father was an engineer. All I wanted that first Christmas after she left was for her to walk through the door on Christmas Eve so that we'd be a family again. Every year, I wished for the same thing until I realized I was making the wrong wish. Even if my mother came back, that doesn't mean my parents would be happy. Instead, I had to wish for something else: for my father to fall in love again, and for my mother to find the life she wanted.

"That wish came true. My father has a wonderful wife and children, and my mother loves the man she later married and she adores Argentina." She fiddled with her parka. "It took longer for me to be happy; I didn't feel like I belonged in either of my parents' new lives. But I loved college, and then I met Ben. Each Christmas, I didn't know what to wish for, I had everything I wanted.

"Except I wasn't looking at our relationship closely enough. Until now." She glanced at Zach. "You're the one who helped me see it clearly."

Rebecca looked so lovely in the afternoon light, with the snow falling softly outside the window. He wanted to take her in his arms and kiss her. To show her that even if neither of them had recognized it all those years ago, they were meant for each other.

"It was watching the footage of myself." Rebecca kept talking. "I thought Ben loved me for myself. But really, he loved me because he could see in my eyes how much I loved him, and it made him feel good about himself. Even though we were equal partners at work, and he showered me with presents, I never came first." She paused. "If we stayed together, I never would have grown."

"You're a special woman, Rebecca. You deserve much more."

Rebecca stood up and paced around the room. Her eyes were bright. She walked back and stood close to him.

"You were such a good friend to me in film class. It's hard

to find friends when you're older. Kimi is the only close friend I have. Ben and I mainly have couple friends, and there's never been time outside of work to make friends of my own." She smiled at Zach. "Now that we've reconnected I hope we can stay friends forever."

Zach swallowed. All his warm feelings, the possibility of things to come—strolling hand in hand with Rebecca along Main Street, ice-skating to slow songs in the village square—dissolved like when the screen turned to black at the end of a movie.

When Rebecca agreed to meet Zach for burgers all those years ago, it had only been as a friend. She never had feelings for him and she never would.

"Of course we'll be friends." He pasted a smile on his face.

"I've been doing all the talking," Rebecca said. "I haven't even asked about the film."

Zach stood up. He zipped up his jacket.

"It's almost done. I should go and work on it. Unless you need some help."

Rebecca shook her head.

"I'm going to finish decorating the Christmas tree." She reached forward and kissed him on the cheek. "I really can't thank you enough. I wouldn't have gotten this far without you."

Zach walked miserably down Main Street. He turned down a lane until he reached the community kitchen.

Jerome was standing at the sink, scrubbing a pot.

"Hey, what are you doing here?" Jerome turned around. "I thought you had a deadline."

"I brought you a belated wedding gift." Zach set his package on the table. "Where's Alesha? You got married two days ago. Shouldn't you be spending all your time going on romantic strolls?"

"No wonder you make movies for a living," Jerome joked. "In real life, we both have to work. Alesha is getting ingredients for her first cooking class. She's already made friends with all the shop owners in Christmas Cove. Everyone loves her."

"I can see why, she's pretty great," Zach said, determined not to spoil Jerome's good mood.

"You look like someone just told you Santa's factory stopped making toys." Jerome studied his friend. "Do you want to talk about it?"

They sat at the table and Zach told Jerome about Ben and Rebecca. Zach had been about to admit his feelings for Rebecca, but Rebecca only saw Zach as a friend.

"There's nothing wrong with being friends before you're romantically involved," Jerome said when he finished. "Alesha and I were friends for years."

"You were twelve years old when you and Alesha met," Zach pointed out. "You were still reading comic books."

"I'm just saying you can change the way Rebecca sees you. Tell her how you feel."

"I've tried a dozen times." Zach shook his head. "But I can't get the words out of my mouth."

"Then tell her the way you do best. Record it on film and show her the footage."

Over the years, Zach often turned the camera on himself. He recorded videos at Christmas and on birthdays for his family when he lived in Europe. And when he applied for grants, he sent a clip of himself explaining how much filmmaking meant to him, and how he would use the money for important projects.

He could put it all in a film. That he knew immediately Rebecca was special when she appeared in class, with her ponytail and bright, summery dress. How he had enjoyed shooting on location with her, and was going to admit he had a small crush when they met at the Burger Shack. That they lost touch, but when he saw her again all the old feelings came back. And they'd only grown over the last few days. Rebecca was warm and compassionate and he wanted to get to know her better.

"That is a good idea," Zach said cautiously. "But I don't have anything to offer her. She's a hugely successful CEO and I'm one step away from living with my parents."

"You're too hard on yourself," Jerome counseled. "And you're probably going to win the contest, you've put your heart into it. I'm sure it shows."

"You're like my own personal Santa Claus." Zach jumped up, beaming. "I came in here thinking my dreams were over and I leave with a brilliant new plan."

Jerome punched Zach on the shoulder.

"I'm glad I helped. That's what friends are for."

Chapter Twenty-four

A few hours later, Rebecca sat on the sofa in the suite's living room. Outside the window, the sun was setting and the pine trees were heavy with fresh snow.

She had loved decorating the boathouse for the party. The Christmas tree was hung with cowboy ornaments, postcards dotted the walls, and the rug was warm and cozy under her feet.

Standing there in front of the boathouse window, she had remembered the first time she stepped into the penthouse of the Four Seasons. She stood with her notepad and pictured how it would look for the wedding. Gold and silver lights twinkling down from the ceiling, and the stone fireplace hung with stockings. There would be nutmeg-scented candles and Christmas tree ornaments that Rebecca and Ben had collected for the past eight years.

She wouldn't let herself think about that now. There were still things to do. She knew now that not marrying Ben was the right thing.

It had been a shock to see Zach walking down Main Street. At first, she had been hesitant to tell him that she and Ben broke up, but then they were sitting together in the boathouse and it had all spilled out. She hadn't told him everything—that Ben had been having an affair with Natalie for months and he left Rebecca hours before the wedding—but that wasn't important anymore.

There was a moment when she reached up and kissed his cheek that she wondered if there really could be something between them. But she couldn't tell Zach about the feelings she had been developing for him all week. It would be too awkward. Then he abruptly left. It was probably for the best. Despite what Kimi said, it was too early to think about someone new. And besides, Zach was probably about to leave for some exotic film location and they'd never see each other again.

She pulled out the next postcard. It was a photo of an ice cave. The caption read: *Explore the ice palaces in Bern, Switzerland.* She read the journal entry below.

December 1990, Bern, Switzerland

We were supposed to be in Brussels by now, we even had tickets to a Christmas concert at the Royal Palace. But we're in Bern, Switzerland, instead. This time, I can't blame Kat for our change of plans. We met some Americans in Paris who said missing the ice palaces would be the biggest mistake of our trip.

So we decided to take a side excursion to Bern, and I'm glad we did. Every building is decorated with colored lights and there are so many cozy cafés, it's impossible to feel cold even though the city is surrounded by snow-covered Alps.

We've already taken a cheese fondue tour, where you sit in a special car called a tuk-tuk and dip bread into a fondue pot while the driver tells you facts about the city.

The ice palaces are magnificent. They were created by a local artist in the village of Schwarzsee. Some of them were fifty feet tall, with turrets and drawbridges made of ice. In the evenings, they're lit up with pink and yellow and green lights, it's the most magical place I've ever seen. After we wandered around, we sat by the fireplace in the bar and drank glühwein, spiced red wine cooked with oranges and molasses.

Kat and I joked that we should publish a recipe book with the different kinds of mulled wine served in Europe at Christmas.

Even better than the mulled wine, even better than the ice palaces, is that I came to a decision. It isn't anything I planned, at least not for right now. But I made up my mind, and now I can't imagine doing anything else. It started yesterday, when Kat decided to go skiing in Grindelwald. It's only an hour away by bus, and one can rent skis and boots at the base of the mountain. But I couldn't face sitting on a freezing chairlift, and suggested Kat go by herself. We hadn't spent any time apart and I didn't mind having the afternoon alone. I was going to catch up on my reading and buy Christmas presents.

Then two things happened. The first was that I missed her. It sounds silly, but at the Christmas market, I couldn't decide whether to buy my mother a candle or a jar of Swiss cloves. And when I ordered the most popular dish at the café, the Berner Platte, which is smoked pork and beef cooked in juniper-flavored sauerkraut, I couldn't finish it and left half of it on my plate. I even missed exploring Bern together. Kat would have insisted we sneak into one of the hotels and use the sauna. It would have been so much fun to sit with the steam rising, sipping hot chocolate and hoping we didn't get caught.

The second thing that happened is I met an Australian named Bruce who owns a tour group. He needs tour guides for his tours in Thailand. Six months of showing tourists the ancient temples of Bangkok and the beaches in Koh Phi. We'd ride elephants and see statues of Buddhas, and sample chicken satay and fried bananas at the markets.

We talked for hours and he offered me and Kat jobs. They come with a salary including lodging, and he'd even pay for our flights to Thailand. I accepted for both of us, as neither of us had any plans when we returned home. And this would be a way for Kat and I to be together while we figured out what to do next.

I was so excited to tell her. I suggested we go to one of the bars opposite the ice-skating rink for dinner. Kat looked radiant after a day's skiing, in a blue turtleneck and beige slacks.

"You should have come skiing." She dug into a bowl of raclette—Swiss cheeses melted over ham and potatoes. "I met some Australians who are skiing in every country in Europe. Australia is so far from everything, when they travel they stay away for months."

"I met an Australian too." I sipped a glass of hot apple cider. For some reason I was nervous. Kat and I had only known each other for a few weeks, and I had planned the next six months without consulting her. But Kat loved adventure, I was certain she would be thrilled.

I told her everything. The job started on New Year's

Day. We'd leave for Thailand from Brussels the day after Christmas.

I finished talking and she didn't say anything. She just kept taking bites of melted cheese and roasted potatoes. Finally, she put down her fork.

"I can't go."

"What do you mean, you can't go?" I asked, puzzled. "We both said we don't have any plans." My voice dropped and I clutched my glass. "Unless you've heard from Stewart . . ."

"Of course I haven't heard from Stewart," she cut in. "I can't go, but you have to accept. It's the chance of a lifetime."

"It's the chance of a lifetime for both of us," I snapped. I don't know why I was angry, it was the way Kat said it. Her face closed up as if it wasn't open for discussion. "There isn't one good reason why you have to rush home."

"There is one good reason why I can't go to Thailand." She fiddled with her napkin. "They have dengue fever, and if I get it I could die."

I'd never heard of dengue fever. It's a disease carried by a certain kind of mosquito found in various parts of the world. Kat got dengue fever on a trip to the Bahamas during college spring break. She had a fever of 105 and couldn't get on a plane for days. When she finally returned home, she missed the rest of the semester because she was still recovering.

"That's why I came to Europe in the winter. I can't go to Hawaii or Mexico or parts of Asia. If I get dengue fever a second time, there is a high possibility that I wouldn't survive."

I felt like a complete idiot. I had assumed that Kat didn't

want to go because she didn't want to be with me. I even accused her of corresponding with Stewart.

"We'll only be apart for six months. It will be good for us. I need to focus on my career. I'm going to send résumés to art museums in New York."

"We don't know if we want to live in New York!" I exclaimed, frustrated.

Kat was pulling away from me and I didn't know how to get her back.

"We haven't talked about the future," she reminded me. "Maybe I'll go to Boston, I've always liked New England." She pushed away her chair. "I'm going to ice-skate. When you finish your raclette, you can join me."

It was the first night we didn't sleep in the same bed since St. Anton. When I woke in the morning, I'd never felt lonelier in my life. The plane tickets arrived and I tore them up in front of Kat. Then I called Bruce and declined the offer.

Kat said I was crazy, and if it was her, she'd be on the next flight to Thailand. She went off to do some Christmas shopping and left me at the hostel.

That's when I made my decision. If I can't bear to be away from Kat for a few months, how can I envision my entire future unless I know she's by my side?

I'm going to ask her to marry me. We may be young, and I may not have a career, but I've never been more certain of anything in my life. Our train leaves for Brussels this evening. When we arrive, I'll buy an engagement ring, and I'll propose on Christmas Day.

The journal entry ended. Rebecca peeled off the postcard and slipped it in her purse.

She wanted to ask Howard what happened between him and Kat. But he was still in Sacramento, and wouldn't return until later in the day.

Her phone rang.

"Rebecca, it's Zach."

"Hi, Zach." Rebecca pulled her mind back to the present.

"I wondered if you'd like to have an early dinner tonight. Nothing fancy, I was going to order room service in the suite. I'd like to show you more of the film."

It was still snowing; it would be nice to eat dinner at the lodge. Zach considered them to be just friends, there was no reason not to dine in his suite.

"I'd like that," she accepted.

"Excellent! I'll see you in an hour."

Rebecca wondered if she had time to take a bath. It felt odd to be having dinner with someone other than Ben. Then she reminded herself that she and Zach had eaten plenty of meals together all week. The only difference was that now he knew she was single.

There were new notifications in her e-mail. They were responses to Meredith's dating profile. Meredith wouldn't know how to reply. Rebecca could weed out the ones that were hopeless: the men who said they were answering for a friend, or the ones with photos that you could tell were taken years ago, because the guy was standing in front of a sports stadium that now had a different name.

Rebecca ignored the one from a guy standing in front of a red electric car, who said he lived in Bermuda. Hardly anyone lived in

Bermuda. He probably took the photo while he was on vacation in front of a car that he rented for a few days.

The next match had a photo of an attractive man in his late forties. He loved Sunday brunch and European football. It was the last line in the comment box that caught Rebecca's attention. "Like you said in your profile, I couldn't be with anyone who didn't believe in herself. But the real dealbreaker would be if she didn't believe in me."

Isn't that what all women wanted? Rebecca had believed in Ben for so long, she hadn't needed anything else. Once she stopped believing in him, there was nothing left between them.

Before she could stop herself, she replied. She and Meredith hadn't agreed that she could respond for her, but she liked her and it was Christmastime. Maybe she had done a good deed and it would change Meredith's life.

An hour later, Rebecca knocked on the door of Zach's suite.

"Please come in," Zach said. He was casually dressed in a green crewneck sweater and corduroys.

"Something smells delicious in here." Rebecca followed him inside.

The lights in the living room were turned low and the Christmas tree twinkled at the window. A white tablecloth covered the dining table, and there was a serving cart with silver domes.

"It must be the French onion soup," Zach said, sitting on the sofa.

"Ben and I used to eat French onion soup every night when we started the company," Rebecca recalled. "They came in those little packets and I only had to add boiling water."

She stopped awkwardly. She hadn't meant to talk about Ben and Dealbreakers.

"I'm sorry, it's been a long time since I had to make dinner conversation with someone new," she apologized. "I'm not very good at it."

"You don't have to apologize." Zach handed her a glass of wine. "I know the feeling. The subjects that were so easy to talk about during the day seem to vanish when the sun sets." He sipped his wine thoughtfully. "I know Meredith told you that we broke up. She's seeing a Christmas musical at the playhouse right now."

"Are you upset?" Rebecca asked.

"Meredith is a wonderful woman, but we're very different," Zach acknowledged.

"I miss Ben, we had great years together," she said truthfully. "I never thought I'd be single at thirty. I've always wanted a family."

"You have everything else," Zach reminded her. "Your own company and an apartment. You're even getting a dog."

"I keep looking at photos of Oliver on my phone." Rebecca grinned. "I'm not sure I want to stay at Dealbreakers, but I don't know what else to do. Today I watched the boathouse transform into a party destination and it felt so satisfying. Even if I'm able to just bring joy into people's lives for a few hours, they'll keep those memories forever."

"I'm sure you're wonderful at it," Zach said.

"I'm sorry, I'm rambling on. You've heard enough about me in the film." Rebecca gulped her wine.

If Kimi was here, she'd take away Rebecca's glass and tell her to pull herself together. An attractive man had asked Rebecca to dinner and she was behaving as if she was talking to a therapist.

"Why don't we keep talking over dinner." Zach stood up. "The room service waiter gave me strict instructions to serve the soup before it gets cold."

They moved to the table and ate soup with sourdough baguettes. There was roasted chicken and green beans and scalloped potatoes. They talked about work and college, and the differences between Berkeley and San Francisco.

With every bite, Rebecca enjoyed herself more. It was like one of those montages in a romantic movie, where at first the couple is so nervous, they don't know what to say. But with every course they become more relaxed, until they don't even notice that the candles have burned down to the wicks and their wineglasses are empty because they're too busy learning about each other's lives.

By the time Zach served dessert—Swedish creme made with heavy whipping cream and strawberries; Zach's favorite because it had so much sugar in it, it kept him awake better than coffee—she felt she knew everything about him.

And she told him everything about herself. That after her mother left, she didn't have anyone to talk to. The girls in high school were in cliques and, even in college, the school was so big it was hard to make friends. It wasn't until she'd hired Kimi at Dealbreakers that she had a best friend.

"Even though I didn't have many close friends at Berkeley, I still loved it. Being there helped me mature," Rebecca said, drinking the brandy they had switched to with dessert. "The campus was so beautiful. I used to sit in the eucalyptus grove for hours, studying."

"I remember you sitting under that tree on the first day of film class," Zach said. "I didn't think you were coming back. I was afraid we'd chased you away."

Suddenly, Rebecca wanted to say that even on their first meeting, she felt that Zach was special. He was passionate about his work, but easy to talk to at the same time. She developed a small crush on him and was disappointed when he never showed up at the Burger Shack.

She opened her mouth, but Zach was standing up. He cleared the dessert plates.

"Do you want to look at that footage?" he asked.

Zach pulled out his laptop. Instead of seeing her own face on the screen, Zach came into focus. He was framed beside the Christmas tree at the window.

"'This film is about first love and happy endings. We've all seen Hollywood movies with the same theme. The male lead plays a fireman who never went to college. He meets a female cardiologist who's stranded on a roof garden in New York. They have a whirlwind romance and get married at Christmas at the fire station on Fifty-Eighth Street.

"'Or she's a small-town veterinarian and he's a developer buying up all the land. She refuses to sell her practice until she discovers he's building a wildlife preserve to protect endangered species in the area. They fall in love and live in a beach house with a menagerie of pets.

"'In real life, first loves don't always end with the couple kissing, while the camera moves in circles around them. In some cases, the girl he's in love with doesn't notice him at all, or only sees him as a friend.

"'When I was a senior in college, I met someone who was different from any girl I knew. She was interesting to talk to, and she had this vitality, like a champagne bottle that has just been uncorked. We were thrown together for a film project, and I'd never had so much fun in my life. But then the project ended. I had to tell her how I felt, or I'd never get another chance.

"'So I invited her to meet for burgers at the local burger place. I said I wanted to talk about the film, but I was going to tell her my feelings. All morning, I was nervous and excited. I changed my shirt three times. I even took out the last thirty dollars in my bank account because I wanted to pay for both of us.

"'Then my roommate borrowed my bicycle, and he was late returning it. By the time I jogged across campus to the diner, the girl was sitting in a booth with another guy. The type of guy every girl wanted to be with. Good-looking, an athlete, in a fraternity. A guy who was perfect for her.

"'I didn't need a scriptwriter to write the ending. She and the guy fell in love, and had the golden future she deserved. We completely lost touch. She never knew I was there that day and I never told her.'"

The camera faded to black. Zach closed the laptop.

The living room was completely quiet. Zach sipped his glass of brandy.

"Ever since you appeared in Christmas Cove on Christmas Eve, I've been wanting to tell you about that day." Zach broke the silence. "But there was no point—you were on your honeymoon. And it was so long ago, it would only embarrass both of us. Then you and Ben broke up and I still didn't know how to tell you." He rubbed the rim of his glass. "It was Jerome who suggested I say it on film . . ."

Rebecca crossed the room while he was talking. She reached up and kissed him tentatively on the mouth. It was only a small kiss, but then he kissed her back. He pulled her close and put his arms around her waist.

"I'm glad you told me," she said.

"Would you like to have lunch tomorrow before you finish getting ready for the party?" he asked.

Rebecca nodded. "I'd like that very much."

"I'll meet you in the lobby at noon." He pushed his hair over his forehead and grinned. "Rebecca, I promise I won't be late."

Chapter Twenty-five

The boathouse was almost ready for the party. A long table was covered with a blue linen tablecloth, and highback chairs were adorned with satin bows. A mirrored bar took up one wall, and there was a sitting area beside the picture window.

Rebecca loved the small touches the most. The silver-and-gold star on top of the Christmas tree, the horseshoe-shaped mistletoe dangling from the ceiling. The florist had delivered huge urns of Christmas chrysanthemums, and there was a round table scattered with photos of Christmas Cove.

She still couldn't believe that Zach had a crush on her all those years ago. What would have happened if he'd told her while they were in college?

Then there was the kiss. When she woke up, she expected to feel it had been a mistake. It had been the brandy after all that wine, or she was lonely and not thinking clearly. She and Ben had only broken up a few days ago, and she shouldn't be thinking about other men. And Zach didn't live in San Francisco, so there was no way for them to be together. She'd make it easy for both of them, and tell Zach the kiss should never have happened and that she hoped they would remain friends.

But instead, lying under the soft, white comforter, the winter sun streaming through the window, she felt a new excitement. It wasn't just the kiss that was lovely, the whole night had been amazing. She felt light and happy when they were together.

It was too soon to know if the kiss would lead to anything. But even if they went back to their separate lives, and their relationship became a series of cute texts accompanied by photos of Oliver and the places where Zach was filming, she still didn't regret it.

She had been developing feelings for Zach all week, she couldn't make them go away.

Rebecca moved to the storage room and rummaged through the boxes. The wedding dress hung in the closet. It really was beautiful. The Belgian lace was soft under her fingers and the satin hem was stitched with silver thread.

Before she could stop herself, she slipped off her jeans and sweater and tried it on. The appliquéd bodice was a little tight, but the rest of it—the white satin sash, the full skirt—was even prettier than it had been on the hanger.

She twirled in front of the mirror and imagined what it would have been like to have had a dress like that for her own wedding. Would she have left the dress in the bridal suite of the Four Seasons after Ben walked out? Or would she have packed it up carefully, hoping that one day she'd meet someone new? Someone who didn't insist that her gown came from the most exclusive bridal boutique in San Francisco. Someone who only cared that she joined him at the altar.

A tag was attached to the hem. There were only two words.
For Kat.

So Howard had proposed. Kat even bought a wedding dress. Why didn't they get married and why did Howard have the dress after all these years?

She hung it back in the closet. Maybe the answer was in Howard's journal. She'd read it later. First she had to finish decorating the boathouse, then she had to meet Zach for lunch.

"I never usually have an appetite at lunch, but today I'm starving," Rebecca said, studying the menu.

They were seated at a window table in the lodge's restaurant. Zach was dressed in a ribbed turtleneck, and Rebecca wore jeans and a pink-and-white sweater.

She told him about her morning at the boathouse and the wedding dress hanging in the closet.

"I feel guilty reading Howard's journals, they're quite personal," she said. "But I can't wait to read why they didn't get married."

"He wouldn't have given them to you if he didn't want anyone reading them," Zach reasoned. He paused for a moment. "About last night. I didn't mean to make you uncomfortable with the footage . . ."

"You don't need to apologize," Rebecca interrupted. She grinned mischievously. "Remember, I'm the one who kissed you."

Zach picked up a bread roll and pulled it apart.

"Yes, you did."

Rebecca put down the menu. She felt braver and more confident than she had in ages. She looked at Zach steadily.

"And I would do it again."

Zach spread butter on the bread roll. He looked up at Rebecca and smiled.

"Well, I can't think of better news than that."

They ordered omelets and talked about Christmas Cove and Howard's party. A man in his early fifties approached their table. He was tall and thin, and wore a dark suit and navy tie.

"Zach! I'm glad to see you, I was going to give you a call," he began. "You can have your job back. My nephew is leaving and I'll need another waiter. You can do room service too, the tips are excellent."

Rebecca glanced from the man to Zach.

"A waiter, here?" she repeated, puzzled.

"I'm Edward, the restaurant manager," Edward said by way of introducing himself. "I had to let Zach go, he was sitting with a guest at her table. But it seems I acted too hastily. The woman delivered a card to my office explaining everything. She said you were an excellent waiter and I shouldn't be hard on you." Edward turned to Zach. "I always tell my staff, it takes a big man to admit his mistakes. I made a mistake by firing you."

Zach's face had turned pale.

"When did this happen?" Rebecca asked.

Edward rubbed his chin while he thought about it.

"It was Christmas Eve. I've got to go. I'll be in my office, Zach, tell me what you decide."

Rebecca put her napkin on the table. Her hands were shaking and there was a pit in her stomach.

"I thought you were in Christmas Cove to make a film."

Zach's cheeks turned red. His eyes were giant pools.

"I can explain," he began. "I am making a film, but it's for a contest. My grant money ran out, and I'm broke. You came into the restaurant. I thought you had just gotten married and you looked so self-assured and successful, I couldn't admit that I was a waiter. So I sat at a table and pretended I was having dinner. I didn't even know it was Meredith's table. She came back from the bathroom and pretended we knew each other, so I played along." He hung his head. "Edward saw me and fired me. The staff isn't allowed to dine with guests. Meredith and I met at a film festival a couple of years ago, though I didn't remember her. She felt sorry for the trouble she caused and offered to let me stay in her suite."

Suddenly Rebecca couldn't bear it. She couldn't listen to someone lie to her again.

"There's nothing wrong with being a waiter. And I can't believe you and Meredith spun such an elaborate lie. You had eight days to tell me the truth, but you never did." She pushed back her chair. "Put the omelets on my bill, and happy new year, Zach."

An hour later, Rebecca sat in her suite, stirring a cup of hot chocolate. She was still hungry, but the thought of putting anything in her stomach was impossible. Even the hot chocolate didn't help. It smelled wonderful, but it was too hard to swallow.

Zach had lied about being a waiter, he had lied about being involved with Meredith. Meredith had been so friendly, and she had lied to Rebecca too.

If only Rebecca hadn't kissed Zach. That one kiss had been warm and soft, and opened up so many possibilities: the chance of having someone new in her life, someone she could share things with, someone she cared about.

But she couldn't change anything that happened. The only thing to do was concentrate on Howard's party.

She studied the last postcard. It was a picture of a giant Ferris wheel. The caption read: *Winter Wonders in Brussels, Belgium*. Underneath the postcard, the journal entry began:

December 1990, Brussels, Belgium

It's the day after Christmas and I'm sitting in a hostel in Brussels, staring at a bottle of jenever gin. Sometime yesterday I switched from vin chaud to gin. I've found that it goes down as smoothly as childhood cough syrup.

Our stay in Brussels started out wonderfully. At Christmastime, the city center is transformed into a Winter Wonderland with an ice-skating rink, and Christmas stalls, and amusement rides. Kat and I both love the Ferris wheel. From the top, you can see the churches and cathedrals. At night, the whole city is lit with Christmas lights, and it's the most breathtaking view I've ever seen.

And we both loved the food. In Brussels, they eat waffles almost at every meal. With fresh fruit and syrup for breakfast, and whipped cream and melted chocolate for dessert. The national dish is French fries served with steamed mussels. Kat had never eaten mussels. Once she tried them, she couldn't get enough.

The only problem was keeping my wedding proposal secret. Every time we passed a jewelry store, I wanted Kat's opinion on the diamond rings in the window. The first night at dinner, I was staring at her hand, trying to figure out her ring size. She gave me this puzzled look, and I blinked and said I had something in my eye.

On Christmas Eve, I went out by myself for a couple of

hours and visited a jewelry store in Place Sainte-Catherine. I couldn't afford a new diamond ring, but they had a case filled with secondhand engagement rings.

"Would your girlfriend like something modern or a more classical style?" the saleswoman asked. She was in her forties and wore a severe black dress.

"I'm not sure, perhaps you can show me some of each."

She took out two trays of rings. Some had round diamonds, other were rubies, and there was an emerald with a platinum band.

"What kind of jewelry does she wear?" the woman prompted.

"Kat doesn't wear jewelry. We're staying at hostels, jewelry would get stolen."

"Well, what kind of jewelry does she wear at home?"

"I have no idea." I rubbed my forehead. "We only met a month ago."

She looked at me like I was a crazy American tourist.

"You're proposing to a woman that you've known a few weeks?"

"What's wrong with that?" I asked stiffly. "Anyway, we've been together every day. Traveling is the best way to find out if you're compatible."

"How can you buy a ring that she's going to wear for the rest of her life if you don't know her taste?"

The saleswoman was right. What if Kat hated the ring? She'd have to wear it forever. To PTA meetings when we had children, and at family gatherings during the holidays. I could tell Kat that if she didn't like the ring, I'd buy her a new one. But I know Kat. She'd think somehow the marriage was a failure.

Christmas was the following day and I couldn't propose without a ring.

"What should I do?" I asked plaintively.

"Find out her taste and come back." The woman put the trays in the case. "We close at five p.m."

When I got back to the hostel, Kat wasn't there. Kat's clothes were all different styles. There were sweaters she found at vintage clothing stores, and jeans she'd probably had since high school. I had no idea what her taste was in anything else, she didn't even wear perfume.

I walked to the Christmas market and browsed around the stalls. There were so many people buying last-minute gifts and souvenirs, no one volunteered to help me.

That's when I saw it. The most beautiful wedding dress I'd ever seen. Not like a traditional wedding dress I'd seen in movies, with a huge skirt and long train. This dress was knee-length. It was made of lace, with a wide sash and satin hem. I only knew it was a wedding dress because it was paired with a pair of ivory satin slippers, and it had a short veil.

The best part was somehow the dress looked exactly like Kat.

Every guy proposed with a ring. What if I proposed with a wedding dress instead? If we didn't get married right away, we could get one of those garment bags for the plane. I'd get her a diamond ring eventually. Later, once we were married and I knew what she liked.

Once the idea took hold, I couldn't shake it. It was the kind of thing Kat would love. Something impulsive and original.

I paid for the dress and took it to the hostel. Kat wasn't back, so I hid it in the closet, behind my clothes. I was going to propose on Christmas morning, after a big breakfast of waffles and sausages.

That night, instead of going out to dinner, we joined all the tourists to see the light show in the Grand Place. Every half hour, royal blue and silver lights shine down from the town hall and sweep over centuries-old buildings that once housed blacksmiths and weavers. In the middle of the square, there's a giant Norway spruce tree decorated with lights and ornaments. People stop to see the Nativity scene and to take photos of themselves in front of the Manneken Pis—Brussel's famous peeing statue that every December for the last four hundred years has been dressed in a different costume.

I've never had so much fun. Just knowing that the wedding dress was in my closet, and that Kat and I would be together forever, made me happy. We drank Glühwein, which is mulled wine made with cloves and spices, and rode the carousel and Ferris wheel.

It was almost midnight when we returned to the hostel. We sat in the main room, in front of the small Christmas tree.

"When I was a child, I never liked Christmas Day; Christmas Eve was much better," Kat reflected, pulling off her gloves.

"How can you say that? Christmas is the best day of the year," I protested.

"That's the thing. On Christmas Eve, it was all ahead of me. In just twenty-four hours, I would open presents and eat turkey and stuffing, and go caroling.

"But on Christmas morning, I always woke up with a feeling of dread. For the previous month everything had been about Christmas: seeing *The Nutcracker* at the local playhouse, performing the Nativity play at church, and exchanging gifts with my friends," Kat continued. "But at the end of Christmas Day it would all be over, there would be nothing to look forward to for a whole year."

"When we have children, we'll save our presents to each other for the day after Christmas. Then we'll have something to look forward to." I leaned forward and kissed her.

Kat had a funny expression on her face. We were both a little tipsy from the Glühwein. She jumped up and went upstairs. When she returned, she was holding a box.

"What's this?" I asked.

"I almost forgot. Our family has a tradition of giving each other one present on Christmas Eve." She handed it to me.

"But I don't have anything for you!" I exclaimed, admiring the red-and-green bow.

"It doesn't matter, open it," she prompted.

Inside was a snow globe. But there was no scene, only fat, white snowflakes.

"I got it from a fortune teller at the Christmas market," she explained. "You imagine what you wish for and shake it. If you wish hard enough, the thing you wish for appears in the snow globe."

Kat had never looked more beautiful. Her reddish hair fell in waves down her back, and her green eyes were bright and sparkly.

I kissed her again.

"I don't need to wish for anything, all I want is right here."

On Christmas morning, when I woke up, Kat had gone out to get coffee and pastries. At first, I was grateful to have extra time to rehearse my proposal. But two hours passed and she hadn't returned.

I began to worry that something happened to her. I went down to the receptionist.

"Did you see Kat this morning?" I asked.

He was just a college kid, I doubted he could help me.

"She left a couple of hours ago."

"Did she say when she was coming back?"

He shrugged and turned the page of the book he was reading.

"It didn't look as if she was coming back. She had her backpack and suitcase."

Kat and I were staying in separate rooms. But I didn't believe him. Kat couldn't have left without telling me.

"You must be thinking of someone else," I insisted.

"She signed the guest book and left a tip." He showed me the guest book.

My head was pounding and my veins felt like ice.

"Did she say anything or leave a note?"

He searched around the desk.

"Nothing here." He looked at me and shrugged. "The same thing happened to me last summer in Madrid. She's not the first girl who walked out on a holiday romance."

I ran out the door and walked all the way to the American Express office. I didn't know what I was hoping to discover, but I cajoled the woman into telling me there had been no urgent telegrams for Kat from America.

I had no way of getting in contact with her. We hadn't exchanged home addresses and phone numbers. Why should we? We were together every day. All I knew is that Kat was from Chicago and her mother worked in a hospital.

That's when I started drinking. At the moment, I have no plans other than switching from gin to beer when the gin bottle is empty.

I'll have to go back to America when my tourist visa runs out. But right now, the thought of maneuvering through airports and making polite conversation on a plane for ten hours is about as possible as seeing Santa Claus fly across the sky on his sleigh.

I'll never look forward to Christmas Day again. Instead, I'll be like Kat, I'll dread it every year.

Rebecca closed the journal. That's why Howard had kept the snow globe and wedding dress for thirty-three years. He had been in love with Kat and she had disappeared on him.

She closed the journal and slipped the postcard in her purse to take to the boathouse. Outside the window, it was snowing again. Big, fat flakes fell on the ground and then disappeared.

Christmas Cove seemed like a fairy-tale destination, with its quaint main street and skating rink in the village square. But right now, sitting in her suite, it felt no different than the bridal suite at the Four Seasons when Ben walked out, or the restaurant at the lodge when Zach admitted he lied to her.

Love was an illusion. Anyone who fell in love was going to get hurt.

Chapter Twenty-six

Zach paced around the suite's living room, going over his lunch with Rebecca earlier that afternoon. What had he been thinking, eating at the lodge's restaurant? He should have known there was the possibility of running into Edward.

If only he had told Rebecca about being a waiter and everything else he had lied about after he showed her the film footage. But they had kissed and everything else fled from his mind.

Now Rebecca would probably never talk to him again. He couldn't blame her, he had lied and ruined her trust. And he couldn't even distract himself by editing. Something in the film wasn't working. He knew what it was, but he couldn't figure how to fix it.

The door opened and Meredith entered.

"Oh dear." Meredith studied Zach's drawn cheeks and blood-shot eyes. "You look like a figure at a wax museum. You and Rebecca were going to lunch. I thought afterward, you'd be cozied up by the fireplace for the rest of the day.'"

"Lunch didn't go quite as I had imagined," Zach said darkly.

He told Meredith about Edward offering him his job back, revealing that he had been a waiter.

Meredith unwrapped her scarf and sat on the sofa. "I really did create a mess. I'll go to Rebecca and explain it was all my fault."

"It isn't your fault, I could have told Rebecca the truth a dozen times," Zach sighed. He sat on the sofa opposite her. "It's too late now. She'll never speak to me again."

"Everyone makes mistakes in a relationship."

"That's the thing, we don't have a relationship, we had one kiss."

He remembered Rebecca crossing the room and kissing him. At first he was surprised, and he didn't know how to respond. Then he kissed her back, and it felt so right. He wanted to wrap his arms around her and kiss her forever. Now he never would.

"On top of that, I'm sure I'm going to lose the contest. There's something missing from the film."

"What do you mean?" Meredith asked curiously.

"I've been rewatching the footage. Each story has a happy ending. There's no drama," he explained. "I can't ask Rebecca to do another interview, and Jerome and Alesha are madly in love. If a movie doesn't contain some kind of dilemma—a betrayal that can't be resolved, an affair that ends in tragedy—the audience is unmoved. A great film makes its audience feel pain as well as joy. You can't have one without the other."

"I hadn't thought of that." Meredith scooped up Buttons. "I haven't told you how my first marriage ended."

Meredith was right. He only knew that she had been married twice. Meredith was so confident and secure, he assumed that she ended her marriage to Phillippe.

"Why don't we record that now?" she suggested. "It might be the footage that you're looking for."

"'It was springtime, Phillippe and I had been married for eight years. Spring was my favorite season in New York. Everyone came out of hibernation. People sat at outdoor cafés and made plans for summer shares in the Hamptons and the Catskills. College students filled out business school applications. It was as if the whole city was looking forward to what was coming next.

"Phillippe's restaurant was doing wonderfully. It had been reviewed in *The New York Times* for the third time, and each review was more glowing than the last. He had decided to get a business partner. He wanted to expand to more locations.

"I wasn't thrilled about being a therapist, but I was good at it and the practice was doing well. And I loved our neighborhood and friends. We attended dinner parties and on Sunday nights, I cooked for both of us. Phillippe taught me to make quiche, and I quite enjoyed it.

"It was a Saturday in April and we were having brunch at Sarabeth's on the Upper West Side. It was our favorite restaurant. Phillippe declared their lemon and ricotta pancakes were better than the crepes his mother made when he was a boy.

"'I have news,' Phillippe said when the waitress set down our plates. 'I signed the papers with Henri. We're partners.'

"Phillippe had known Henri when they worked at the same restaurant in Paris. Henri was very successful and wanted to invest in French restaurants in America.

"'Are you sure that's what you want?' I asked.

"'I'll be forty soon, I can't work restaurant hours forever.'

Phillippe spread butter on his pancakes. 'And I'm ready for new challenges.'

"Phillippe worked long hours. He often started at the fish markets at five a.m. and didn't get home until after the restaurant closed. But we were both used to it. I worried that he wouldn't know what to do with his free time.

"'You won't be forty for five years,' I corrected. 'I don't want you to get bored at night. I'm often asleep at ten p.m.'

"'I'll be busy with new restaurants,' he replied. There was a twinkle in his eye. 'And I have an idea of what we can do with our nights.'

"I blushed, wondering if anyone had heard him. Even though our hours were different, our lovemaking was as pleasurable as when we were newly married. We made up for the nights when I went to bed first, by staying up until midnight on weekends and spending Sunday mornings in bed.

"'I thought we were happy in that department,' I remarked. 'I can buy some new lingerie . . .'

"'You don't need lingerie, you'll always be the most beautiful woman in the world,' he said gallantly. 'I was thinking, it might be time to have a baby.'

"We hardly ever talked about having children; the restaurant had always been like a child. And I discovered I wasn't maternal. I'd see women pushing strollers, or I'd notice the pink sweaters in a baby store, and wait for something to twist inside me. The feeling that I was getting older, if we didn't start soon, we'd miss out. But nothing happened. I was content with my life.

"'You want to have a baby?' I repeated, putting down my fork.

"'With Henri as a partner, it will be hard, but I can create my own schedule.' He placed his hand on mine. 'I can't think of anything better than making a new person with the woman I love.'

"It wasn't a bad idea, I still had plenty of time, and I only worked three days a week. And even if I wasn't crazy about babies, I liked children.

"We talked about it more until he convinced me.

"'All right.' I nodded, smiling. 'If that's what you want.'

"'You'll want it too.' He kissed me eagerly. 'It will be a new adventure.'

"I wondered if Phillippe would say the same thing when our pristine kitchen was overtaken by baby bottles and jars of pureed squash, but I didn't say anything. Every couple survives the baby stage and we would too.

"For three months, we had sex often, but nothing happened. A friend suggested we see a fertility doctor, but I refused. I didn't want to become one of those wives who's always whipping out a thermometer and calling Phillippe at the restaurant to come home because I was ovulating.

"We spent August in the Hamptons and I was confident I'd get pregnant. We made love almost every day, and the rest of the time, we lolled around the house, eating healthy meals.

"Toward the end of our stay, I developed an aversion to coffee. I'd read that's a telltale sign of pregnancy, but I didn't say anything. Phillippe was so eager. If I was wrong I didn't want to disappoint him.

"Then in September, I got my period. I had to tell Phillippe. He merely kissed me and said we'd try harder.

"It was the beginning of October, and I was standing in the kitchen, heating up a bowl of soup.

"Phillippe appeared and tossed his jacket on the table.

"'When were you going to tell me?' he demanded.

"I'd never seen him look so angry. His dark eyes were hooded, and his shoulders were hunched.

"'Tell you what?' I wondered.

"'That you lied about being pregnant before we were married,' he replied. 'Or maybe you were telling the truth, and the baby's father was someone else.'

"'I don't know what you're talking about,' I said.

"I kept my expression calm, but there was a prickle on my neck. Like when a spider crawled down my back once when I was getting dressed.

"'I went to a fertility doctor,' Phillippe said. 'I know we agreed not to, but I had to know if it was my fault.'

"Phillippe went to the fridge and took out a beer. He never drank beer, it was only there for guests.

"'I have a low sperm count. There's a five percent chance I could father a child.'

"I started to say that perhaps his condition started recently, that I had gotten pregnant eight years ago. But I couldn't lie to Phillippe again. So I told him the whole story. He was going to lose his work visa, and he'd have to go back to France. I was afraid I'd never see him again. He saw the second pregnancy kit on the counter and assumed I was pregnant. I didn't mean to lie, I just didn't correct him.

"'I couldn't go through with it. Remember? I told you that the doctor said the home pregnancy test was wrong, I wasn't pregnant after all,' I finished. 'I was young and immature. I'm so ashamed, it was a terrible thing to do.'

"His eyes flickered. I could tell from his expression that he knew I was telling the truth.

"'I have to meet Henri. We'll talk about it when I get back,' Phillippe said.

"They were going to Philadelphia to look at a restaurant. The trip had been planned for days.

"I waited anxiously for Phillippe to come back. I kept telling myself it would be all right. I'd even suggest we adopt; I knew how much he wanted a baby.

"Except Phillippe didn't come back. Instead, Henri delivered a letter.

"I opened it when I was alone.

Dear Meredith,

I have gone back to France. Please don't follow me.

It isn't because you lied about being pregnant. You wouldn't have been the first woman to trap a man into marriage. Many of those marriages lasted happily forever.

It's because I realized you don't know me at all. You didn't believe in me enough to know that I would have done anything so we could be together. You've had eight years to tell me the truth, and you never did.

That might seem like a small thing to you, but to me it's everything. Love comes before anything. If we don't believe in each other, we don't have a marriage.

Henri is going to run the restaurant in New York and I'll take over his restaurant in Paris. I'll file divorce from France, or you can file in New York. It doesn't matter to me. Perhaps you can send my books and my clothes.

Phillippe

"I ran to the desk in Phillippe's study. His passport was gone, along with a copy of our marriage certificate. I called his cell phone, but it went straight to voicemail. Then I called his mother and anyone else I could think of in France.

"For the next month, I tried to get in contact, but Phillippe never replied. I booked airline tickets to Paris and then canceled them. Finally, I received divorce papers just after Christmas. I signed them, there was nothing else to do.

"I got a smaller apartment and starting working for a friend's catering company in the evenings. That's how I met Josh, my second husband. For some reason he fell in love with me. After a few months, he asked me to marry him.

"Josh was charming and handsome, I couldn't think of a good reason to refuse. I was sure that in time, I'd forget Phillippe. But you never forget your first love, it becomes as much part of you as a childhood scar from falling off a bicycle. The best one can hope for is that over time it becomes less painful and fades away."

Meredith stopped talking. She scooped up Buttons.

"I didn't mean to say all that," she said. Her eyes were dangerously bright.

Zach pressed Stop on the camera. "I don't have to include it."

Meredith stood up, and she put on her jacket.

"Of course you do, now you have your ending. Buttons and I are going for a walk." She walked to the door and turned around. "And Zach, I don't know how to thank you. I feel much lighter. I've been bottling up those emotions for years."

Chapter Twenty-seven

On New Year's Day, Rebecca was putting the finishing touches on the boathouse for the party in the early evening.

It snowed during the night and when she arrived, the path from Howard's chalet was blanketed with fresh powder. Rebecca had never experienced such stillness. Everything around her was white. The boathouse's wooden roof was white, the stone steps leading down to the lake were covered with fat snowflakes, and the pine trees were heavy with new snow.

Then she entered the boathouse, and the contrast—the bright postcards on the walls, the Christmas tree twinkling with ornaments—made her feel almost giddy.

In the afternoon, the florist and caterer would arrive and the air would smell of roses and spices. She couldn't wait to show Howard the old-fashioned popcorn machine set up in the corner, and the jukebox that would play during the DJ's breaks.

The door to the boathouse opened. Rebecca thought it was Howard, but it was Meredith.

"Meredith," Rebecca said in surprise. "What are you doing here?"

"I wanted to send you a photo for my dating profile, but I realized I didn't have your phone number, and I stopped at the bakery and got you a cup of coffee." Meredith held up a cup.

Rebecca studied Meredith warily. She hadn't spoken to Meredith since she discovered that Zach had lied about everything.

"How did you know about the boathouse?" Rebecca asked.

"Zach told me. He doesn't know I'm here." Meredith handed Rebecca the coffee. "Please, take the coffee. You have been working so hard on this party. It's a special Christmas Cove blend."

"Thank you." Rebecca accepted the cup. "But that doesn't mean I want to talk about Zach."

"It's all my fault." Meredith unwrapped her scarf and took the lid off her own coffee. "I'm the one who pretended we were a couple, Zach just played along. And then I got him fired. I felt terrible, so I offered that he could stay in my suite."

"He could have told me the truth," Rebecca said. "There's nothing wrong with being a waiter."

"Of course there isn't," Meredith said slowly. "Unless the girl you've been in love with since you were twenty-two is standing before you. And she's a hugely successful CEO with a giant diamond ring on her finger."

Rebecca looked up sharply.

"How do you know Zach is in love with me?"

"I've been with him all week," Meredith said. "At first, it was nothing he said. But every time he came back from being with you, there was a sparkle in his eye, and he walked with a bounce in his step."

"He may have had a crush on me in college, but that was ages ago," Rebecca protested. "We didn't even stay in touch."

Meredith raised her eyebrows.

"Since when is love rational?" Meredith asked. "When I met

my first husband, Phillippe, I thought he was overbearing and pushy, I didn't even like him. But I fell in love with him anyway."

"Why would you think I have feelings for Zach?" Rebecca wondered.

She wasn't ready to talk about Zach, but somehow she couldn't help herself. Ever since she ran out of the lodge's restaurant she hadn't stopped thinking about him. And she went over her own actions the night they met in Christmas Cove. She had lied to Zach about being married and about being on her honeymoon with Ben. But she couldn't admit that to Meredith now. It was too embarrassing.

"Let's just say I'm good at reading people," Meredith said, interrupting her thoughts.

"None of it matters." Rebecca shrugged. "Howard's New Year's Night party is tonight. Tomorrow, I'm leaving. Zach and I will probably never see each other again."

Meredith sipped her coffee thoughtfully.

"Give Zach another chance. If you still can't get over that he lied to you, at least you'll know you tried."

Rebecca wavered. Zach shouldn't have lied to her. But she had been lying to him too.

"When Phillippe left, I didn't try hard enough to win him back." Meredith kept talking. "I was confident I'd meet someone new that I loved just as much. But I never did. My second marriage was a mistake; I knew it the minute we moved in together. True love is unpredictable. The important thing is knowing when it happens. If you ignore it, you could miss the best thing in life."

Rebecca pictured sitting in the bridal suite of the Four Seasons and Ben telling her he was going to St. Barts with Natalie. She thought about Kat disappearing and Howard keeping her wedding dress for thirty-three years.

"What if I've stopped believing in love?" Rebecca asked.

"That's like refusing to believe in Christmas." Meredith wrapped her scarf around her neck. "Christmas will still happen every December. The only difference is when everyone else is opening presents and going caroling, you'll be alone."

After Meredith left, Rebecca finished arranging the place settings. She couldn't stop thinking about what Meredith had said. She did have feelings for Zach, or she wouldn't have kissed him. He lied to her about being a waiter, but she had kept the truth from him too.

She went into the storage room and cleared the boxes from the floor. The wedding dress was hanging in the closet. There was a rip in the hem that hadn't been there before. It must have happened when Rebecca tried on the dress. She'd take it to the bridal shop in Christmas Cove and ask them to fix it.

She stacked the boxes in the corner. There wasn't time to think about Zach. The party was in eight hours and there was so much to keep her busy.

"Excuse me, I brought in a wedding dress earlier today," Rebecca said, entering the bridal shop. "The salesgirl who was here said it would be ready by two p.m."

The saleswoman took Rebecca's name and went into the back room. An older woman appeared. She wore a navy dress and her auburn hair was worn in a bun.

"Miss Huntley, my name is Janice, I'm the owner. I'm afraid there's been a mix-up. The dress isn't here."

"What do you mean, it isn't here?" Rebecca asked.

She had dropped it off a few hours ago, on her way back to the lodge from the boathouse.

"I'm afraid my salesgirl thought the dress was for resale and sold it to a customer," Janice said nervously. "How can we compensate you?"

"You sold the dress!" Rebecca repeated in horror.

Howard had trusted her with everything in the boathouse. And the wedding dress must be important to him, he'd kept it for thirty-three years. He'd be furious and it was all Rebecca's fault. She should never have tried it on in the first place.

"I'm terribly sorry, I don't know what to say. I've owned the shop for twenty years," Janice said, apologizing. "Nothing like this has happened before."

"You must have the contact information for the woman who bought it," Rebecca said urgently.

Janice opened the cash register and riffled through the sales slips.

"There's no phone number. My salesgirl did say the woman mentioned where she was staying. But I can't give out that information."

"Please. It's a very special dress," Rebecca insisted. "I have to get it back."

"All right." Janice nodded. She handed Rebecca the sales slip. "Here's her name. She's staying at Fir Tree Inn, on the other side of the lake."

Rebecca spent the next hour trying to find a way to get to Fir Tree Inn. First, she went to the community kitchen, but Jerome was out in his car making deliveries. Then she tried the car services in Christmas Cove, but they were all booked. She even considered taking a horse and buggy, but she wouldn't be back in time for the party.

She was standing in the lodge's lobby when Zach appeared. She hadn't seen him since she walked out of the restaurant.

"Rebecca." He approached her. He wore a navy parka and jeans. "Are you all right? You look upset."

Rebecca moved away. "It's nothing, I'll figure it out."

"Please. Maybe I can help."

Rebecca turned around. Zach looked so concerned and sincere. And there were only a few hours left until Howard returned for the party. Perhaps Zach could help her get the dress back.

She told Zach how she had tried on the wedding dress, and it had gotten a small tear in the hem. She'd taken it to the bridal shop to be repaired and the salesgirl had sold it to someone else.

"Howard kept that dress for decades," she finished. "I have to get it back."

"I have a car, I'll take you," Zach offered. "The transmission makes a coughing sound, and the heating can be temperamental, but it will get us there."

"I can't let you do that." Rebecca shook her head. "It's New Year's Day and a lot of people are leaving. With traffic, it could take ages. You must have better things to do."

"Please, Rebecca. I know how angry you are because I lied, and I don't blame you," Zach urged. "I'll do anything to make it up to you. At least we can be friends."

If they left now, they'd be back by 5:00 p.m. She could text Howard and say she had to pick up a few things. The party didn't start until 8:00 p.m., there was plenty of time.

"All right." She nodded.

"Excellent! Just don't ask me to sing along to the music." Zach grinned. "I don't even sing in the shower, in case anyone hears me."

Fir Tree Inn was a two-story wooden building with floor-to-ceiling windows. Fir trees lined the entrance and there was a boat dock and a stone balcony overlooking the lake.

"Excuse me." Rebecca approached the front desk. "I'm looking for a guest, Ms. Katherine Chapman."

The man clicked through his computer screen.

"Ms. Chapman is staying with us," he confirmed. "But I can't give out her room number."

"Could you tell her that I need to talk to her." Rebecca scribbled her name on a piece of paper. "Please, it's extremely urgent."

The man picked up the house phone. He spoke for a moment and hung up.

"Ms. Chapman said she'll meet you in the lobby."

Rebecca and Zach sat on opposite armchairs in the lobby. The car ride had been easier than Rebecca had imagined. She thought they wouldn't have anything to talk about, but they had a spirited discussion about music and how so many young artists were discovered on TikTok. And Zach was a good driver. He took the curves around the lake with confidence and Rebecca allowed herself to relax and enjoy the view.

An attractive woman in her late fifties approached them. She had dark reddish hair and wore a stylish, long skirt and a cashmere sweater.

Rebecca jumped up.

"Ms. Chapman, I'm Rebecca Huntley and this is Zach," she said. "It's about the wedding dress. There's been a terrible mix-up."

"It's nice to meet you." The woman held out her hand. "Please call me Kat."

Rebecca gulped and her heart seemed to flutter in her chest.

"Did you say your name was Kat?"

"It's short for Katherine." The woman nodded. "Why don't we go somewhere quiet, where we can talk?"

Zach went for a stroll along the lake, and Rebecca followed Kat into the inn's library.

Rebecca told her everything. About Howard's New Year's Night party and the wedding dress hanging in the boathouse storeroom. How Rebecca had torn the dress hem by accident and had taken it to the bridal shop to be repaired. When she'd returned, it was gone. She even told her about the postcards and Howard's journal.

"Goodness," Kat said when she finished. "That's quite a story. I saw the dress through the window and had to go inside. It looked so familiar. At first, I thought I was imagining it. At my age, I'm always seeing things that remind me of the past. But then I saw it up close and it was the same dress that Howard bought all those years ago in Brussels. I had to buy it. You don't know how many times over the years I've thought about that dress. My life would have been so different if I'd accepted it in the first place."

"Howard never gave you the dress," Rebecca countered, recalling the last journal entry. "You left Brussels before he could propose."

"On Christmas Eve, I went into the closet in Howard's room at the hostel. I bought him a sweater for Christmas and wanted to make sure it was the right size," Kat said, remembering. "The dress was hanging in the back. I guessed what it meant; Howard had been hinting about marriage. I loved Howard, but I got scared. We were so young, neither of us had careers. If he proposed and I said we should wait, he'd be so hurt. So instead, I made up a family emergency and left a note and his present with my roommate."

"I doubt he ever got them," Rebecca said. "The journal entry ends the day after Christmas."

"I thought he read the note and didn't want to see me again," Kat sighed. "I got a job at a museum in New York. Eventually I moved to San Francisco and got married and opened an art gallery. The marriage didn't work out, but I kept my married name." Kat paused reflectively. "How funny to think that Howard and I both live in San Francisco and only crossed paths again in Christmas Cove."

"Howard never married. His whole life has been about his travel company."

"He was a wonderful travel companion." Kat's eyes had a far-off expression. "We had so much fun together. I missed him terribly, but there was nothing I could do. We never exchanged addresses or phone numbers and I didn't know how to reach him. Things were so different then. Now you can find anyone in a few minutes online. Then so much time passed, I never looked him up."

Rebecca suddenly had an idea.

"You should come tonight," Rebecca suggested.

"Come where?" Kat frowned.

"To Howard's New Year's Night party," Rebecca urged, excitement growing in her chest.

"We haven't seen each other in decades! I can't just show up at his party."

"I'm sure Howard isn't seeing anyone special. Most of the guests are people he knows through his company," Rebecca said. "You can drive to Christmas Cove with Zach and me. Trust me, it will be a wonderful surprise."

Kat's green eyes twinkled. For a moment, Rebecca saw the impetuous young woman Howard had described in his journal entries.

"I don't have any evening plans and it does sound like fun." Kat hesitated, smiling. "But I don't have anything to wear. I only packed casual clothes."

"I know just the dress." Rebecca smiled back. "It's hanging in your closet."

"You want me to wear the wedding dress?" Kat's mouth dropped open.

Rebecca nodded. All the uncertainty and humiliation of the last week rolled away, and she felt a wonderful jolt, like drinking the perfect cup of coffee. Christmas was about helping others. She was doing something to make two people happy.

"I can't think of anything better."

Chapter Twenty-eight

Rebecca stood near the bar in the boathouse while Howard greeted his guests.

Standing there, the picture window strung with colored lights, the Christmas tree glittering with ornaments in the corner, it was impossible to believe that a few days ago the boathouse was just bare floors and concrete walls with rowboats hanging from the ceiling.

Every inch of the interior had been transformed. The floors were covered with thick wool rugs, the long table was set with blue-and-white china, and there were flowers everywhere: Christmas chrysanthemums in giant urns, and crystal vases of red and white roses, and succulents and cacti artfully arranged in the cowboy boot centerpieces.

The pin spotlighting gave the room a warm glow, and the air was scented with cloves and pine needles. There was an old-fashioned stagecoach where guests could take photos, and Rebecca had created sitting areas with cowhide sofas and armchairs upholstered in rich-smelling, buttery-textured leather.

Howard was thrilled with everything she had done. He spent ages going over the postcards on the wall, and he sampled so many desserts before the guests arrived, he groaned that he wouldn't have an appetite for dinner.

Rebecca listened to the DJ and was overcome with happiness. Nine days ago, she had been sitting in Kimi's SUV, surrounded by Leila's stuffed animals and wondering how she would survive Christmas. Now she had new friends, and she'd done something satisfying. She had created an experience that the guests would remember forever.

Kat was getting her hair done, and would arrive any minute. Rebecca couldn't wait to see Howard's expression when she stepped through the doors in the wedding dress. And Zach was on the other side of the boathouse, filming the party. Howard decided at the last minute to record the night, and Zach was happy to offer his services.

On the drive back from Fir Tree Inn, Rebecca had told Zach about Ben and Natalie, and how she had lied about being married. They agreed to start fresh, with no lies, and when Zach arrived at the boathouse, handsome and fresh-shaven in a black suit and white shirt, the giddy feeling had welled up inside her.

Every now and then he looked up from his camera and they shared a smile.

"You've done an amazing job," Howard said, joining Rebecca at the bar. "I was gone for so many days, and we only had a brief conversation before I left. I worried that you wouldn't know what to do."

"I do think the western theme fit perfectly," Rebecca replied. "It takes a pioneering spirit to start your own travel company."

"It's uncanny." Howard sipped his champagne. "You seemed to know what I wanted better than I did myself."

"A party should reflect the host's personality," Rebecca reflected. "Reading your travel journals helped me get to know you."

"Those journals are so old, they must have been quite boring."

"Not boring at all." Rebecca shook her head. She was about to say something when Kat appeared at the entry. Her red hair fell in soft waves to her shoulders and she wore a pearl necklace and pearl earrings.

Rebecca couldn't take her eyes off the dress. It fit Kat perfectly. The pleated skirt stopped just below her knees, and the wide sash circled her small waist. The cap sleeves looked lovely and the appliquéd bodice twinkled under the lights.

Kat gave a little wave and Rebecca watched as Howard turned and noticed her. His cheeks went white and, for a moment, Rebecca worried that she'd made a mistake. She should have given Howard some warning, or made sure they met when they were alone.

But then his expression changed and his face lit up in a smile. His eyes crinkled at the corners and his mouth wobbled.

He started toward Kat as she walked over to them.

"Howard," Kat said simply. She held out her hand. "Rebecca told me about the party. I hope you don't mind that I crashed your celebration."

Howard glanced from Kat to Rebecca.

"I don't understand, what are you doing in Christmas Cove?" Howard asked, his eyes traveling over the wedding dress. "And where did you get that dress?"

"That's a long answer," Kat said, a smile playing over her lips. "Do you think I might get a glass of champagne first?"

It was almost midnight and dinner was over. Howard had insisted that Rebecca prepare a plate for herself. The honey-glazed ham and potato casserole were delicious. After dinner there had been a few speeches and then everyone took to the dance floor.

Howard and Kat didn't leave each other's side all night. They danced to almost every song and they even went to the dessert table together, exclaiming over the same desserts they had eaten all those years ago. The apple pastry with whipped cream in Copenhagen, and the strudel they had in Vienna and the bûche de noël and chocolate Arc de Triomphe they had seen in Paris. Now they sat on a sofa next to the window and waited for the fireworks to begin over the lake.

Zach came over and joined Rebecca.

"I got a lot of great footage," he said, putting down his camera. "I should stop recording. People get drunk toward the end of a party and don't like the way they look on camera."

"It was nice of you to do it. Howard is so happy."

"I've filmed a few weddings and parties over the years," Zach replied. "It's always fun. People are in a great mood and I usually get a free dinner."

"There are still plenty of desserts." Rebecca waved at the dessert table. "Help yourself."

Zach selected a slice of cheesecake and stood beside Rebecca. Lights flickered over the lake and there was the scent of chrysanthemums mixed with cloves and cinnamon.

"I know we said we're starting over and we haven't been on a proper date. But it's New Year's Night and we're standing underneath mistletoe," Zach said, pointing above them.

It had been Rebecca's idea to hang mistletoe even though Christmas had passed. It made the space look so festive.

"Are you saying you want to kiss me?" Rebecca raised her eyebrows.

Zach put down his plate. "That's exactly what I'm saying."

The DJ played the next song and guests drifted onto the dance floor.

"Then you'd better hurry," she said playfully. "I have to make sure that everyone has enough champagne before Howard's fireworks are set off."

Zach took her in his arms. His mouth found hers and he wrapped his arms around her. Rebecca kissed him back. His breath was sweet and he smelled of soap and aftershave.

The popping sound grew louder and neon-colored rockets shot into the sky. Fireworks shaped like snowflakes scattered over the lake, and a set of gold-and-silver fireworks that resembled Cinderella's carriage made everyone *ooh* and *ahh* in astonishment.

After the fireworks display was over, the DJ played a slow song, and Zach led Rebecca onto the dance floor. She rested her head on his shoulder and he pulled her close against his chest.

For a moment, Rebecca closed her eyes. She couldn't remember a better New Year's party.

The next morning, Rebecca rose early and jogged one last time around the lake. Then she joined Zach and Jerome and Alesha at the community kitchen for breakfast. They talked about Alesha's cooking classes and Rebecca's new idea.

It had come to her while she was cleaning up after the party. So much food was left over, she'd wrapped up most of it and taken it to the community kitchen.

She was going to start her own party-planning business in San Francisco. After each event, she'd donate the leftover food to schools for children who couldn't afford lunches. And she'd take all the flowers to retirement homes throughout the city. The thought of brightening up the rooms of the elderly made her so excited. She couldn't wait to get home and figure out a business plan.

Zach had his own plans. He was going to stay with Jerome and Alesha for a few days until he finished editing the film. Then he was going to move to Berkeley. His old film professor had a small production company and was looking for an editor. It didn't pay much, but Zach could use the equipment to edit his own films.

Rebecca teased him that he shouldn't rush into anything. He'd probably win the contest and then he'd be in great demand. Zach had leaned over his plate of scrambled eggs and said even if he won the contest, he'd need a home base and he knew exactly where he wanted to be. In Berkeley, on the other side of the Bay Bridge from Rebecca's apartment in San Francisco.

Now Rebecca had finished packing her suitcase. She glanced at the series of texts from Kimi on her phone. Kimi had sent a dozen photos from the ship's New Year's Eve celebration. There were pictures of Leila with tinsel in her wispy brown hair, and photos of Kimi's parents wearing party hats and waving streamers. Rebecca liked the photo of Kimi and Andy the best. They were standing arm in arm at the edge of a dance floor. Kimi wore a floor-length silver dress that was probably from the ship's gift shop, and Andy wore a tuxedo and bow tie.

Kimi seemed more relaxed than she had since Leila was born, and they both looked so happy.

There was a knock at the door and Rebecca answered it. Meredith stood in the hallway. She wore a blue parka and held Buttons in her arms.

"Buttons and I wanted to say goodbye," Meredith said.

"Please come in," Rebecca greeted her. "I was packing."

Meredith followed her inside. "We are flying to Los Angeles, then I'm packing a bag and we're going to Paris."

"Paris!" Rebecca exclaimed.

"You'll never guess what happened," Meredith said. "Phillippe replied to my profile on Dealbreakers. We started chatting online and this morning he sent me a ticket to Paris."

"He must have seen your photo in your profile," Rebecca suggested.

"That's the strange part. He said he responded before there was a photo, and that I replied to his post," she said meditatively. "But I never did."

Rebecca recalled replying for Meredith to an attractive-looking man in his midforties.

"Dating sites are always a bit mysterious," Rebecca answered, folding a sweater into her suitcase. "I'm glad it worked out."

"Phillippe never married again. He owns two restaurants in Paris." Meredith kept talking. "Who knows if anything will come of it, but the chemistry is still there. And it's Paris!" she said happily. "I'm going to eat soufflés, and walk on the Champs-Élysées in the rain, and shop in the grand department stores." She stroked Buttons's nose. "I've heard the French love little dogs. Buttons and I will have a wonderful time."

Meredith left and Rebecca pulled on her boots. There was another knock and Zach stood at the door.

"Are you sure you don't need a ride to San Francisco?" he asked when Rebecca ushered him inside.

Zach had volunteered to drive her to the city, but Kat had called earlier and offered her a ride. Kat and Howard had stayed up most of the night talking. They were going to spend a month traveling together. Howard called it a prewedding honeymoon and Kat didn't argue with him.

"There's no point in you driving all that way when Kat lives close to me," Rebecca said. "Anyway, we'll see each other in four days after you finish editing the film."

"I brought you something." Zach gave her a small bag. "I bought it a few days ago and forgot to give it to you."

Inside the bag was a snow globe of Christmas Cove.

"I wanted to give you something to remember Christmas at the lake," Zach said, kissing her. "It's not much, but I hope you like it."

"It's perfect." Rebecca shook it and watched snowflakes settle over Main Street. "Thank you."

She remembered the empty snow globe that Kat had given Howard. If you shook it and wished for something hard enough, the thing you wished for appeared in the snow globe.

It was the first week of the new year. She had Zach, her new business idea, and soon she'd have her puppy, Oliver. She closed her eyes and made a wish. Anything could happen, all she had to do was believe.

Acknowledgments

Thank you to my wonderful agent, Johanna Castillo, and my fabulous editor, Sallie Lotz, for everything you do for me and my books. Thank you to the team at St. Martin's Press including Jennifer Enderlin, Alexis Norville, and Brant Janeway for getting them out there. Mostly, thank you to my children, Alex, Andrew, Heather, Madeleine, and Thomas, and my daughter-in-law, Sarah, for bringing me so much joy all year round.

Sheri Geoffreys

Anita Hughes is the author of *Rome in Love* (adapted into a Hallmark movie in 2019) and *Christmas in Vermont* (adapted into a Lifetime movie in 2019). She is also the author of *Market Street, Lake Como, Santorini Sunsets, Christmas in Paris, Monarch Beach,* and other titles. She attended UC Berkeley's Masters in Creative Writing Program and lives in Dana Point, California.